NATHAN

JOHNSON FAMILY RULES BOOK 2

CARLY MARIE

Editing Services: Jennifer Smith

Proof Reading: Charity VanHuss

CONTENTS

PROLOGUE

ELLIOT

I'd never been so glad to see our Fifth Avenue apartment building since the day I'd moved in. If I heard another *Congratulations* for the rest of my life it would be too soon. Hours of smiling and pretend happiness had worn on me. All I wanted was a cold beer and to forget about the day.

Emma hadn't fared much better.

We hadn't spoken much on the ride back home and we rode the elevator up to our apartment in silence, both of us lost in thought. As soon as the doors opened on our floor, Emma let out a sigh. "Thank fuck."

The only reason I laughed was because she'd voiced what I'd been feeling. "Longest day in history."

Her response was pure Emma. "I need a drink."

That made two of us. We walked down the hallway to our door. Thanks to the large box filled with unopened champagne, leftover cake, and a few gifts, I had to wait for Emma to fish the key ring from my pocket.

The box was getting heavier by the second and the open door was a welcome sight. We walked into the apartment, not bothering to stop to take off our shoes, and headed toward the kitchen.

I slid the box onto the counter and turned to see Emma standing behind me, her lips pressed into a firm line. Her immaculately styled hair from hours before had become unraveled in places, but the hair product the salon had used kept it at unnatural angles. The makeup that had been perfect at one in the afternoon was splotchy and smudged twelve hours after it had been applied.

To me she was still beautiful, and she looked a lot more like the woman I'd known for eight years.

Even rolling out of her room first thing in the morning, no caffeine in her system, hair rumpled, with sheet creases on her cheeks, Emma was beautiful. The professional makeup and hairdo had only accentuated her natural beauty, but I liked her more like this. Like this, she was my Emma. My best friend and confidant.

After shucking my tuxedo jacket, untying my bow tie, and popping the top three buttons of my shirt, I pulled the box of cake off the top of the pile. Below it sat one of the bottles of champagne we'd escaped with. Emma was still in her dress but had headed over to the silverware drawer and pulled two forks out. "Shall we eat our feelings?"

The first genuine laugh I'd had in hours bubbled from

my chest. "God, that sounds like a perfect way to end this day. Can I interest you in champagne?" I held up the bottle of champagne that had caused me to nearly choke on my water when I'd heard its price at the tasting six months earlier.

"Skip the glass." She reached into the fridge. "Beer?"

"Please." I might have been wearing a custom-tailored tuxedo and had spent the last week rubbing elbows with New York's most elite attorneys and socialites, but I still preferred a cold bottle of beer to any glass of wine or champagne offered, and Emma knew it.

I popped the cork just as Emma took the cap off my beer. We traded bottles, and I grabbed the cake box, following her into the living room where we promptly collapsed on the couch, wedding attire and all.

Because, somehow, we'd gotten married that day.

Emma propped her Converse-clad feet onto the coffee table, took a long swig of champagne, then stabbed a bite of cake.

I wasn't as anxious to eat the cake but sighed in relief as the cold beer slid down my throat. "How did we even get here?"

Emma's laugh was sardonic, and she shook her head. The motion caused the loose strands to move, but it wasn't a natural movement, and I found myself staring at it. "I think it started with us drunkenly deciding to date to get people off our backs about not being settled down and nearing our mid-thirties."

I nodded at the memory. "Right, because we're far more valuable partnered up or some such shit."

Another long pull from the champagne bottle later, Emma narrowed her eyes at me. "No, *I'm* apparently worth more partnered up. Partnered, but god forbid I have children... You needed someone so that people stopped questioning why you weren't dating."

My cheeks flushed but I didn't say anything.

"Elliot Mitchell, you're thirty-five years old and aside from a drunken half-confession to me that night, you've never said the words out loud."

I drained my beer too quickly and went to get another. There was no point in pretending this was going to be a one- or even two-beer night. "It wasn't supposed to get this far," was the only defense I had as once again I took my seat next to her.

She left half the slice of chocolate cake with raspberry filling uneaten and started on a slice of lemon sponge cake. I couldn't remember the filling in that one, but then again, the cake had been huge, with multiple layers and just as many different fillings. The only one I'd cared anything about was the layer with German chocolate cake, dark chocolate ganache, and the sweet coconut filling that had nearly given the baker a heart attack when I asked for it.

Eventually, Emma sighed. "Who'd have thought your bringing me coffee one morning would end up with us walking down the aisle?"

I poked at my cake as I thought about that fateful day.

She'd been exhausted after having not slept much while preparing for a trial that was starting. I'd stopped by her favorite coffee cart on my way into work to pick us both up coffee, then swung by her firm on the way up to my own office.

Emma's eyes had widened when she spotted me walking toward her, and a genuine smile spread across her face. She'd pulled me into her office and given me a giant hug and kiss on the cheek. As she sipped the double shot mocha, she sighed. "I'm so glad I've called keeps on you forever."

We'd both laughed, and I'd given her another hug and headed up the elevator to my own office, the law firm her dad had started thirty-some years earlier. I hadn't thought a thing of the morning detour until Emma flew into my office unannounced at lunchtime, panting as she closed the door, her eyes wild with panic. "Think fast! I don't know how—" But the knock on my office door cut her sentence off and she groaned. "I'm so sorry," she apologized as she opened the door to both her mom and dad.

Her mom, Michelle, looked over the moon while her dad—my boss—looked like he'd swallowed a lemon. "Why didn't you tell us?" Michelle gushed as she continued to speak. "When did it happen?"

"I'm sorry?" I couldn't figure out what they were talking about.

Michelle carried on like I hadn't spoken. "An engagement! How exciting! When's the wedding? Oh, we have so much to plan!"

The ringing in my ears was nearly deafening. My eyes shot to Emma's but she was pale and offering me no help, so I did the only thing I could think of. I smiled and went for as close to the truth as I could without having any idea what the actual truth was. "Oh, well, it's kind of new."

It had snowballed out of control from there. Before we could right the misunderstanding, Emma had been dragged to a dress fitting. When she'd come home shell-shocked to inform me that her mom had purchased her a wedding dress, we talked about it and had decided to go through with it.

The most mature decision ever? Probably not.

The easiest? Well, looking back, no, it hadn't been.

But hindsight's twenty-twenty.

Over the last few months, Emma and I had nearly lost our friendship over the wedding stress. We'd both argued about calling the entire thing off. In the end, we'd followed through with it, but the last week had been a special form of hell.

Emma gave up on the sponge cake and went for a direct kill. "Did you ever talk to your brother?"

I shoved half of the remaining slice of cake into my mouth.

She shook her head. "What am I going to do with you, Elliot? That was half the reason we went through with this insane thing. You two need to talk."

I washed the bite down with a swallow of beer and glanced over at her. "Do you really think Rand would let him anywhere near me? God only knows what that man knows. He's huge and kinda scary."

"And you've been an absolute asshole to him all week."

I made to open my mouth to refute it but Emma held up her hand and glowered at me. "Do not make excuses to me. I get it. Your parents are stressful. He's in a nontraditional relationship. You're so vanilla you couldn't even be considered French vanilla. This *year* has been stressful and you've been on edge. But Jesus, Elliot, you went through so much trouble to get your brother here so you had a chance to talk."

"That was before I knew he was going to have his Daddy with him! Seriously, I really didn't think he'd have a Daddy! How the hell do you go to a ranch in Middle of Nowhere, Tennessee, and end up hooking up with your gay boss?"

Emma let out a snort of laughter that told me she was probably tipsy by that point. A glance at the bottle said the champagne was half gone. It was going to be an interesting night. Despite her intoxication, her words were clear and precise. "He told you he was bringing Rand. He gave you warning. And they were sweet together. No offense, but if I could find a man to look at me the same way Rand looks at Kyle, I'd consider dating."

My eyes fell closed and I stifled a laugh at her statement. "None taken. Truthfully, if a guy ever looked at me like that, I'd consider it too."

Emma let out a gasp. "I think that was the closest you've ever come to admitting your sexuality."

If only I wouldn't lose the only family I had if that happened. I pinched the bridge of my nose, trying to figure out a way to change the subject before things got more uncomfortable. "You know it was faked?" I winced at my own words. "I mean, I think it was faked? But now it's real? At least I think it's real?"

Emma's eyebrows made a weird succession of movements before settling on a confused arch. "Well, if they faked it, they faked it well. Your brother is genuinely in love with that man, and Rand looks at him like he hung the moon. And that protective streak he has for Kyle couldn't possibly be fake."

I waved my empty bottle around in front of me. "It's not fake now! It was when we first invited them to the wedding. He didn't want to come."

"Imagine that."

"Hey, we didn't want to be here either," I shot back defensively.

Emma leaned over and rested her head on my shoulder. "We've fucked up, El."

Tell me something I don't know.

"Your dad hates me. Your mom thinks I'm an idiot. My brother hates me. My parents aren't happy with me... but there's nothing new on that front."

"My dad doesn't hate you. And my mom will cool off."

The headache that always hung out behind my eyes threatened to turn into a migraine. "We kept this up, thinking it wouldn't be that bad. Maybe I'd finally make partner out of it; you'd move up in your firm as well. Well, you're about to be made partner, but your dad made it clear that that isn't in the cards for me. Fuck." I scrubbed my free hand down my face.

Emma hummed, that patient understanding way I'd come to know and love about her. Yes, I loved Emma but not in the way a husband was supposed to love his wife. "Did you really want to make partner?"

I lifted a shoulder. "Honestly? I don't know. It's just what's expected, right?"

"There are plenty of attorneys who never want to become a managing partner in a law firm."

I thought about her words. Did I want to be a partner? If I really analyzed it, I hated my job. I loved the law, I liked family law, and I loved being an attorney. But did I want to bring even more work home every day? Did I want the responsibility of managing other people? Probably not. Hell, I was quickly proving I could hardly manage myself.

I felt my body sink back into the couch as the weight of the realization fully hit me. I didn't want to be a partner. At least not in Richard's firm. I'd wanted it because my parents expected it. *Fuck.*

Emma stayed silent for so long I thought she'd fallen

asleep. When she spoke, I jumped slightly. "It was a helluva party, though."

I couldn't help my chuckle. "That it was. Too bad we were too angry to really enjoy it."

We sat in silence for a long time before I came to a decision. "I'll take the fall for this."

Emma's head shot up and she swayed slightly. "What?"

"Em, this is your apartment. This is your life. You're NYC born and raised. You love your job, you love the city, you love your friends. You're about to make partner. What do I have? A law degree and eight years in a firm that isn't going to make me partner? You can still be happy. We'll file for an annulment on Monday. I'll find something else. You'll move on."

Emma scooted closer. "If I move on, then you have to too. You need to stop trying to please the two most vile people on the planet. If you hadn't made Nancy and Edward Mitchell happy before this week, you never will. They are truly the nastiest people I've ever met, and if you keep trying to please them, you're going to turn out the same way."

I winced at her scolding. She wasn't far from the truth. I hadn't laughed since their plane had landed. I'd been a fucking nightmare of epic proportions, even worse than normal, and I could admit that. "And how will I do that?" The defeat in my voice was depressing even to me.

Her warm hugs and steady presence would be the worst loss from this entire disaster. I wasn't going to be able to stay in New York, and I knew that. A city of eight million wasn't very big when lawyers started to talk. I was going to be blacklisted from every firm in the city. The weight of the last week was nearly crushing.

"You're going to be true to yourself."

I took it back. *That* was the most crushing thing of the last week. My eyes went wide and my newest bottle of beer paused halfway to my mouth. "I-I what?"

Emma poked me with a flawless French-manicured finger. "It's time for you to live for you. You're going to find a job you *like*. You're going to come out."

When I went stone-still beside her, she backpedaled slightly. "I'm not telling you to take out a billboard in Times Square. I'm telling you that you're going to tell at least one person the truth."

Sweat trickled down my back. I was thirty-five and the closest I'd ever come to saying what Emma was asking—no, telling—me to say was that I didn't like women in *that* way. She'd gotten it without my needing to say more. It was what had made our "relationship" work as long as it had. Emma didn't want to be married or dating; she was happy single. I was tired of dodging attempts at being hooked up with everyone's friend or sister. With us dating, she hadn't been pressured to find a man, and I hadn't been pressured to find someone to date.

Then it had gone sideways.

"I'm not trying to send you into a panic attack, Elliot. But you're not getting any younger. If you are willing to take the blame for this mess that *we* got ourselves into, then I'm going to demand that you find happiness. You're not going to do that until you admit to yourself that you've lied to everyone for the last twenty-plus years you've known."

That last piece of cake was not sitting well in my stomach. "Look what happened to Kyle when he came out."

Emma squeezed my arm. "He found a job he loves, a home he loves, and a man who loves him every bit as much as he loves him."

"Before that, Em. The hell he went through at home. The hell he went through at school. The hell he *still* goes through." I groaned as the weight of it all really sank in. "The hell I've put him through so no one looked too hard at me." I'd been an asshole to him since he came out, but I'd never been there for him before that either. That was on me, but the way I'd treated him since he'd come out was what really bothered me.

She wrapped me in a hug and held me tight. "And it's time to make that right. Call him in the morning. Without your mom and dad and grandma around. I won't go if you don't want me to, but meet up with him, grovel, and apologize. It's not going to fix it, but hopefully it will set the wheels in motion. Maybe you can salvage something from this disaster of a week."

"I'll call him," I promised after a few moments of silence. "But the odds of him agreeing to meet me are infinitesimal at best."

We spent the next few hours discussing what steps we

needed to take, how we'd move forward and onward, and what we'd do without the other. In the eighteen months we'd lived together, our lives had become intertwined even without the romance. It was going to be an adjustment to not have the other just a door away.

"Where are you going?"

I shrugged. "Back to Chicago, probably. The house is big enough that my parents likely won't even remember I'm there after a few days. I'll find a job."

She chuckled. "Is Chicago really big enough for you to live that close to your parents?"

My dramatic sigh was answer enough. "Fuck if I know. I've got savings—I just don't want to dip into them. Maybe I can find some place less expensive to live? Maybe find a job outside of Illinois."

"I'm here for whatever you need. Always. I hope you know that." She pinched the bridge of her nose. "Fuck, I'm drunk. And champagne hangovers *suck*. I'm going to head to bed."

"Need help out of that dress?"

Emma looked down at her attire. "Ha! Wedding dresses aren't made to be gotten out of on your own. They assume the spouse will do that."

I grinned. "God, I'm going to miss you."

She got a little teary-eyed. "Same. But you're going to finally fly. And I'm not going to let you retreat again. You're free now."

Instead of acknowledging her words, I did what I did

best and changed the subject. "Let's get you out of that dress."

She saw through my misdirection but thankfully didn't push harder. "And in the morning, you're going to call your brother."

Five sleepless hours later, I could honestly say I'd stuck to my word. I called Kyle as soon as I thought it was reasonable, but the call went straight to voicemail. So I did the next best thing and sent him a text.

Me: *Want to do breakfast?*

The text back came about two hours later. Short and to the point.

Kyle: *Already home. You can't use me as your token gay brother anymore.*

I read the text a number of times. He was gone, and he was rightfully angry. There was no salvaging this mess, and I had no one to blame but myself. And for the first time in I couldn't remember how long, I cried.

CHAPTER 1

NATHAN

Six Months Later

Elliot Mitchell, Esq., graduated New York University, top five in his class, 2012. Eight years at Pierce, McClain, and Marisol, New York City, New York.

The Pierce, McClain, and Marisol. They were one of the top family law firms in the city. I knew this because I'd graduated from NYU myself, though a year after Elliot, and I'd contemplated throwing my resume to them before I'd landed a job perfectly suited for me in an area of town much more affordable than Central Park.

I sometimes missed my old brownstone, even with its drafty windows and cold floors. The neighborhood shops and restaurants had made the imperfections of the building well worth it, until I'd moved back to Nashville the year before to help my mom out.

And now she was retiring in a few months and had hired an attorney behind my back. One I had not personally vetted. I didn't have the budget at the moment to hire a second attorney, so I needed to make sure that this was going to work out before I offered the job to another attorney, a guy I'd been talking to for a few weeks now and had a good feeling about.

There was a small chance that I'd been playing my cards too close to the vest because my mom hadn't realized I'd been close to offering the job to someone. Now I had this Elliot guy who had been thrown in front of me, and I needed to figure out what to do with him.

I waited for the phone call to connect while I read the resume again. In the twelve hours since my mom had dropped the bombshell on me that she'd hired a new attorney behind my back, I'd read and reread this sheet of paper. I felt like I could list everything about Elliot Mitchell, but I didn't *know* the man. I hadn't met him. I hadn't talked to him. This was all my mom's doing.

"Pierce, McClain, and Marisol." The woman who answered was every bit the crisp New Yorker I'd expect to be answering a phone in a large New York City law firm. "How may I direct your call?"

I sat up straighter in my chair. "Mr. Richard Pierce, please." I'd been practicing for an hour to say his name and not laugh. I really hoped he didn't go by Dick in his personal life.

"Please hold." The line went silent and I sat back while being connected with his secretary. I knew better than to assume I'd get directly in touch with the head partner on the first shot.

I propped my feet up on my desk and leaned back in my chair as the phone rang three times. "This is Richard," a strong voice answered, and I nearly fell off my chair.

"Good morning, Richard. My name is Nathan Johnson, with Smith-Johnson Family Law in Tennessee. I was hoping to speak to you about a former employee." I gave myself a pat on the back for how quickly I'd pulled myself together.

He hummed in acknowledgment. "Yes, Elliot." I obviously wasn't the first one to contact Richard.

"Yes, sir," I confirmed. "I'm taking a guess that you spoke with my mother, Connie Smith-Johnson?"

"She's a force to be reckoned with." His chuckle was warm, and I got a good vibe from him.

I laughed despite the tension in my shoulders. "That she is. Then again, you've not met my brothers and sisters. We got it honestly."

His booming laugh caused me to pull my phone from my ear, but I broke out in the first genuine smile I'd had since dinner the night before. "What questions might you have that your mom has not already grilled me on? I'm telling you—she would have made a great prosecutor."

He had no idea. "The truth is she hired Elliot without speaking to me. She has the best intentions, but now I'm stuck looking at a sheet of paper and trying to figure out if Mr. Mitchell will be a good fit to work closely with."

As I thought about what I'd said and how preposterous this call had to be to him, I knew he had every right to tell me to speak with my mom and that he didn't have time for this. I held my breath until Richard began to speak. "Elliot is a very bright young man."

Cautious.

Alarm bells were ringing.

"But?" I inquired when he didn't volunteer more information.

I could hear the humor in his voice as he spoke. "There are privacy laws in place to protect this type of conversation."

We could go around like this for hours. I'd gone to school in New York, and I'd faced some of the harshest family judges in the city. He wasn't going to scare me away. "I'm well aware. However, in this case Mr. Mitchell has already been given a job at Smith-Johnson. Consider me a colleague you are venting to."

"Yes, I see what you mean. You are much like your mother."

In spite of myself, I smiled. "That I am."

The sound of Richard's grin through the phone as he answered was infectious. "I really should have let Libby pick up this call. This is what I get for arriving before my assistant."

I looked out my own door to my brother's vacant seat, wondering when he'd show up for the day. I didn't say anything to Richard, though. Silence made even the most experienced lawyers nervous. And just like I'd hoped, Richard took a breath in and began to speak. "Elliot is incredibly intelligent and driven. However, I think he's been driven by the wrong factors his entire life. He resigned after I refused to offer him a partnership."

This was interesting. I was scratching notes rapidly on the legal pad in front of me as Richard spoke, and I gave a hum to let him know I was listening.

"Truthfully, if I thought that being made partner here was truly what Elliot wanted for himself, I would have done it."

I hadn't been expecting him to say that.

"I worked with Elliot for eight years. He was nearly part of my family." His laugh said there was something more to that statement, but he didn't elaborate and I didn't ask. "However, he's never been truly happy, and I don't know why." He hummed quietly to fill the space, but I could tell he'd gotten lost in his thoughts. "I sort of pushed him out the door, if you will."

I wasn't stupid. There was something that Richard wasn't telling me, but I got the impression it wasn't about work.

Now I was at a crossroads. I could either move forward and take a chance on Elliot or tell him to take a hike. I looked down at the sheet of paper in my hand again. *What's your story, man?* "Thank you for your time, Richard. I appreciate it."

"Not a problem, Nathan. I hope I've given you some clarity."

Yes, in the form of mud. I didn't say that and instead told him goodbye. All that was left to do was wait for Elliot to show up in two weeks. I wasn't sure when it had happened, but at some point I'd decided to give the enigma a chance.

A bundle of wild brown hair and indigo eyes nearly tumbled into my office holding two cups of coffee. His black pants were nearly painted on, his crisp fuchsia dress shirt not much looser, and the ridiculous striped bowtie was obnoxious around his neck.

"Hey, I'm so not late." Then his eyes narrowed as he set one of the coffee cups on my desk. "Did you sleep here again? I'm going to tell Zander on you."

"I went home." And it was the truth. I'd gone home, gotten a shower, and collapsed into my bed when my phone had pinged with an email notification. I knew I shouldn't have looked, but curiosity and all that. So I'd rolled over, grabbed my phone, and saw it was an email from my mom with Elliot's resume and an apology about how she shouldn't have sprung it on me.

The apology was nice, but the thing that had caught my eye was his impressive resume. On paper he looked like a good fit. But there hadn't been enough there to really know if he would fit with my vision for Smith-Johnson Family Law.

I'd spent most of the night tossing and turning, only to finally give up around four. That being said, I'd been here since just before five pondering the best next steps.

Austin narrowed his expressive eyes. "You look like you need a double."

"Probably a triple if I'm being honest."

"Conveniently, that's exactly what I got you." His grin was mischievous, but I could see concern in his eyes. "After you stormed out last night, I was worried about you. You've been really uptight lately."

Some of my frustration at the last twelve-plus hours drained at the sincerity in Austin's voice. He was a ball of energy who could just as easily be at pole dancing lessons as chasing our brother Seth down the ice in full hockey gear, but he was also incredibly in tune with everyone in the family. He felt it deeply when we were upset, and he worried about us all.

"I don't like surprises." Scrubbing my face with my hands, I pointed to the seat across from me. "Sit. I've got a story to tell you."

Austin's indigo eyes turned nearly purple as he approached cautiously. "This sounds serious. Like, is this a coffee or a whiskey conversation?"

My bark of laughter surprised me. "It's barely eight a.m."

"Whiskey goes great with coffee," Austin responded. "And you've got a really nice bottle in your cabinet."

I narrowed my eyes at my brother. "Stay out of my liquor stash, pip-squeak."

Austin snorted. "I remember when you used to *actually* scare me. So, no liquor?"

"No liquor."

He sighed and settled into the seat. "Fine. You really do take yourself too seriously."

"Do you want the story or not?"

Austin made a zipping motion over his lips and held his hand out to me in a gesture to continue.

Where did I begin? I hadn't actually told anyone what had been going on in my head. The best place was probably the beginning, so I started there. "When I first moved back, Dad came to me to vent. He'd just discovered that there was a member at the club who was at risk of losing his kids when his husband died suddenly. The in-laws had somehow discovered that they were members of DASH and threw a holy fit that started even before the death of his husband."

Austin's hands balled into fists and he growled, his eyes turning a dark, stormy blue. I simply scoffed because that hadn't been the half of it. "Being ultra-religious conservatives, when their son died, they decided that the son-in-law was not fit to be a parent and would corrupt the children, despite them having almost no contact with the family for years before then."

"Closed-minded pricks." The storm that had settled in Austin's eyes spoke of his contempt as much as his voice.

I couldn't disagree with his statement. "Very long story somewhat short is that the guy was one court date away from losing the kids. His attorney was totally ignorant about BDSM and unwilling to learn anything about it. I got the impression he wasn't much better than the guy's in-laws. It took me all of ten minutes talking with this guy to realize he was seriously fucked if he kept his attorney. He fired the attorney, I took the case on, and after a number of sleepless nights, a few delayed court dates, and a lot of arguing, my client got to keep the kids."

Austin let out a breath he'd been holding and sank into his seat. "And they say you're an asshole."

I chuckled. "I *am* an asshole. But I'm not unreasonable. I know the law, and I know BDSM. Being a Dom who's active in the local BDSM community allowed me to gain his trust as well as know how to handle this case. There was no learning curve for me in regards to their relationship. The guys had kept their D/s relationship behind closed doors, and he was a doting father who'd just lost his submissive and was near losing his kids. He was a mess and the potential of losing his kids was making a shitty situation worse. This should have been a cut and dry thing, the judge should have thrown the custody dispute out as soon as it came across his desk. Except the first attorney had fucked it up royally and nearly cost the guy his kids."

"I could only imagine how stressful that would be.

Damn, I'm glad you took the case."

"Me too. But afterward, I realized we could be doing a lot more for the community. Mom's not as active in DASH. Sure, she's around for a scene here or there, but she's a silent partner, and not everyone knows her or is comfortable talking with her. They see me around a lot: at munches, in the club, doing scenes. They know I'm a safe person to talk to."

It was just something that happened when your parents owned Dom And Sub Haven, the only gay BDSM club in middle Tennessee. Our dad was known as Master Zachary in the community and was a well-respected man. I'd been involved in the scene since I was in college but had jumped into the DASH community with both feet when I'd moved back.

Austin's head bobbed up and down. "Yeah, I get that. It makes total sense. Besides, no matter how open and nonjudgmental Mom is, it's different to talk with a sixty-five-year-old pansexual woman who's married to a man and talking with a gay guy in his mid-thirties. Like it or not, there's going to be a bias there."

I grunted. He was unfortunately right, and I'd witnessed it firsthand over the last few years. People really liked my mom, but they didn't think she'd understand. "I've been taking cases for members on the side since then. But I want to shift focus to more of the BDSM and LGBT side of things."

Austin's eyes widened with the knowledge. "Ohhhh.

Oh, that makes sense!"

"And I've been looking for a lawyer who will mesh well with that. It's not been easy. Mom took it to mean that I *haven't* been looking."

Austin was understanding the problem more as I spoke. "And she took it upon herself to find an attorney, thinking she was helping you out."

"Yeah. This might be a time I've kept things too close to the vest, but I didn't want to rock the boat all at once. I do enough of that without telling her I'm changing my focus when she retires. I flipped when she told me that she's leaving this year because I wanted to have more time to get *my* shit in order and be ready to switch gears."

Austin's eyes were as big as saucers as he processed the information. "Yeah. I totally get it. What do you think about this guy, though? He's from New York and Chicago. He's got to be open-minded, right?"

I bit my lip. "I hope. I won't lie—I tried calling, but his phone went right to voicemail and I was worried that I'd scare him off if I just flat out left a message."

"Definitely leave message delivery to me, please."

My stony veneer cracked at Austin's words. "Deal." I took a sip of my coffee. "Thank you for this. I really needed it. Anyway, I spoke with his old boss, and there's promise there, but I'm not completely sold."

Austin raised a shoulder as he sipped his own coffee. "I guess time will tell."

Yeah, time would tell.

CHAPTER 2

ELLIOT

The boxes piled up by my hotel door were overwhelming. "What the hell am I doing?"

Emma's voice was a calming presence I desperately needed right now. "You're taking control of your life."

"I moved to Tennessee!" Tennes-fucking-see. The same state as my brother. I was working for a person I'd only met on a video conference. This was by far the most insane, asinine thing I'd ever done in my life.

"You're closer to your brother."

I winced. Yeah, about that. I knew he lived in Winchester, or at least that was where he got mail, but I had no idea where that was in Tennessee. "I still haven't spoken to him. He could literally live on the other side of the state. You know, over the mountains and through the woods!"

"I'm pretty sure the saying is 'over the river and through the woods.' And I looked it up. It's about an hour and a half southeast of you." Rustling sounded from the other end of the line. I guessed Emma was getting into bed. It was an hour later in New York, and she'd have an early morning the next day. "You still haven't called him? It's been over six months."

"I've called a few times. He hasn't answered."

She sighed. "Oh, Elliot." After a pause, she continued, though she sounded disappointed in me. "You know what? We're going to focus on happier topics. Are you looking forward to tomorrow?"

How was that happier? "I think I might puke."

"How'd your parents handle the move?"

I couldn't remember the last time I'd seen either of them. "Well, the housekeeper told me goodbye as I packed the car. And the chef gave me a breakfast sandwich and a bagged lunch." It had been my favorite when I was a kid: a peanut butter and jelly sandwich, a package of fruit snacks, a handful of cheese cubes, an apple, and a bag of baby carrots. The juice box had been replaced with a canned coffee. I'd been halfway through my lunch before I realized that neither my mom nor my dad had ever made me a lunch. I couldn't even remember the last time I'd seen one of them actually cook.

Truthfully, my parents were still pissed about how things ended with Emma. The wedding had been a disaster of epic proportions and all they could see was that their son was now unwed, unemployed, and living at home while he found a job. When they found out that I took a job in Tennessee, my mom had scoffed and informed me that I was throwing away my career. My dad had looked at me dumbly and asked why I'd want to go *there*.

Would it have been better to stick it out at Richard's firm? Maybe.

Would I have been happier in the long run? I honestly didn't know.

"Your family is a piece of work." She was quiet for a few seconds, then a small hum came from the other side of the line and fingers worked furiously at the keyboard. "You know, there's a place in the city called Vortex." She paused for a response, but I had no idea what she was talking about.

"What's Vortex?"

She sighed. "A really popular gay club. There's pictures here of a few musicians going into it."

The phone tumbled to the bed and I scrambled to get it. Why was I shaking? "What?" And the way my voice cracked did not help matters.

"It's time. Remember, we set each other free. If that means I have to come down there when you're settled and drag your ass to that club, you're going."

"One thing at a time. Please? Dammit, you're a force of nature."

"We've been talking about this for nearly seven months now, Elliot. You're going to take control of your life. You did something your parents didn't support. You're in

Tennessee; we're not together. There's no pretending anymore. You're free."

"I'm going to go try to get some sleep."

Emma actually cackled at me but let me go. "I expect a call tomorrow night."

Sleep didn't come easily, but sometime in the wee hours of the morning it found me. Several hours later when my alarm went off, it wasn't a welcome sound. Of course, I was going to be grateful for the fact that I wasn't fighting New York City traffic at seven in the morning. I was far enough outside of Nashville proper that at quarter to nine, there was some traffic but nothing unbearable.

And how weird was it that the office was nine-to-five? I'd been assured on Friday that no one would be there before nine and to not bother arriving before then. But there was no way I could wait that long, so I was anxiously waiting in my car in the parking lot at ten minutes to nine.

The only car in the parking lot when I'd arrived had been a black Mercedes G-Wagon. I didn't know a lot about cars—I'd been living in NYC since I was eighteen and hadn't needed a vehicle until I'd moved back to Chicago—but I knew a G-Wagon when I saw one. And even parked half the lot away from it, the thing looked pristine. I could only imagine what the inside looked like.

At 8:59, two more vehicles pulled up. A guy with brown hair juggling two coffees, a messenger bag, and a phone popped out of a newer SUV, nowhere near as expensive as the Mercedes. I then watched in horror as the guy walked over to the G-Wagon and ran his finger along the hood.

"Austin!" A gray-haired woman scolded. I recognized her from the interview. Connie Smith-Johnson, my new boss. "Do not piss your brother off before we've even walked in the door."

The guy shrugged a shoulder. "He needs to get the stick out of his ass. Besides, I brought him coffee."

My stepping out of the car caught Connie's attention. She spun and her face broke out into a broad grin. "Elliot! So glad to finally meet you in person. Austin, this is Elliot Mitchell, the new attorney."

The guy who had just swiped his finger across the gorgeous SUV looked over at me with wide eyes and a wicked grin. "Oh, he's going to be great."

I had no idea what that meant, but I was too drawn to the way the sun was hitting his eyes. They were nearly purple. I'd never met someone with purple eyes before. Even in the romance novels Emma and I had read in New York, I'd never heard of a character with purple eyes. "Your eyes are purple." My own eyes widened in surprise. "Shit, I'm sorry."

Austin grinned even bigger. "In the sun they do look purple. Wilder tells me they're indigo or cornflower blue. They change in different lights."

My mouth flapped open and on some level I knew I was bungling this first meeting, but I was totally in awe of his eyes. "They aren't contacts?"

"Nope!" Austin popped the *p* but was grinning as he did so. "Au naturel! Something with Mom and Dad's genes gave me and Wilder these eyes. Though Nathan, Heather, and Seth didn't get them. Neither did Zander and Mallory or Larson and Brian." He shrugged and I was left confused as to what I'd just been told.

Connie laughed. "I hope you're a coffee drinker because you'll need it around here. And, for a little background, Austin just listed off all our kids."

Now I really was confused. "That was a lot of names."

She grinned in a way I'd seen very few people do when talking about their family. "It is. You'll never keep them all straight, but I had two kids from a previous marriage, my husband—Zachary—had two kids from a previous relationship, and together we have five. You're going to get tired of seeing us around, hate to say it. This office is pretty central to everyone, so it tends to be a meeting ground for the family. Come on in, I'll introduce you to Nate. He's really the one you'll be working with most often."

Austin was already at the door, balancing the cups on top of one another. His phone was tucked under his chin, and he was working to unlock the door. "Nate!" I heard him yell as he entered.

"Austin's a morning person."

I finally laughed. "I can tell."

"Nathan is a..." She trailed off as we entered the building to a booming voice echoing down the hallway.

Austin was running back toward us, only one coffee in his hand and already down his messenger bag.

"Save me!" Austin gasped as he hid behind his mom.

Connie swiped at him. "In the mood you're in, you probably deserved it."

"Austin Cooper Smith-Johnson, what the shit is this? Chocolate and whipped cream! I know that I told you a double shot when you texted!"

Connie sighed. "Please tell me you didn't fuck with his coffee. He's going to kill you, and I think I could argue to the judge that it was justifiable."

Austin handed his mom the coffee he was holding. "Here, it's the right one." Then he was gone, dashing down another hallway, his laughter following him.

"Where the fuck did he g—" The man, Nathan, stopped bellowing as he stepped into the lobby and saw me standing with his mom. His perfectly tailored suit looked to belong on a Fashion Week runway, not in a law firm in Tennessee. It hugged every muscle in his legs and arms, and the unbuttoned coat showed off a trim waist and broad chest. My eyes kept going upward until I reached his face, where I was met with a strong chin set in annoyance, a very short and well-maintained beard covering his jawline, and a gold hoop in one ear.

Then I caught sight of his eyes. They were the color of a hurricane. Was that even possible?

Well, before that day I might not have thought it possible, but given that I was seeing it, it must have been. Gray and green twisted and intermingled within his irises, just like the skies over Manhattan when a hurricane blew in.

I was so mesmerized by his eyes, I almost missed taking in the close-cropped hair on the sides of his head or the longer, spiked portion at the top. *Almost*, not *didn't*. There was a distinction there that was important, but at the moment, I couldn't figure out why.

Nathan hadn't uttered another word once he'd spotted me, but if possible, his eyes turned even stormier.

Connie thrust the cup of coffee into his hand, and for some reason, I found myself surprised he didn't crush it. "Don't kill Austin. How long have you been here? Your engine is cool."

He narrowed his eyes at her, though he didn't look as angry with her as he did with the rest of the world. The man I was going to be working for looked more on edge than I felt. This was going to be a disaster. "Couldn't sleep."

"Usually helps if you get into your bed," his mom responded without missing a beat. Then she waved her hand between Nathan and me. "Nate, meet Elliot. Elliot, this is Nate."

Emotions flew across his face, and I did something I rarely did. I took a step back. He had a few inches on me, though I was used to that. I wasn't the tallest guy at just shy of six feet, but it was the intensity of Nathan that drew me up short.

"Nathan," he said by way of greeting.

It wasn't easy, but I forced myself to keep my voice

steady as I spoke. "Nice to meet you." My voice hadn't broken and I hadn't stuttered, but he still looked like he could break me in two.

"I'll be in my office." Nathan turned and walked away.

Connie pinched the bridge of her nose and sighed. "He'll warm up. He's not usually such a grumpy ass... Wait, I take that back. He is. It's been worse since I told him I was retiring at some point this year."

My eyes popped open wide. "Retiring?" She was retiring and was going to leave me with him?

She smiled fondly. "I'll still be around. I can promise you that no one will get rid of me that easily. Nate will relax once he sees that you're a good fit."

I hoped that would be the case, but judging from the brief encounter we'd had, I wasn't so sure that would actually happen.

Austin appeared from a different hallway. "Is he gone?"

Connie sighed. "Yes, he's gone. Couldn't you have waited to torment him until after he'd met Elliot?"

The young guy grinned broadly. "He takes himself way too seriously."

Connie didn't respond to the statement, and I suspected she got into the middle of way too many arguments with nine kids. "Austin, please show Elliot around. I think there's some more paperwork that needs to be sorted out as well." She turned to me and offered a bright smile, nearly identical to Austin's. "I'm around. If my door's open, I'm available to chat. Come to me with anything you need."

I began to nod my head, but Austin cut me off. "Let's get you to your office. Don't worry—my desk separates your office and Grouchy's."

My smile couldn't have been more forced as I spoke. "Great."

Austin saw through my smile and chuckled as he began to walk. "Nate's a control freak. We love him, and he's a damn good lawyer. Be open and honest with him and things will go well. I'd say his bark is worse than his bite, but I've seen the marks he's left on guys."

It was a good thing I was behind Austin because I could feel as my eyes bugged slightly at the comment. He'd just outed his brother like it was no big deal. I could already hear Emma in my head screaming, "I told you so."

My heart was still pounding uncomfortably in my chest as he stopped in an open doorway. I couldn't figure out what was making my pulse ratchet up or my palms sweat, but I found myself drying my hands on my pants. Nathan wasn't the first gay man I'd encountered. Hell, he wasn't the first gay man I'd worked with.

I was going to blame it on lack of sleep and being on edge in general. It was just one more thing to add to my ever-changing life. Today had already thrown me a number of curveballs and it was only twenty past nine in the morning.

"Your office," Austin announced proudly, his hand waving grandly at the blank canvas. There were a few bookcases against the wall and a large desk sat in front of them, but otherwise it was truly a blank slate. Nothing but a few law books on the shelves. "Mom said to take you out later today to pick out a laptop for you. We'll do that at lunchtime. How long have you been here anyway?"

Information was coming rapid fire and I barely had time to process it all, and I was still trying to settle myself from the encounter with Nathan. I settled on the one thing I could answer. "I got in last night."

Austin's brows pulled together. "So, where are you staying?"

"For now, a hotel. I need to find something this week."

Expressive eyes showed surprise, but then joy. "Oh! I can take you around."

I wanted to decline, but the truth was I had no idea what I was doing or where to look. "That would be great. I'm a fish out of water. I'm guessing the housing market is a little different here than in New York."

Austin snorted a laugh. "Yeah, just a bit, but in a good way. We'll make time in the next few days. Hopefully, get you out of that hotel before you go bankrupt."

I walked in and set my bag on the desk. "It definitely costs more than an apartment."

"I've got a few ideas already. Let me make some calls."

A shadow filled the doorway, and the two of us looked upward to see Nathan filling the frame. He still didn't look amused, but he didn't look downright murderous anymore, and his eyes softened slightly when he saw his brother. "Thank you for the coffee—the right one—pip-squeak."

Austin rolled his eyes, but the grin belied any annoyance at the nickname. "You should know by now that I always keep you well caffeinated." He reached up onto his tiptoes to give his brother a smacky kiss on the cheek, which Nathan growled at. Then Austin turned to me and grinned. "I'll be back in time for lunch. Don't let the bear scare you."

Easier said than done. And what was that about the marks he left on guys? Jesus, what had I walked into?

Before I could figure out what to say to keep Austin around, he was gone, making an excuse about some filings and phone calls.

Nathan might have been pissed earlier, but now that he'd had some coffee, he just looked stern. "My office, now."

I'd never been a pushover, and despite the guy looking like he could eat me for lunch, I wasn't going to be his doormat. Yet, despite my brain's desire to tell him to fuck right off, my feet were moving before he tacked on a belated "Please."

CHAPTER 3

NATHAN

Elliot's eyes flashed with all sorts of colors at my words. Anger had burned clear at first, and I'd fully expected him to tell me to go fuck myself. I realized what an asshole I sounded like. Elliot wasn't a little green attorney that didn't know a complaint from a deposition; he was actually a year older than me. He'd graduated from the same law school I had, and he'd been working at a top-tier firm for years.

Before I could soften the words, he started toward me. As fast as the fury in his eyes had appeared, it was replaced with confusion. I still added a "Please" in hopes that it would make the following conversation more comfortable for both of us.

Thanks to my mom springing this hire on me, and his phone always going to voicemail, I hadn't had the luxury of feeling him out before he started. Maybe I should have left that voicemail I kept contemplating, but it had never felt right at the time. Now I needed to have a very blunt—

likely uncomfortable—conversation with him. It was better to have it now, especially since I'd already overheard that he didn't actually have a place to live yet. If he was going to freak out about my plans for the firm, it was better to do it before he had a lease, or worse yet, purchased a home.

I pushed the door to my office open. It was nearly identical to Elliot's office but fully furnished, and pictures of my siblings and parents seemed to grow by the week. I swore someone took pleasure in driving me insane by adding shit while I wasn't around.

Elliot looked around the office as we made our way to a small table and chairs I kept for more informal conversations. I needed him to feel like a colleague, an equal, not a client.

Swallowing my pride, I began with an apology. "Sorry for how you met me this morning. I'm not a morning person. Hell, sometimes I don't feel like an afternoon or evening person either, but I'm really not functional until I get coffee. Austin knows that and pushes my buttons. Do you have siblings?"

He replied with a small nod, then seemed to realize words were probably necessary in this situation. "A brother."

I chuckled. At least he'd get it. "Ah, so then you know."

His eye twitched in a way that told me there was a story there that I didn't have. "We-we're not close." After a pause, he added quietly. "At all."

There was definitely a story there, but it wasn't my

place to press. "Sorry to hear that. My siblings—my entire family, really—are tight-knit. Sometimes, I think it would be nice to have some space, but I couldn't imagine not having them around. Now that I'm back, I realize how much I missed them while I was gone."

Elliot's answering scoff spoke volumes. "My family isn't close. It's not just my brother and me. It's who we are as a family and there's not much that I can do about that."

Right, touchy topic. Time to change gears. "I know that my mom hired you and she was trying to help me out, but there are some things we need to talk about before you really settle in here." I sounded like an asshole, but he was going to have to get used to it if he was going to stay here long term. I wasn't one to mince words.

Elliot's back stiffened at my words, and his eyes dropped subtly. He was putting on a good show of being stoic, but there were nerves below the surface that I could read like an open playbook.

"You're going to find this out soon enough, so I'm just going to lay this on the line now. My parents own DASH—Dom And Sub Haven. It's a BDSM club that caters to the gay community here in Nashville. The entire state, really." I watched as his eyes widened to the point that I could see little flecks of gold in what I'd originally mistaken as dark brown eyes.

I pushed ahead. This was going to be a good test to see if Elliot had a snowball's chance of making it here. "Much of the family is part of DASH and involved in the BDSM community in one way or another."

Elliot swallowed, his Adam's apple bobbing hard in his throat, but he didn't say anything. If Elliot was anything like me, it was hard to stun this big city lawyer into silence, but I'd done it. The question I had was simple: why? Unfortunately, the answer wouldn't be so simple, and I knew that.

"I've read your resume countless times over the last few weeks. You and I are pretty much cut from the same cloth, at least in terms of education and work experience. I graduated from NYU a year behind you."

The surprise was back in Elliot's face and he finally found words. "I don't remember you at all."

I grinned. "Likewise. We must have run in different circles."

It was his turn to laugh, but it was humorless. "That's not hard to believe. I didn't run in many circles. Law school was a means to an end for me. I didn't get involved in much more than I absolutely had to in order to graduate with a job." He winced at his words. "That didn't come out right. There was a lot of pressure on me to succeed in law school. My parents expected good grades and for me to graduate in three years with not just any job lined up. They wanted..." He trailed off for a moment as he thought. "That's wrong. They expected it, really."

I leaned back in my chair and studied the man in front of me. Definitely a different experience than mine. I'd worked hard, but I'd played hard too. I'd been involved in a number of clubs but had also been part of the local kink community. I'd had my first true taste of the lifestyle while I was in college here in Nashville, but while at NYU, I'd gone to one of the local BDSM clubs and joined. I'd learned all about D/s relationships and power exchange. To say I'd been busy in law school was an understatement, but I credited my success afterward to my experiences at the club.

Simply understanding my need to be in control usually helped me temper the urge to argue over everything that didn't go my way. As a lawyer in the city, that happened frequently. I also understood the importance of negotiations.

"I couldn't imagine trying to live up to that pressure." It was an honest assessment of the situation. My parents had never pressured me into law school; they'd never pressured me to find a good job. They just wanted me happy. I was the one who pushed myself.

My drive was what led me to the place I was at today. With the ability to continue to work hard and play harder. I glanced out my window to see my baby: a brand new Mercedes AMG G-Wagon. Obsidian black metallic, chrome accents, twenty-two-inch rims. She sparkled in the morning sun. And I couldn't help but grin at the sight.

Turning my attention back to Elliot, I cleared my throat in an attempt to bring my mind back to the topic at hand. "I'm going to be blunt with you because you deserve that honesty from me. I haven't talked to my mom about this, mainly because I've been working the details out in my head, but when she retires, I plan to expand the focus of the firm."

I could tell I had his attention because he'd leaned forward on the table and a furrow had formed in his brow as he listened to me speak. "Explain."

Short and to the point, an air of confidence radiating off him. It was the first moment since I'd met him that I saw the hint of a big city lawyer shine through his generalized nervousness.

"There is a need in the BDSM community for a law firm that can represent and understand them. Now, I don't expect that my entire business will be built off the BDSM community. However, I want to make it a more well-known part of the firm."

Elliot had gone completely unreadable. Everything from his mouth to his eyes was completely blank.

I went out on a limb. "I gather you are not part of the BDSM lifestyle."

The statement startled an uncomfortable laugh out of Elliot. "As my ex pointed out to me, I'm vanilla as they come. There's not even flakes of vanilla bean in me."

And that left me in a pickle. "I don't need you to be in the lifestyle, but I need to know that you're going to be okay with who we represent."

Elliot chewed on his bottom lip as I spoke. It was a nervous habit that drove me insane. My older brother had a tendency to do the same thing when he got nervous and I always had to try to keep myself from reaching over and pulling his lip free. The only reason I managed to stop myself from doing so to Elliot was that we barely knew each other and I was at work.

His eyes clouded over as he thought, then blew out a breath, his lip coming free on its own. "Can you break down what you see this representation looking like? Pretend I'm a total idiot. Which in this particular case, I am. And it kills me to admit that."

"I can respect that." I liked that he wasn't shooting me down, though I'd seen in his eyes the desire to tell me to take a long walk off a short pier as he'd thought about what I was telling him. "About a year ago, I helped a guy retain custody of his children when his husband passed away unexpectedly. The shortened version is his husband's parents had major issues with the lifestyle and had felt that my client was abusing his husband, despite it being a consensual relationship. His first attorney knew nothing about BDSM and had clearly felt the same as the in-laws. I stepped in at the last minute and managed to successfully argue the case."

Elliot's eyes had gone wide as he listened and he hung on my every word. As I finished, he seemed to withdraw in thought. "I'm not as closed-minded as I likely appear."

Those were not the words I had expected to hear from him, but really looking at him, I suspected he wasn't fully talking to me. He was lost somewhere in thought, and I had a feeling it was a million miles from my office.

He blinked back to the here and now and seemed completely pulled together. "I personally do not have experience with BDSM, but my brother and his boyfriend are in a... well, a unique relationship, for lack of better words. I've never thought about it before, but it probably is BDSM, and I could see how, on the outside, it is something that would be hard to talk about."

I liked this side of Elliot more than the one who looked two seconds away from bolting at any given moment. "For most of us, it is incredibly difficult to be authentic in our daily lives while kink is such a huge part of who we are. I have never met any self-respecting member of the community who would expect a non-kinky person to be kinky, yet vanilla—as you called it—people often refuse to see past their own perceptions of what a relationship *should* look like and try to force *their* view of relationships on the kink community."

Elliot paled noticeably the longer I spoke, though his voice gave nothing away. "I could understand that."

The extended pause afterward told me that he wasn't going to say anything else, so I pushed ahead. At the current time, I figured I had a fifty-fifty shot of scaring Elliot right out of Tennessee before lunchtime. "Ideally, I want an attorney who is open and accepting and even willing to get involved with every aspect of representation. Quite frankly, I want someone working with me that isn't going to have a problem with it. You don't have to be in the lifestyle, but I expect... no, wait, I demand, respect and understanding from any attorney who will be working here."

Elliot was quiet for a long time after I spoke. When he finally found words, they weren't the giant *Fuck you* I'd almost expected. They were carefully thought out. "I have no experience with the BDSM community. Like I said before, I'm as vanilla as they come. Like I also said, I have a brother in a nontraditional relationship, so I can't say I have no knowledge of it. What I can tell you is that I need time to really think about how I feel being involved with the..." He trailed off as he gathered his thoughts, the first real time he'd shown any hesitation to speak of since he'd begun his reply.

Once he found the words he wanted, he continued just as professionally as before. "With the community. I don't want to do a poor job representing someone simply because I can't or don't understand the lifestyle or connect with it in any meaningful way. That isn't fair to them, and in the end, it's not fair to you. So I'm going to ask for some time."

Diplomatic, concise, well thought out. Even though I didn't like his words, I knew that I couldn't have expected more. This would either work or it wouldn't. I couldn't lie—part of me hoped like hell it would work. Elliot might not have been the person I'd hired, but I could easily admit that I was tired of looking for an attorney. I needed someone soon if I was going to get them up to speed with everything before the end of the year or whenever my mom decided to finally retire.

I found myself nodding to his request. "Yes. Of course. I'm here to answer any question you might come across while you're making a decision."

Elliot gave a wry smile. "I figured you might be able to do that."

CHAPTER 4

ELLIOT

I'd made it through the rest of my first day. Not entirely certain how I'd managed or even what I'd done for the remainder of Monday. All I knew was that Nathan was gay and part of the BDSM community. His family was not only a part of it but what sounded like a driving force behind it. And then, in all of that, he'd also told me he wanted to represent clients from the BDSM community.

That was a lot for a first day.

And I'd been kicked out of the office at five on the nose, being told that the office was closed and it was time to go home. So it wasn't even six, I'd ordered takeout and had a shower, and was left with absolutely nothing to do for the rest of the night.

I needed to talk this out.

Me: *You home yet?*

Emma: *Just got out of my car. What's up?*

Me: *Call me when you're settled. My day was... weird.*

I'd barely hit the send button and my phone was ringing in my hand.

Putting the phone to my ear, I hadn't even said hello and Emma was talking. "Good weird? Bad weird? Weird weird? Spill! The suspense is killing me." A door clicked behind her and a bag hit the floor, along with the distinct sound of her heels thudding against the floor as she kicked them off.

For a moment, I was back in the apartment with her, making dinner while she sipped a glass of wine and I had a beer. Homesickness like I'd never felt before hit me in the pit of my stomach.

"You okay, El?"

Her sincerity threatened to break me, but I swallowed hard a few times before I spoke. "Yeah. I'm okay. Just miss you right now."

"I miss you too. I can't believe we haven't seen each other since January. But you've gotta tell me, how was it? I've been dying to know!"

"Do you want the long or the short version?"

Emma laughed, a warm sound that wrapped around me like a blanket. "Tell me everything."

I collapsed back onto my bed, ignoring the dinner on the desk across the room, and began to tell her everything. "They're nuts. The entire family. Well, at least the three I work with. There's apparently a small army of them, from what I gathered. The woman who hired me, Connie, sprung on me this morning that she's retiring at some point this year. That leaves me to work next to her son Nathan. Oh, and I can't forget Austin. He's her youngest, and Nathan's assistant... and apparently mine too."

I heard a cork pop from a bottle of wine, then Emma sigh as she finally sank into the couch. "And?"

"Let's see. Nathan's scary. Oddly enough, he graduated from NYU a year after me, though I don't remember him at all. He worked in the City for a long time before coming back here to work with his mom. He's got Big City Attorney confidence out the ears and a stick up his ass."

Emma barked out a surprised laugh. "Sounds like you two should get along great. You're the most serious man I know at work. Hell, at home too."

"But I'm not scary."

"No, you're more like a mountain lion cub. You've got a lot of bravado but not so much a real bite to back it up."

Had she just compared me to a Disney cartoon? "I'm not sure exactly how to take that, but the truth is he's flat-out horrifying. First time I met him, he was coming down the hallway threatening to kill his brother for switching his coffee at nine in the morning."

Emma laughed so hard she snorted. "Oh my god, so much better than what happens at my work."

At least she was getting a kick out of this. "I barely made it to my office and he was in there demanding to speak to me."

"I'm sure that went over well."

Better than she'd have assumed. I didn't like being told

what to do, but I'd been powerless to stop my feet from reacting to him. I ignored the statement and continued. "He then proceeded to tell me that his dad owns a BDSM club in Nashville and most of his family is involved in some way or another."

Silence. Emma didn't say a damn thing as I spoke. I actually paused and checked the connection when she'd been quiet for so long. "Did I mention it's a gay BDSM club? And that he heavily alluded to being a member?"

That got Emma responding in a hurry. First it was a gasp, then a quiet "Ohhh," then an all-out delighted giggle. "Only you, Elliot."

"I need advice here, Emma!" I needed a hug and for someone to tell me I wasn't insane for wanting to run the other way. I was going to have to settle for Emma's brutal honesty, because she'd give me nothing less. That's what best friends were for, right?

I heard clicking on a keyboard at the same time she began speaking. "Okay, BDSM one-oh-one."

"What?"

"We're going to learn about BDSM. We can't make a decision unless we have all the information. Neither of us is knowledgeable about the BDSM community. So, let's learn."

My phone pinged, alerting me to Emma trying to connect with a video call. I switched over and was immediately greeted with a screen share. "You're taking this quite seriously."

"This is so much better than reading the brief that got sent over today that I've been dreading. Anyway. Let's get to work."

Emma already had five different sites up before I'd connected, and she was clicking on the first link as she spoke. I winced when I saw the man suspended by hooks through his back. "Too much!" My yelp was far from masculine, but thankfully Emma didn't call me out on it as she quickly flipped tabs.

"Okay, we'll come back to that one later."

I shook my head. "We really don't have to."

She sighed over the line. "This isn't meant to be a 'Can we make Mr. Vanilla turn into Mr. Cookies and Cream.' This is meant to be educational, to see if Mr. Vanilla can be comfortable talking to Mr. Rocky Road and Mr. Moose Tracks."

"You're making me hungry."

"You know what sucks? You're not here to stop me from eating the entire tub of ice cream for dinner. I've had to start buying pints. Okay, let's figure this shit out, Elliot."

The site she had pulled up that time was more like an introduction to various forms of BDSM. The definitions helped a lot. Everything from the *B*, *D*, *S*, and *M*, to terms and kinks. My brain was already overwhelmed when Emma scrolled down the page to an article about common misconceptions of submission and domination.

"Oh, that's interesting," Emma noted as she scrolled

through the pages. "I think I knew a lot of this stuff on an intellectual level, but I never really thought of it."

I'd been caught up in reading about how submissives were never fully out of control. The night was already shaping up to be eye-opening. "Submissives have control of how much control they give up," I read from the website.

Emma hummed. "The Dom is only as powerful as the submissive allows."

She began to scroll and a section caught my eye. "Wait, wait, go back." Emma reversed course and we read together.

"Whoa," she breathed over the line, clearly reading what I was. "That's crazy. BDSM scenes actually decrease psychological distress."

Not what I'd expected, and I was jotting notes down as quickly as I could to reread the information later. The preconceived notions I'd had of BDSM were quickly proving to be unfounded. My shoulders were beginning to relax as my confidence returned. This wasn't feeling as scary and overwhelming as I'd thought.

Then Emma switched tabs again. That time, she'd landed on a page with different forms of D/s relationships. The world of BDSM was far more varied than I'd ever expected it to be. Dom and sub relationships came in every shape and size.

"Awww, look how cute that puppy and his Master are!" Emma's squeal of delight was the same one she made when we came across a puppy in Central Park, and for a moment, I was expecting to look at the screen to see a fluffy ball of fur. When I looked at what she'd seen, my eyes widened in shock.

"That man is wearing a hood that looks like a dog's head."

"He's a puppy! I love that orange color!"

I was more caught up in the strong lines of the puppy's back and thighs. He was clearly muscular and took good care of his body. He looked a lot like the guys I used to see at the gym in New York. His tail was obviously a butt plug that was keeping his arousal evident through the skimpy jock he was wearing.

My dick stirred in my boxers, but I couldn't figure out why. Sure, the man was attractive, but there was nothing about him that drew me to him. I didn't know what it was or why. I was just beginning to figure out that it was something to do with the look in his eyes when Emma scrolled down the page.

The erection that had been threatening deflated quickly when I saw the Daddy and boy in the picture. It wasn't in disgust—it was pain, almost like my worst nightmare had come true. I muttered a curse as I stared at the screen.

Emma was silent. I didn't need to see her face to know she was thinking about my brother as well. She scrolled much slower through the section about Daddy Doms, and I knew she was reading just as closely as I was. Neither of us needed anywhere near that much time to take in information. We were well adept at scanning and skimming, but sometimes that just wouldn't cut it.

I didn't want to know much about my brother's sex life, but reading about the lifestyle in black and white gave me a better understanding of why Kyle was drawn to it. Safety, security, acceptance, unconditional love. We hadn't had much acceptance or unconditional love growing up. Hell, Kyle had bucked the conventionality our parents valued so heavily that I wasn't sure he'd had much safety or security at home either. They couldn't wait for him to leave, and they'd made sure I'd known how disappointed they'd been in him.

Not like they'd needed to tell me. I'd figured that out quickly. Being a few years older than Kyle, I'd seen how they treated us differently. Even as a child, I'd known it was wrong, but when they'd begun to hold tuition and money over my head as a teenager, I hadn't been strong or confident enough to stand up to them.

Long minutes passed before Emma finally uttered a sound. "Huh" was all she said, but it said enough.

I watched the cursor hover over the *next* button for a few seconds. I suspected she was waiting for me to tell her to stop or to click one of the multiple links that had been within the article. I did neither, and she eventually clicked over.

That time, the picture that greeted us was a man naked and on his knees. His hands were clasped behind his back, his erection visible between his legs, while he looked at the man standing in front of him with the most peaceful, blissed-out expression I'd ever seen. Similar to the pup's but so much more... something.

My breath caught in my throat and my heart rate quickened as all the blood in my body rushed south. He was gorgeous. Not necessarily *him* but the way he looked. Had I ever felt peace like that? My eyes flicked up to the man standing over him, his hand crooked and holding the submissive's chin upward. I had no idea who these people were or who took the picture, but it was gorgeous.

I could see Nathan standing in the Dom's place. Not that I was particularly skilled at reading people, but he was a Dom—there was no question in my mind. I didn't know much about the guy, but nothing about him said he'd be the person on his knees.

The real question was why did that thought turn me on more?

Emma began reading about more traditional Dom/sub relationships, oblivious to the way my body and brain had reacted to the picture. "That's interesting. Could you imagine giving control to someone like that?"

Could I? Well, no.

Would I consider it? The thought drew me up short.

Looking back over my adult life, I'd been pushed by my parents and myself to do everything by the book. To be nearly superhuman and excel at everything I tried. And when I failed, when I didn't meet those expectations, the disappointment in myself was near crushing. What would it be like to have someone tell me to stop? To remind me to take care of myself? To not overdo it?

What if that person told me I wasn't good enough? That I needed to do more? That I wasn't enough?

What if I disappointed Nathan?

The thought caught me off guard and my dick deflated.

"No. I couldn't." My voice hadn't come out right, but it was the truth. I couldn't handle disappointing someone else or knowing that I still wasn't enough.

"You okay, El?" Emma's voice was imploring, genuine concern evident in her words, and the screen share ended to show her face staring at me in concern. "You look like you're about to puke."

I shook my head. "I can't do this. I need to cut my losses now. I've still got savings. I can go somewhere else and find work."

Her brown eyes went wide in surprise. "What the hell happened? You were doing fine. We were learning."

My head seemed to be stuck going back and forth. "No. I'm not the right person for the job. He told me he needs someone who can be understanding of the community. Someone who won't judge. I'm not the right person."

Emma's lips had long lost their signature pop of red lipstick, but there was enough color left that even as she pressed her lips into a thin line, they didn't turn white. "Elliot Mitchell, that is not the man I've known for damn near nine years. With the exception of the wedding, I've never seen you treat anyone any differently, no matter who they are. I know you can do this."

And there my head went, once again shaking side to side. I didn't have the words to explain to her that I couldn't face disappointing Nathan. He obviously cared a lot about his clients and about the BDSM community in general. He had genuine goals and wishes for the firm, and I wasn't positive I could be that person. "I can't. Fuck, Em, he has these grand visions of doing all these great things for the BDSM community. I have no experience in that. Until tonight, I didn't even know there were different forms of domination and submission. I can't be this knowledgeable person. I can't disappoint someone else."

Emma's face softened. "Oh, you sensitive oaf. You can't disappoint people."

I snorted. "Top five at NYU? Should have been top. Landed a job with your dad's firm? Should have had a girlfriend to go with it. Get a boyfriend instead?" I shuddered at the thought. "Well, you can guess how that would have gone. Get the girlfriend?" I used air quotes around the word *girlfriend*. "Should have already made partner. Our sham marriage collapsed, I moved back home, and I didn't find a job for six months. Jesus, I've disappointed everyone. You, your dad, your parents, my parents, my brother. I just can't keep disappointing people."

To my surprise, Emma's voice rose in volume as she spoke. "Don't you dare include me in the list of people you've disappointed. You and I, we were all appearances, but what we had—still have—is real, true friendship. We could never have made a marriage work. I can't believe we made a *fake* relationship work as long as we did. We both knew that before we walked down the aisle. And truthfully, I don't think you disappointed my dad either, but you'd have to ask him directly."

I visibly recoiled at the thought of speaking to Richard again. Not after how it had all ended.

"Your parents are assholes. You could settle Mars and they'd tell you that you should have aimed for Jupiter. You'll never be able to please them." She came up for a breath. "You've got work to do where your brother is concerned, and I'm not going to pretend otherwise. You fucked up. You had a chance to make it right and you let your parents get in your head. That need to please them has got to stop. You've got to start living for yourself."

My head hit the headboard and I groaned. Frustration boiled in my stomach and the room felt much too small for the space.

"What did I tell you when you told me you'd take the blame for the wedding disaster?"

I scrubbed at my face, not wanting to relive the moment.

"Elliot."

Her snapped word had me answering. "You told me I had to be honest and be happy."

"Have you been honest with anyone since then? Hell, have you been honest with yourself?"

My silence said more than any words could.

She slapped the end table beside her and I jumped. "That's what I thought. I swear to you, Elliot, I held up my end of the bargain. I told my parents I don't want to date or be married. I told them I'm happy being alone, and that I don't want kids." She allowed a shiver to run through her body at the mention of kids and I felt myself crack a smile. "I made partner, and *dammit*, I'm happy! But you." She pointed a perfectly manicured finger at the screen. "You ran. You ran home to the worst two people I've ever met. You didn't make a true effort to reach out to your brother."

"I called."

She snorted. "And you probably didn't leave a message. You never admitted *your* truth to anyone. You never told your parents, your brother—hell, you probably didn't even tell the fucking bedroom wall! Who are you really disappointing right now, Elliot? Everyone else, or yourself?"

My mouth flapped open and shut a number of times. I didn't have a good answer to her rapid-fire accusations or questions. Fuck, I had no idea what was up at this point. All I knew was that I was miserable and I was seeing failure signs flying at me from every direction.

"That's what I thought. You are going to take this job. You're going to do it because it's a challenge and you're going to learn something new and it's going to give you the opportunity to be part of a community of people who will get you."

She held up her hand. "I did not mean kinky people,

because god forbid you be anything more than vanilla. I mean people of similar sexual orientation." She shook her head. "I really wish you'd fucking admit it because I'm not going to be the first one who says it, and with that, I'm not going to be the one who gives you an out. But dammit, you have to be honest with yourself at some point."

"Fine." My whispered resignation at my next steps seemed to be enough to burst her angry bubble.

"Good. And just remember I'm here for you, Elliot. You're not a disappointment. And I'm going to make sure to hold you to all these things that you've been denying yourself."

My shoulders slumped and I let out a breath. "Fine. Okay. I can do this."

She smiled. "Yes, you can. And you can also go eat that dinner I know you forgot about in order to call me. Love you, Elliot."

I grinned. "Love you too, Em."

I closed my laptop and looked over at the bag of food. "Fuck my life."

CHAPTER 5

NATHAN

I'd been more than a little surprised to see Elliot's car pull up outside on Tuesday morning. Yet there he was, fifteen minutes before nine, sitting in the parking lot. My phone buzzed on my desk and I flipped it over to see who was texting me.

Zander: *How's the new guy?*

Me: *Well, he's in the parking lot again this morning. I guess I didn't scare him off yesterday. Mom told him not to get here until 9, but the last two days he's been here at 8:45.*

Zander: *Try to give him an actual shot. I keep worrying that you're going to stroke out.*

Me: *There's a lot going on here, and I don't know much about him. I thought I scared him half to death yesterday when I spoke with him.*

Zander: *You catch more flies with honey than vinegar.*

What if I didn't want flies? Besides, I was looking for an attorney, not a partner. And I definitely didn't want a fly for a partner. I was pretty sure any partner for me would have to be a unicorn.

I glanced at the family schedule on my computer.

Me: *What are you doing up? You worked the night shift, you're usually dead by now.*

As the chief deputy sheriff in Williamson County, Zander worked weird hours and his sleep schedule was erratic at best. But the fact was, for all the unpredictability in his schedule, Zander predictably crashed hard as soon as he arrived home.

Zander: *I'm making breakfast for Noah. Trying to coax him out of the bedroom with pancakes and bacon. He's going in at ten this morning. I'll sleep when he goes to work.*

I smiled at the text. Zander had been convinced he'd never find a boy. When Noah entered his life, he'd quickly become smitten, and I'd never seen him happier.

Me: *Have a good day.*

Zander didn't respond, but I figured he'd probably gotten sidetracked with Noah. I glanced back outside to see that Elliot was still there, and Zander's words bounced around in my head. Was I being a petulant child and punishing Elliot because my mom was trying to help?

I scrubbed my hands over my face. I hated when I was wrong, but even I could admit that I'd been needlessly blunt with Elliot. I hadn't tempered myself after I'd noticed I was overwhelming him either. Part of me had likely wanted to stick my tongue out at my mom and say *Told you so!* but I was a thirty-four-year-old man and needed to act like it. Mom's heart had been in the right place, and I hadn't even given Elliot a chance to get in the door before I'd been looking for ways to get rid of him.

It was time to admit that I'd judged him based on my initial impression. I'd been so frustrated with my mom that I hadn't given him a chance. After one glance at Elliot, I'd decided he was a straitlaced straight guy who wouldn't get kink or BDSM. Given the chance, I'd gone straight for the shock factor, figuring he'd be back in Chicago before the sun set.

I really was an asshole.

The least I could do would be to go outside and offer him an apology and a key to the office. If I was quick, I might be able to make it to the break room and nab one of the donuts I'd brought in for him. Before I could push back from my desk, the door clicked and I heard Austin's voice filtering down the hallway.

"Seriously, I'll get you a key. Nate's just a grouchy pants. I told you yesterday, ignore him."

I wanted to be annoyed at Austin, but I found myself smiling. Calling me a grouchy pants was a very Austin thing to say. Any of my other siblings would have flat out called me on my shit.

Elliot's voice was quieter, and even from thirty feet away I could hear the hesitancy in it. "He's intense, yeah."

Nice way of calling me an ass.

Austin hadn't seemed to notice anything was off in Elliot's voice. "Wilder says that he's wound so tightly he's going to stroke out before thirty-five. That's only six months from now."

"Wilder?"

My brother was going to overwhelm him in very short order if this kept up. "My older brother." From the sound of his voice, I was pretty sure he was literally bouncing down the hallway. "You'll figure us out soon enough."

They'd been talking as they walked and I could hear them right outside the doorway. Knowing they were there, I started to walk from my desk, hopeful that I could catch Elliot and talk. I'd made it all of a half step when Austin continued. "Oh! Let's do lunch. I called my other brother and I think I found a place for you to live. Even if it's temporary, until you can find something else that suits you. I can take you by on our lunch break. There's an amazing falafel place over there."

The only falafel place in driving distance was right outside of Seth's neighborhood, and Austin loved it.

"Really?" The relief, paired with shock, was evident in Elliot's voice. "That would be awesome. The hotel I'm at is nice and all, but it's going to get pricey. And I haven't had falafel since I left New York."

Seth hated strangers at his house, even at his guest house. The guy valued privacy, which I got. He'd been playing hockey since he could stand and had played all over the US, Canada, and even the world at various levels. His life had been anything but normal once he'd reached the Juniors. He'd lived in Ontario one summer in high school, then moved to Europe to train his junior and senior years of high school. He got drafted out of the European league at eighteen, played a few games with the minor league team, got called up to the NHL, and had never gone back down.

At twenty-five, Seth had been around the block in the hockey world. He'd had fans hounding him at every turn for seven years already and he'd had reporters following him around for a decade. He liked his privacy and rarely let people he didn't know near his house, so I couldn't help but wonder what Austin had had to do to convince Seth to offer up his guest house.

"Okay, I'm going to go poke the bear."

Elliot let out an honest laugh at Austin's antics. "Good luck. I'll be in my office. Please don't rely on me to help. I think Connie dropped some files off she wanted me to look over anyway."

Austin appeared in my doorway not even a second later, his hand fluttering in a dismissive gesture at Elliot's door. He never missed a beat as he stepped into my office, all signs of the jovial man from a moment before gone. "Hey, want to come to lunch today?"

My mouth hung open for a moment as I tried to figure out how to respond. "You just made plans with Elliot."

"You can come with us. We're going to go to Seth's place to see the guest house. I called him last night and he said that it's fine if Elliot crashes there."

I scoffed. "I highly doubt it was that easy."

Austin flashed me a toothy grin. "I like Elliot a lot. He seems really nice, and I think he's going to fit in well here. I told Seth that he's staying at a hotel and could use a place to crash. You know how insane this time of year gets for him. He's rarely there, even if he's in town. Elliot can be there to make sure the house is safe but not be in Seth's personal space either. The odds are he'll find a place before Seth gets back anyway."

It had to be exhausting living in Austin's brain. I couldn't figure out how he got from one topic to the next. "What makes you say that Elliot will fit in here?"

"Have you seen those big brown eyes? He's going to have everyone eating out of the palm of his hand before long." At my eye roll, Austin shrugged. "Hey, you catch more flies."

"Are you and Zander conspiring against me?"

Austin furrowed his brow. "What?"

I waved a hand dismissively in front of my face. "Zander seriously said the exact same thing to me not five minutes ago."

"What can I say? Great minds... well, great minds and Mom and Dad, who pounded that into our heads."

I groaned at Austin. You'd think that after growing up and moving out, the family rules would be forgotten, yet we were reminded of them every time we turned around. Though I could begrudgingly admit that the advice was usually sound, even as an adult. Which was what was leading me to seek Elliot out that morning.

Which really meant that I should be talking to our newest attorney, not my brother. "I'm not going to lunch with you today. Don't railroad Seth into something he's not ready for. I don't care if you two shared a womb; you don't have control over his life. And maybe a little less caffeine in the mornings. If Seth doesn't like it, you and Wilder have an extra room at your place."

I edged around Austin on my way out of my office, ignoring his glower.

In my haste to get away from Austin, I'd forgotten that Elliot's office door was only about ten steps from mine and found myself standing in his doorway before I had my thoughts in order. I wasn't good at apologies and I wasn't good at small talk, but I needed to manage at least one of those things to bridge a gap I knew I'd created on my own.

Any question about the way I'd left things the day before was dashed when Elliot looked up and his eyes widened noticeably. The early morning sun was beaming in through the windows of his office and reflecting off his eyes. I understood what Austin meant by Elliot having people eating out of his hands. His eyes were the most amazing honey brown color with flecks of gold and chocolate. Of course, that only served to remind me just how spooked the guy was. If he could have gone out the window to escape me, I was pretty sure he would have.

I cleared my throat in an attempt to buy another second, but as it turned out it didn't take very long. "Um, hey. Do you have a moment?"

Elliot blinked at me. When he didn't say anything for a long beat, I repeated his name. "Elliot, may I come in?" I hadn't intended to make my voice drop. It was something that happened naturally when I was being assertive. To my surprise, Elliot snapped back to the present, those mesmerizing eyes boring into me, and he finally found his voice.

His back had subtly straightened, and he was watching me closely as he pointed to the chair in front of his desk. I had to give my cock a firm reminder that I'd only shocked him and it had taken Elliot a moment to process my arrival in his office. The reaction had not been the same as a submissive reacting to my growly Dom.

"Have a seat. I was just going through some files Connie left."

He pointed to a small stack of files. For the first time since he'd arrived, he looked confident. It reminded me that he'd been an attorney longer than I had. Different office, different position, same damn job. He'd made it at a top firm in NYC for over eight years. He would be fully capable of handling the stuff my mom currently did, probably more than capable, even if he didn't get involved in the direction I wanted to go. There was nothing wrong with having two attorneys who could divide and conquer.

I sat down faster than was warranted, but my cock wasn't getting the memo that those eyes weren't meant to be flirting with me, and his stiffened back was more from being on high alert than submission. For a second, I seriously contemplated yelling at him in an attempt to get him to leave. There was no way I could work with him if my cock kept thinking it was playtime.

Work and play didn't mix... at least not for me.

It was Elliot's turn to clear his throat and draw my attention toward him. "You wanted to talk? At least I'm guessing that's why you wanted to see if I had a moment. Well, that or you're just trying to imitate a creepy stalker and stare at me while I work." He paused for a moment, then smirked. "Might I suggest calling my phone and breathing deeply instead of speaking? That usually helps the stalker vibe."

The words startled a laugh out of me. I hadn't expected witty snark from him, but if this continued, I might have actually found someone to verbally spar with. And that thought gave me more satisfaction than it should have. If finding someone snarky was enough to get my motor running, it had likely been too long since I'd had a satisfying hookup.

And I needed to stop thinking about those things at work, or that uncomfortable situation in my pants was going to get a lot worse.

"I wanted to stop in and talk with you about the conversation we had yesterday."

Elliot bristled, his jaw locking, his eyes cooling noticeably, and his fingers tightening on the file he was holding. When he spoke, his tone was flat and I knew then that he'd had a lot of practice concealing his emotions. "Yes, I've done both research and thinking on that. I'm sure that the knowledge I gained last night is not enough to be considered anything more than rudimentary, but I did learn a lot. There was a considerable amount of information to take in, and it really challenged my previous views on the lifestyle. I guess you could say that it was enlightening."

I had a feeling that was an understatement, but I didn't interrupt.

He drew in a deep breath and let it out slowly. "If you can be patient with me while I gain more understanding of the lifestyle, I'd appreciate it. I hope to be able to serve you in the ways you need."

I thanked the stars for the black dress pants I'd put on that morning because there was no way in hell he'd have missed the way my cock was straining against my pants otherwise. Did he have any clue how those words sounded? It was pure fucking evil and showed just how green he was to the lifestyle.

My head wouldn't even nod in acknowledgment of his words. Every ounce of blood had rushed to my cock and I found myself wondering just how quiet I could be while jacking off in the bathroom stall.

I still hadn't figured out what to say to him when Elliot's face flared an angry tomato red and he closed his eyes for a moment. "That came out wrong. I'm sorry—what I meant to say was that I want to be an asset to the firm, and I don't think alternative lifestyles are going to be a problem, but I need more time to understand them." There wasn't a doubt in my mind that Elliot would have crawled under the desk if he thought it would get him out of the conversation.

What I wanted to say was that I'd be happy to teach him all he wanted to know. My mouth had even opened to say it, but my brain kicked in at the last second. "I can appreciate that. And thank you for your honesty. I'm going to leave you alone—I'm sure my mom will keep you plenty busy for the time being."

I stood and adjusted my sports coat, hoping the movement of my hands would draw any attention away from my dick, and made for the door as fast as I could without seeming suspicious or rude.

I didn't even stop when my mom called my name or Austin tried to hand me a coffee. I headed straight for my car to get some space from Elliot. This was going to be torture.

CHAPTER 6

ELLIOT

"This is really nice. Are you sure you don't mind me staying here?"

Seth looked more than a little uncomfortable at the prospect of renting me his guest house. He'd been kind enough, but the conversation I'd overheard in Nathan's office was still replaying in my head. I'd spent more than a few minutes looking between Austin and Seth, trying to spot similarities between the two, but there weren't many.

Seth was tall with dark hair and dark eyes. Austin was shorter, and while his hair was dark, it looked different somehow. His nearly purple eyes definitely didn't look like Seth's. Where Austin was slender, Seth was muscular. He also had a fresh pink scar under his eye and a faded scar on his chin. I was pretty sure that I'd seen him flinch when Austin had hugged him. What had earned him all the scars, I didn't know, but it looked painful. Though, judging by the size of the house, it earned him a lot of money too.

When it came down to it, if I hadn't heard the conversation about them being twins, I wouldn't have known they were even related.

Seth's deep voice brought me out of my thoughts. "No, you're fine. I hate to admit it, but Austin is actually right. I'm going into a period of time that I'm not going to be able to be home much, even when I'm in town. It's better if someone is around more often than one of my siblings or parents stopping by here and there. In the end, this is helpful. Besides, everyone I know lives locally—the team, my family. This place doesn't get used. Ever. It's decorated nicely, but it hasn't been opened, except for the cleaning crew, in over a year."

I found myself nodding slowly. "I think I could see myself here. I don't know anyone, so you don't have to worry about me inviting people over. The only person that might not stay away is Emma, but she lives in New York, so it's not like she'll be around randomly. I'm happy to tell you if she is coming."

Austin and Seth both gave me matching looks of curiosity, and I finally saw the resemblance. "You don't have to ask me if you want friends over or even give me a heads-up. As long as you don't give them the gate code and they stay away from the main house, I'm fine with it."

His words said one thing, but his voice said something else entirely. I wouldn't make a big deal out of it, but there was no reason he needed to worry.

Seth fished into his pocket and produced a key. "I guess

I'll see you around six this evening. That should give you enough time to grab your stuff from the hotel and get back here."

After the brothers shared another hug and Austin wished Seth good luck, we were back in Austin's car. "Seth's leaving in the morning, but he'll be at the arena late tonight. He'll be gone for the week, so you'll hardly see him."

Arena? Gone for a week? The question was out of my mouth before I could stop myself. "What is it that Seth does, exactly?"

Austin gave me an honest-to-god giggle, but his body puffed up in what I could only describe as pride. "He's a forward for the Grizzlies. Finally got traded back here. We're so glad to have him home."

My mouth fell open. "Wait, Seth Johnson is your *brother?*" I didn't follow many sports, but I'd always watched hockey when I could. I'd been to a number of games in New York and Chicago and had kept up with quite a few teams when I had a chance. He looked a lot different in faded jeans and a T-shirt with his hair unstyled than he did in the custom suits he was frequently pictured in or in all of his hockey gear. Until that moment, I hadn't put the two together in my head. Johnson was too common of a last name, and I'd been too shell-shocked for the last twenty-four hours to think about hockey.

Austin's grin was infectious. "*Twin* brother. He's older by eight minutes." Austin huffed dramatically, but I was already getting used to it, so it didn't surprise me. "We were definitely the oops babies. Mom and Dad had Wilder—the OG oops—and were very done having kids at that point, so Dad got snipped a few months after he was born. Turns out, Mom was already pregnant with us at the time. So *surprise,* two more Johnsons made an entrance into the world fourteen months after Wilder. Mom and Dad like to tell people that we were very determined to enter this world."

I found myself laughing at the story. It felt good to laugh like that, as I hadn't been in a particularly happy mood recently.

"Oh, we're here!"

I blinked at the front of the restaurant that sat outside the expensive neighborhood I now lived in. "Falafel House?" It was like... Waffle House, but for falafel. Staring at the building, I admitted to myself that I was overdue for a trip back to NYC.

"Don't let the name fool you. It's amazing. Come on." He was out of the car in seconds and bounding to the door. How did the man have so much energy?

I followed behind more slowly, but the parking lot was small and the front of the restaurant was tiny, so he didn't beat me to the hostess stand by much. I had to give him that the place smelled amazing and felt cozy and welcoming. We'd arrived after the lunch rush, so the place was pretty empty, though I could see signs that they'd been busy recently.

In New York and Chicago, there were rarely downtimes in restaurants, just times that weren't quite as packed as others. In addition to the accents, the far lighter rush hours, and the penchant for country music like I'd never experienced in my life, quiet restaurants were also new. I had a lot of adjustments to make.

At least the falafel selections were standard and I was able to make a decision quickly. I was pretty boring when it came to meals out. I tended to get overwhelmed with all the choices, so I stuck with things I knew. Maybe Austin was the same or he just had a favorite here because he declined the menu altogether.

With our orders placed, we were left with a lot of time to fill with talking, something I wasn't great at. Austin didn't have the same problem and pretty much carried the entire conversation.

"So, Mom says that you're from Chicago?"

I nodded absently. "Born and raised. Went to college in New York, though."

Before I could continue, Austin finished the story for me. "Yeah. You went to NYU like Nate. What part of the City were you living in? I overheard him saying that you worked for a really prestigious firm there. How was that? Did you enjoy your time there? It's got to be a culture shock coming from there to here."

How many questions had he asked? And what did I need to respond to? "From what I gather, I graduated a year before Nathan, though I had never met him before yesterday. And I guess it kind of is shocking. I've been in a really big city for a long time. This is almost quaint. The accents are the hardest to get used to, though. And the politeness. I never spoke to shop owners or pedestrians on the street in Chicago or New York. Here, people just strike up conversations. I was trying to eat last night and some guy just sat down and started talking to me."

Austin scrunched up his nose. "I get the impression that you're pretty private."

To that I nodded. Private was a nice word for being cold, standoffish, and an all-around introvert. Yet Austin was making an effort, and Emma's words about being myself for once were echoing in my head. I didn't know a lot about the Johnson family, but Nathan was gay, anyone who followed sports or current events in the last eight years knew that Seth was gay, and even though my gaydar was nonexistent, I was nearly positive that Austin was gay.

Maybe someday I'd be comfortable enough to become more than work acquaintances with Austin. He was barely in his mid-twenties, but I thought that maybe we could even be friends.

What would it be like to actually go out and do things with someone that wasn't Emma and her friends? When was the last time I'd been out with anyone I knew?

"So, is Emma your girlfriend?"

My response was so automatic that it flowed from my lips without input from my brain. "Ex-wife." I laughed at myself. "No, that's really not right."

Austin's eyes had gone a near midnight blue as he stared at me in confusion. "What do you mean ex-wife but not?"

"It's an insane story."

Austin pulled his phone out and tapped frantically at the screen. A few seconds later, it pinged and he looked down, a wide smile spreading on his face. "We've got all the time in the world. I told Mom that we're out to lunch and won't be back on time."

I chuckled. I'd never been late getting back from lunch since I'd started working. Hell, I couldn't remember the last time I'd taken a lunch out of my office that wasn't a business meeting or Emma bodily pulling me out. Second day on the job and I was not only out to lunch but not going to be back before the end of the hour.

"So, who's Emma?"

"She's my... She's my best friend. She's my best friend, and yes, we did get married, but it was such a disaster that we didn't even have a chance to send the marriage documents to the courthouse."

Austin's mouth hung open as he listened intently to every word I said. "I've got to hear this!"

I rolled my eyes. "It's so crazy I almost don't believe it happened." I'd never told anyone the real story of our dating, engagement, and very, very brief marriage. If I said it out loud, it was going to be true, and I didn't know how I felt about that.

Austin couldn't hide his genuine curiosity. "You don't

strike me as the person to do something crazy or irresponsible. You look like a guy who is put together all the time and has a plan for his plans."

He had me there, and I found myself smiling. "Which is how I ended up engaged to my best friend, then getting married and calling it off before the cake was eaten."

I wished I could take a picture of the expression on Austin's face. He was beyond shocked and equally excited about the story I was about to tell. "This just keeps getting better."

"I'm an asshole, and... and, well, I've been terrified of everything my entire life." When Austin blinked, I knew I needed to continue, so I thought of where to start. "My parents are very wrapped up in appearances. The only option my brother and I had was to go to college to become a doctor or a lawyer. My brother rebelled, and before he even came out, they treated him differently, so I kept my nose in the books and followed what was expected of me."

Austin's eyebrows had drawn together in thought, and he was looking at me the way I'd expect a puppy to. I shrugged slowly and tried to gloss over a lot. "I went to a good college, got top grades, got hired at an *acceptable* law firm. I did everything right. But it wasn't enough. They couldn't figure out why I wasn't settling down."

It was easy to tell Austin wanted to say something, but he didn't. He didn't even prod as our dishes were set down in front of us. He just stayed quiet, focusing his attention more on me than the food in front of him.

"I'd met Emma shortly after I started at the firm; her dad was the head partner. She's fierce and confident and outspoken. She's a lot like my brother in some ways." I hated talking about Kyle, but it was the truth, though I was just beginning to see that. "When her parents started pushing her to find a guy and her friends kept pushing her into blind dates, we'd ended up really bonding over others' desires to see us partnered up. We decided to tell everyone we were dating."

"But you weren't?"

I shook my head. "Aside from a few pecks on the cheek, we never even kissed until our wedding."

Austin's mouth hung open and the falafel ball he'd stabbed with his fork fell into the tzatziki sauce without his ever realizing. "You never kissed her?"

This story sounded more insane coming out of my mouth than it had in my head, and I'd *lived* it. "Not once. After about eighteen months, we'd gotten into a good routine. We could be just sweet enough around family and friends that they thought we really were together.

"Then it all went to hell one day when I brought coffee to her on my way into work. Someone overheard her—jokingly—tell me that she was so glad she'd chosen me for forever, or something along those lines. Next thing either of us knows, everyone thinks we're engaged. Before we could straighten out the mix-up, her mom had her shopping for a wedding dress and planning the wedding. God, it snowballed so fucking fast. It was like being in the middle of a whiteout; we'd gone from friends and roommates to planning a wedding neither of us wanted, and we couldn't figure out how to stop it."

"This is a real life made-for-TV rom-com. The only thing missing is, like, if you're gay."

I laughed. "Yeah, I'm gay."

The words were out for the first time ever. The falafel burger I'd just eaten was threatening to come back up. I didn't know what crossed my face, but Austin sobered immediately. His eyes were wide with surprise, but they'd seen enough to know I was beyond shocked myself.

There were a million things I thought he might have said in the moment, but he set his fork down and reached across the table to rest a hand on my arm. "I'm so sorry—I hadn't meant that seriously."

Embarrassment, shame, and humiliation all roiled in my gut, but there was a sense of peace that was fighting the feelings just as hard. I'd said it. I'd come out, *for real*, for the first time in my life. My brain kept screaming at me to say something, anything, but the part that connected to my voice box was completely detached.

While in the midst of my own freak-out, I still found myself feeling bad that I was worrying Austin. He'd been staring intently at me since my admission, but neither of us had said anything since he'd tried to apologize. He'd apologized for my outing myself. What a fucked-up day.

The quiet finally got to be too much for him because

he spoke, but it was quiet and uncertain. "And you're closeted?"

The absurdity of the statement snapped my brain back into working and I snorted a laugh. "That's an understatement. I've... I've never actually said it out loud before."

Austin's eyebrows met his hairline and I found myself wondering if I'd ever met someone as expressive as him. "You've... never?"

I shook my head. "Not even Emma. God. That's insane, isn't it? I've known since I was a teenager, shortly before my brother came out. When my parents took it so terribly, I knew I just couldn't come out to them. Then they paid for college, and my first apartment while I got my feet under myself, and then they were always prodding into my life. Even twelve hours away from them, it always felt like they were right there. That's why it was great for Emma and me. She was—still is—happily single and I was deep in the closet."

"In all that time, how didn't you tell her?"

"She knew. I told her I wasn't into women like that, but I never flat out said I... Said I'm..."

After a third try, Austin winked at me. "You never came out and said that you're gay."

"Yeah. That." My head dropped and I felt my cheeks flush. I was nearly thirty-six years old and could not force myself to say it a second time.

Austin waited me out, but when I didn't raise my head, he spoke. "Hey, Elliot." He didn't say anything else until my eyes met his. His smile was kind and understanding and his eyes showed patience. "Conveniently, you landed a job at a very gay friendly office. In my family, only two of us recognize as truly straight. Hell, even my parents are on the LGBT spectrum." His smile turned a little wobbly before he spoke again. "And I'm really honored to be the first person you came out to."

I poked at my burger, the melt-in-your-mouth falafel no longer appetizing, and sighed. "Emma's going to be proud of me."

He blinked in confusion, so I clarified. "After the wedding—drunk and stuffed on leftover wedding cake—Emma made me promise to actually say the words. She's been disappointed that I haven't found a single person to say that to in six months."

Austin stabbed the fallen falafel ball with his fork. "So, you two are still friends?"

I nodded as a dopey smile spread on my face. "She's amazing. I don't think anyone in New York realizes we're still close and talk almost every day. I left right after the wedding. We'd agreed to blame the split on me, so I'm definitely the bad guy there, but those were all her friends anyway. It doesn't really matter."

Austin shrugged a shoulder. "Their loss, we've got you now. And we're going to teach you just how amazing it is to be gay, even in Tennessee."

The groan I let out was completely warranted.

Undeterred, Austin began to probe into my life as he

finished eating. I didn't even bother picking my burger up again. "I get that you're closeted, but in the grand scheme of things, that doesn't mean much. Have you been with a guy before?"

My answering blush gave enough away and Austin practically swooned. "Oh! I've got a baby gay!"

CHAPTER 7

NATHAN

THE WEATHER HAD WELL and truly broken, and late spring had set in hard, but with it, a cloud of pollen seemed to be following my G-Wagon. After washing it three times in as many days, I'd given up and brought my truck to work that morning. I was used to Elliot being early, but when I pulled in at eight fifteen Wednesday, I was still surprised to see him there.

My windows were rolled down, and I heard his voice clearly. I looked over to see him talking on the phone that was connected to his car's Bluetooth. He hadn't noticed me and had his head leaned back, eyes closed, and a soft smile on his face. It was the most blissed-out sex face I'd ever seen. And there I went again. This was becoming way too much of a problem when he was anywhere near. Everything about the man was catching my dick's attention, no matter how many times I told him that we didn't know Elliot.

My brain took control of my dick in time to hear Elliot laugh. It was deep and throaty and it struck me that I'd never heard him give a genuine laugh. "Em, you'd be so proud of me."

Who was Em?

A softer voice filtered over the line. "Yeah? What did you do?"

"I actually told someone."

Told someone what? Dammit, I was getting mostly her side of the conversation over the Bluetooth connection, and since Elliot didn't have a tendency to speak loudly, I could just barely make out his words. *And this makes you a creepy stalker, Nathan.* I told my brain to shut up and continued listening.

The voice through the speaker nearly yelled. "You did?" Wherever she was, I was pretty sure I'd heard it screamed from her home straight to my car.

Elliot scrubbed his hands down his face, muffling the next words out of his mouth, but her voice echoed into my car. "Oh, El! I'm so proud of you! I *told* you Tennessee was going to be great for you. What did he say when you told him?"

What did Elliot tell who? And who is the guy? What was he doing? These questions shouldn't have mattered to me, but they did.

Elliot's smile went fond and his voice was stronger, allowing it to just filter through the window. "I hadn't meant to tell Austin, so I was shocked at first."

Em's voice turned tender and she was no longer screaming. "Oh, El, only you could finally admit you're gay on accident. I'm proud of you regardless, but I want you to be able to tell someone on purpose. This was the goal. Give you space from your family and their expectations so that you can finally become the man you've always wanted to be."

How wide could eyes get before they actually fell out of the sockets? I didn't know, but I suspected I was pushing the limits. Elliot was gay. And he'd told my brother? The brother who had never been able to keep a secret in his entire life, yet hadn't let something this big slip? When did Elliot tell Austin? Jesus, none of this was anywhere near my business.

My logical brain came fully back online and I realized just how inappropriate it was for me to be overhearing this conversation. Logic won out and I rolled my window up before I could hear more and ended up feeling guiltier than I was already starting to. Elliot was gay and had only told my brother—at that, it had been by accident—and now I knew.

Dick move, Nathan.

I turned the truck off and opened the door. Out of the corner of my eye, I saw Elliot's head whip over at the sound of my door shutting and the person he was talking to asked him if he was all right. I didn't take time to look back, no matter how much my body demanded it, and headed straight toward the office.

By the time I sank into my desk chair and booted up my computer, I had managed to convince myself that I needed to stay well away from Elliot Mitchell. Nothing good would come of my pursuing him, anyway.

The front door opened and shut, and voices filtered through the entry. "Lunch today?" That had definitely been Austin's.

I hadn't expected the smile I heard in Elliot's voice when he responded. "Yeah, that sounds great. I'm dying for a good burger."

"Oh! I know a good place." *Of course he did.*

Not even thirty seconds later, Austin appeared in my doorway with a cup of coffee in his hand. "Want to go get burgers with us this afternoon?"

At the risk of seeming like an antisocial ass, I shook my head. "No, I don't think so."

Austin set the cup down on my desk as he shook his head at me. Disappointment radiated off him. "You're never going to get to know Elliot if you keep avoiding him."

Being dressed down by my youngest brother wasn't pleasant. It was especially unpleasant when the man dressing me down was dressed like a clown. Okay, a clown wasn't exactly right, but the pink dress shirt, navy slacks, and navy-and-white polka-dotted tie were bright and vibrant. What really sucked was that I knew he was right.

I MANAGED to avoid Elliot for a week. Well, I hadn't necessarily avoided him, but I hadn't prodded into his life, and I hadn't been in his office since his second day. I suspected I wasn't the only one giving the other a wide berth because Elliot was never in the hallway or break room with me. However, he was certainly spending a lot of time with my mom and Austin. Why it bugged the hell out of me that he was spending time with Austin, I couldn't quite put my finger on.

Try as I might, I couldn't bring myself to get to know Elliot. My body kept reacting in weird ways, and knowing that he was gay, I kept making things awkward. Yeah, that awkwardness was on me way more than it was on Elliot.

He hadn't done anything other than be kind to my family and all the clients. Which pissed me off even more. He was fitting in better than I could have hoped for, making me feel like a bigger asshole for trying to keep my distance.

But I'd simply smelled his cologne in the break room Monday afternoon and had gotten hard in my pants. There was no way I was going to be able to keep myself under control if I stayed around him. What was getting to me was not understanding why that was. Part of me worried that it was only because I knew he was gay and in the closet. And if I was only attracted to him because he was a newbie gay, that wasn't fair to him. I wasn't going to be *that* guy.

There was a smaller part of me that swore my body was reacting to him because I was drawn to him. Elliot was like a magic blue pill that my body reacted to on sight. The one and only interaction I'd had with him in a week had been a quick, "Good job, the case looks great." He'd sat up straight, his head held high, and gave me the most genuine smile I'd ever seen from anyone. And I'd gotten hard in the hallway.

Because that was appropriate.

The longer these feelings continued, the grumpier I became, and the more I was beginning to hate myself. It had gotten so bad that Austin had been keeping a clear distance from me all week. He'd even stopped asking me if I wanted to join them for lunch. That morning, I'd looked over from my computer to find a coffee cup on my desk. Hot, triple shot, no sugar, barely a splash of cream, just enough to take the temp down from scalding. There was no mocha, no hot chocolate, no messed up order, and most notably, no sign of Austin.

How much of an ass had I been that Austin was avoiding me and not intentionally messing up my coffee orders? I kind of missed it.

Unfortunately, there was nothing I could do about it as I sifted through the current case I was working on. Matt, a Dom from DASH, and Maxwell, his husband and submissive, were due to be arriving soon to discuss their will. Matt's mom had died unexpectedly a few months earlier, and the entire process had been a nightmare. It had lit a fire under his ass to get their will taken care of. He didn't have kids, but he wanted to make sure that there would be no question about who got what in the case of one of their deaths.

Austin knew I was expecting them, so it didn't surprise me when Matt knocked on my door a little after eleven. He was smiling brightly but seemed to be alone.

I gave him a bright smile in greeting and half stood. "Hey, come on in." Looking past him, I was surprised to see his husband wasn't anywhere around. "Will Maxwell be joining us today?"

Matt threw a thumb over his shoulder. "Austin and Max disappeared into the office beside yours. I'm guessing he'll return shortly."

Elliot's office? I tried to school my surprise, but I had no idea why Austin would be taking Maxwell to Elliot's office. I guessed I hadn't done a good job of hiding my shock because Matt looked worried. "Is that a problem?"

Shaking my head, I stammered for a second. "Oh-uh, no, not a problem. I was just surprised. Austin is up to something, but I don't know what."

Matt snorted in an attempt to hide his amusement. He'd known our family almost as long as I'd been alive, so he'd known Austin his entire life. "With that boy, it's probably better to not ask."

If that wasn't the truth. I tried to ignore my need to know what the three were up to and focus back on Matt and the will, but it was a lot harder in practice, especially when I heard giggles filtering in through the door.

Matt and I had all but finished, and I needed to go over

the documents with Maxwell before we could wrap everything up. "Excuse me for a moment." I stood. "I'm going to go figure out what's going on next door."

Matt waved me off, an easy smile on his face. "Knowing Max and Austin, they are probably driving the new guy insane."

Part of me had worried about that. I made my way to Elliot's office on autopilot but stopped short when I saw the three men sitting around Elliot's desk in a serious conversation. Sure, they were smiling, but Maxwell had been very seriously discussing why the process of making a will was scaring the hell out of him. I'd only heard a snippet of the conversation, but I could tell that he had been quite honest about the fears he had of losing his husband and Dom.

For his part, Elliot had a notepad on his desk and was jotting notes down as they spoke. "I can't imagine." I got the impression Elliot was speaking more to himself than to the other guys. "Have you talked to your husband about these fears? I basically know enough to know that you're supposed to talk to your Dom about these sorts of things."

Maxwell let out a resigned sigh. "I have. And he's assured me he's healthy. He's been treating me with kid gloves for a few weeks now."

Elliot's eyes softened. "I get that. I'm sorry it's been hard." He was so sincere and had connected with Maxwell on a level I wasn't certain I'd have been able to. I was also positive that this conversation wouldn't have come up if it had just been Maxwell, Matthew, and me in my office.

Austin squeezed Maxwell's arm. "You'll let us know if there is anything we can do for you?"

Maxwell's head bobbed up and down. "Absolutely. Thanks for listening."

I stepped back quickly and gathered myself. I was turning into a massive eavesdropper and that wasn't who I wanted to be. Thankful for the wall outside Elliot's office making it so that he couldn't see me, I took a few deep breaths, then took a few steps back toward his door and knocked on the frame.

Three sets of eyes turned toward me. Elliot's face heated when he saw me and he quickly ducked his head, avoiding eye contact. I cleared my throat and forced a casual tone I wasn't sure anyone bought as relaxed. "Hey, Maxwell, we're ready for you."

He stood abruptly and reached out to shake Elliot's hand. "Thanks again for listening. I appreciate it. It feels good to get that off my chest."

To my surprise, Elliot gave him a beaming smile. "Any-time. Seriously. Oh, hey, take this." He handed over his card. "It's got all my contact info if you ever need to talk more."

Maxwell flicked the card and I could hear the smile and sincerity in his voice as he spoke. "Thanks so much. Austin has all my info. We should get together at some point."

Austin stood and wrapped Maxwell in a hug. "Sounds great. Good luck with Grumps here." He pointed to me and rolled his eyes. "Don't let his growl scare you."

Maxwell laughed and headed out of Elliot's office. When I was certain my client was not looking my way, I flipped Austin the bird, then left to go to my office. I still couldn't figure out what I'd walked into, but the strange sense of pride rushing through me was not what I'd expected.

CHAPTER 8

ELLIOT

After a week and a half living in Seth's guest house, I was willing to admit it wasn't awkward at all. Seth was a lot quieter than I'd expected and while I didn't see him often, he texted me frequently to let me know if and when he'd be back. It had definitely surprised me just how little he was actually home, even when the team wasn't traveling.

I'd settled in nicely and was even beginning to do grocery shopping and cook on my own. Seth had had a few pots in the house but not enough to actually do much cooking, and I'd left all the cookware with Emma when I moved out of our apartment. It had taken me a while to get pots and pans purchased, but once I had, cooking at home became commonplace. I was making a nice routine for myself in the evenings and being home by six every night made it easier to plan meals.

Besides, eating at home eliminated the need for me to decide what to eat at so many different restaurants.

After Connie had caught me leaving the office with a few files the Friday before, she'd put her foot down and told me that work stayed at work, especially on weekends. It was weird to come home without work. I'd spent money on good cookware, fresh groceries, and an online cooking class, and was rather shocked to find that I was enjoying my routine quite a bit.

Learn something new every day.

I'd just thrown a lemon-and-garlic chicken breast topped with fresh rosemary into the oven when my phone buzzed on the counter. It would either be Austin or Emma, since they both spent most evenings texting me.

My phone had never been this active before.

Emma: *Hey, I just found this. I thought you'd find it interesting.*

The link had been shortened, so I didn't have a clue what she was sending me, but I clicked on it anyway. Another text popped up as it loaded.

Emma: *I think it could be helpful, and it's local to you. It looks really low key and interesting, and the place gets great reviews.*

What the hell had Emma found?

I switched back to the browser and my phone slid right to the ground when I figured out what she'd linked me to. Pinching the bridge of my nose, I took a few deep breaths and steeled myself for what was on the screen. It still didn't prepare me for the bold letters exclaiming *BDSM Intro*

Night. What the hell had Emma been looking for to find this? And what did she think she knew?

I tapped back to the text app and responded.

Me: *Um, what?*

Emma must have had the text already in the phone because the response was immediate.

Emma: *I figure this will give you a good feel for the BDSM community there. See if it is something you can see yourself representing.*

Oh. Oh, right. I hadn't told her about the crazy thoughts in my head the night we'd discovered the BDSM websites, and I definitely had omitted the conversation with Max, the sweet guy from work, on Wednesday. I'd thought about that conversation a lot since then. Max had been so sweet and honest as he talked about the way he and his husband had discovered BDSM, and I swore he'd had hearts in his eyes as he spoke about the way submission made him feel.

"Free" was the word he'd chosen. "Uninhibited" and "powerful" had also been thrown out there. But there had also been words like "beautiful," "important," and "special." I'd never felt any of those things before. While the rope play he'd spoken of didn't do much for me, those feelings certainly had my mind wandering back to the articles that Emma and I had discovered the first night we'd gone exploring on the Internet.

It felt like a lot longer than ten days ago.

I switched back to the notice. It was an eye-catching announcement in rich, bold colors. *DASH Presents...*

Me: *Can't go. That's the club Nathan's family owns.*

Emma's response took longer that time. The bubbles started and stopped dancing a number of times before a text finally came in.

Emma: *I can't imagine there are a lot of BDSM clubs in Nashville... hell, in Tennessee for that matter. I figured it was the same club, but it isn't like you have to go to become a member. You just need the research.*

Emma: *Unless you want to become a member, there's nothing wrong with that, either.*

I'd been taking a drink of my beer and found myself choking on it. I wasn't ready to think about joining a BDSM club. Not seriously anyway. The conversation with Max and Austin had been eye-opening, but that was a big step. I wasn't even sure I was interested in it, despite not being able to get the image of that guy kneeling out of my head.

And I'd be lying to say I hadn't imagined the Dom as Nathan a time or two already, especially since Wednesday. There had been a day early on where he'd praised my attention to detail on a case. If I'd internally preened at the notice and my dick had gone impossibly hard, Nathan hadn't noticed, so it didn't count.

I didn't know what it was about Nathan that, even through his growls and scowls, I was drawn to him like a moth to a flame. At least this moth had the common sense to keep ten feet of distance between us at all times.

The grunts and glares he gave me told me well enough that he hated me at the office, even if Austin and Connie liked me. The fact that he'd actively avoided going to lunch with Austin and me every single time Austin had asked let me know he wanted space.

Maybe submission, because I definitely wasn't dominant, was something I could enjoy. I hadn't found the sites Emma and I had looked at all that unappealing. Quite the opposite, actually. I'd found many of the things described quite interesting, hell, almost desirable.

And that had to be weird, right? Wanting freedom from the responsibilities I'd always taken on and the pressures my parents had always put on me to succeed, by allowing someone else to make decisions for me.

Okay, so I was pretty sure I was submissive. But no matter how I cut it, I couldn't see finding a man who would want someone as messed up as me. Sure, there were other people with much bigger problems than mine, but I was a thirty-five-year-old closet case with extreme self-confidence issues and a fear of letting people down. I couldn't come up with a scenario in which I'd be able to relax enough to just *be* and not get lost in my head.

I scrubbed at my face. "You're pathetic, Elliot."

"Why?"

The voice from the front of my house had my phone flying across the room and me squealing loudly.

Seth's face appeared at the open window, a pink blush staining his face. "Sorry, I didn't mean to scare the hell out of you. I just got home and thought I'd see how everything was going. I know you said it's going well, but I wanted to check in."

I went to the door and opened it. Inviting him in turned out to be more complicated since my voice didn't seem to be working right with my heart pounding nearly out of my chest. "C-come on i-in. Sorry, you scared the hell out of me. I didn't hear you coming."

Seth's face was still a little pink, but he was smiling now. "Yeah. I just got home and noticed your car out front, and—oh my god, it smells amazing in here!"

I didn't know it was possible to make me blush so fast. "Want to stay for dinner? I can't promise it's going to be edible, but it will be ready in about ten minutes or so." I had no idea what had made me ask, but I could definitely see that he looked starved.

His eyes got wide. "You don't have to feed me. I have something in the fridge from the trainer."

"You might still need to eat that, depending on how this turns out. I've never cooked much. When I lived in New York, my..." I really shouldn't call Emma my ex-girlfriend anymore. I was trying to move past that and here there was no reason to hide. That left me with a question about what to call her. "My roommate and I usually did takeout on the way home from work. We both worked at firms that kept us busy well into the night. Then when I moved back to Chicago, I lived with my parents and they have a cook. So I'm learning via YouTube and an online cooking class I signed up for."

I clamped my mouth shut. Rambling wasn't an attractive quality, but I'd been so surprised to see the dark-haired man appear in my window that I wasn't entirely convinced my brain had fully kicked back online yet.

Seth's smile was blinding. "There's no way it can be any worse than what our trainer sends home." He shuddered. "I'm too cheap to hire a chef, so I suffer through it, but she's just plain evil. But are you sure you don't mind? I eat a lot."

"I still have leftovers from the last two meals I made. Believe me, you can eat as much as you want. On the plus side, I'm pretty sure it's healthy. It's a chicken breast, but I'll be honest, I was just going to throw a bag of rice and another bag of broccoli in the microwave."

"At this point in the season, I wouldn't care if it was deep-fried pickles and mashed potatoes. I'm hungry, tired, and sore."

That didn't sound pleasant, but I could understand where he was coming from.

To my surprise, conversation flowed easily from there. Once he knew that I was quite happy with the place, he focused in on what he'd walked in on. "So, what's this about you being pathetic?"

My face scrunched up and I waved my hands around

in a vague gesture of nothing. "We can just forget about that."

He took a sip from the bottle of water I'd slid him and shook his head. "That was not a *nothing* exclamation. You sounded legitimately pissed at yourself."

The truth was I had been. "Emma sent me something and it threw me for a loop."

Seth studied me with narrowed eyes. "I see... What was it?"

I dropped my head. "You're just like Austin, aren't you? No matter what I say right now, you're going to find a way to get the answer out of me if it takes two minutes or two hours."

He lifted a shoulder and gave me a lazy smirk. "What can I say? We're Johnsons. The youngest two, at that. We were basically raised to be nosy, and Austin and I learned from the best. My oldest brother is the chief deputy sheriff down in Williamson. You already know Mom and Nate are attorneys. And with nine of us kids, we were constantly butting into each other's lives. We still do." The smirk turned into a devious grin. "So you might as well just tell me. You know I'm not going to give up."

Why did I feel like that was, unfortunately, the truth? Sighing in defeat, I went on a search for my phone. Amazingly, it had landed on the armchair and was waiting for me as innocently as could be. There were four missed texts from Emma, but I ignored them and unlocked the phone to the screen I'd been staring at. No matter how I cut this, it was going to be awkward. At least I wasn't going to have to explain what DASH was.

"This." I flipped the screen around and watched as Seth examined it for a moment.

"Oh! Yeah, Dad does those about every three months. Are you interested in going?" There was nothing in his voice but genuine curiosity and it helped some of my anxiety ease.

Anxiety or not, it didn't help me answer the question. "Emma says I should go. Christ, I don't know what is okay to talk about or not at this point." Did anyone but me know that Nathan wanted to take on kinkier clients? Was it okay to tell his brother?

Seth sat back on the barstool and crossed an ankle over his other knee. "This sounds ominous. Or like you're just really fucking confused. As long as you're open to being with men, and you want to submit or dominate—though I don't see you as a Dom—or if you're just plain kinky and want some like-minded people, DASH is the place to go."

He made that sound so normal, but that really hadn't been why I'd been nervous. However, it was a good out from telling him about Nathan's plans. "I don't know if I'm kinky."

Seth's brown eyes turned soft. From spending so much time with Austin over the last week, I knew nothing good would come of the look. "But you're interested."

"I'm intrigued. And working with your brother, I'm realizing that I'm also very, very naive."

Usually I'd be offended by someone laughing at something I'd said in all seriousness, but the warm sound of Seth's laughter didn't sound cruel in the slightest. "That kind of interest is exactly why Dad does those nights. Not everyone falls into BDSM early on in their lives. Some people learn that they like it but don't like the structure of the club, so they keep it at home only. The beauty of kink is that it's individual. It's not one size fits all, and no one serious about the lifestyle should ever make you think that it is."

The words definitely helped, even though it was up there on the list of strange conversations I'd had since moving to Tennessee.

"You should go. Seriously. See if it's something that interests you. If nothing else, there will be some great eye candy there."

The way my eyes widened must have taken Seth by surprise because he choked on his water. "You're gay, right? Or at least bi. DASH is a *gay* BDSM club. If you want a straight club, there's one I can direct you to."

"No! I mean..." I swallowed hard. "I mean I don't want a straight club." I'd said it. I hadn't wanted to crawl in a hole that time, but I was still stressed, and Seth was studying me way too closely.

"So you're not out?"

How did he and Austin make it not sound like a terrible thing?

"Yes and no?" I hadn't meant the answer to come out as a question, but it had. "I'm pathetic."

Seth reached over and grabbed my arm. "You're really not. Coming out isn't easy, no matter what age you are. And even if it's easy for some people, not every single experience is great. Believe me, I'm definitely not one to hide my sexuality, but not every person I've told has taken it well."

I appreciated his words, but I didn't know if they were helping me or not.

"Unfortunately, we've got a game tomorrow night or I'd take you to DASH myself. Austin and Wilder already have tickets to the game, so Austin's out. Would you want me to ask Nate to go with you? I hate to think of you going to DASH alone the first time."

The horror must have come through on my face because Seth chuckled. "Or not."

There was no way I wanted to go to DASH with Nathan. He barely tolerated me and didn't know I was gay… so of course I was drawn to him like I'd never been drawn to anyone before. Which was why I stayed as far away from him as humanly possible. I didn't want to end up drooling over the guy I was working with and end up with him thinking I was nuts.

Avoiding him had taken skills I hadn't realized I'd possessed before the last week. I'd become increasingly aware of his presence. I could tell the sound of his car engines—truck and SUV—the sound he made when he walked, and I could pinpoint anywhere he was in the office just by the sound of his voice echoing.

With our offices barely ten feet apart, I'd done an impressive job of not seeing him. Going to DASH with him would totally defeat the purpose of staying away. And with my brain the way it had been lately, I'd probably end up saying something incredibly inappropriate and freak him out while embarrassing the hell out of myself. No, not Nathan. I needed to take this step on my own.

If Seth could see the insanity running through my head at the moment, he'd probably worry I was going to have that stroke everyone kept saying Nathan was going to have. Since he hadn't said anything else, I figured it was on me to say something. "Your brother is a little intense."

Seth barked out a laugh. "That's one word for it! Wilder and Zander keep telling him that he needs to find a guy who needs a helicopter Dom."

That was definitely more than I needed to know about Nathan. I'd suspected since the first day that he was a Dom, but having that suspicion confirmed was more than I could take at the moment. If I let myself go down that path, I'd never be able to work with him.

"You okay? You kinda look like you're going to puke."

My nervous laugh said enough, but I forced myself to find words. "I haven't told Nathan I'm gay. Actually, until just now, the only other people I'd said the words to are Emma and Austin."

Seth's eyes widened a fraction before he schooled his

features. "Oh, I can see why that would be a big step then. And thanks for telling me—I feel honored." He gave me a genuine smile, but I wasn't sure it calmed the war in my stomach.

I was beginning to make coming out to Johnsons a habit, and I didn't know how to feel about that. Emma kept telling me I was taking control of my life, but the more people I blurted it out to, the more out of control I felt.

I focused on setting the table and not the insanity in my head and the roiling of my stomach. Thankfully, Seth was content to let me find my equilibrium again without pressuring me, but I also got the impression he wasn't going to go very far until he was certain I was fine.

He didn't say anything until the plates were in front of us. "So, are you going to go to DASH tomorrow night?"

And that was the million-dollar question. I probably should, but I was getting the feeling that it wasn't as much research for my job as it was research for myself.

CHAPTER 9

NATHAN

"Sorry, I'm going to have to cancel tonight."

I looked at my brother in shock. He was at my house nearly three hours before Seth's game was due to start. "What do you mean you've got to cancel tonight?" We always watched the Grizzlies games together.

Zander spread his arms. "Seth called in a favor. I'm going to help him out."

"Volunteer muscle again?" Sometimes things got a little crazy for the hometown hockey hero, and Zander would escort Seth somewhere. I hadn't heard about any drama surrounding Seth or the team, but I wasn't usually the first to know those types of things.

"Something like that."

Well, damn. There went my plans for the night. My brother standing me up for our Saturday night of watching TV didn't speak highly of my social life. Maybe I needed to get out more. "Well, I hope you enjoy yourself."

Zander smirked at me. "Easy work, and I should be home by the time Noah gets off."

I'd tease him about how lovestruck he was by Noah, but love looked good on him. "That's awesome. I'm happy for you." And I was... if not a little bitter as well. "Wait, you came over to my house to tell me you couldn't come over for the game?"

"Actually, I wanted to make sure you were really home and not at the office."

I threw my hands in the air and managed a laugh, despite it sounding a bit off. "I'm not that bad." *Was I?*

The look Zander gave me said I was that bad. "Look, all I'm saying is that I'm glad you're actually home today. Maybe you can mow your grass?"

A thirty-four-year-old man could roll his eyes at his older brother if he wanted to. "The neighbor boy will be over later. There's thirty bucks sitting on the table by the door." Nothing had changed since we were kids—I still hated yard work. Growing up, I would volunteer for any chore in the house as long as it got me out of working outside. Zander never minded it and still mowed his own lawn.

Crazy bastard.

Zander glanced down at the phone in his hand. "I need to get out of here. Sorry I'm going to miss the game. I know it's our thing."

They teased me that I was going to stress to death, but Zander was truly the mother hen of the siblings. He tried to take on all our stresses and fix them, and I was pretty sure I'd personally given him the graying hair at his temples on his head. If he thought one of us wasn't happy, he'd worry about us constantly. Even now that we were grown, he still checked in on us, though he'd taken a small step back with Noah in his life. That didn't change the fact that we all still called him and leaned on him, probably more than most adult siblings leaned on one another.

"I'll be fine." And I would. "One hockey game isn't going to end the world. Seth tells us to miss more anyway. I'd say he's going to be proud of you, but you're probably just going to sit in the family box and watch anyway."

A weird look crossed Zander's face, but he masked it quickly and leaned in for a hug before I could ask. "I'll see you later, Nate."

I waved him goodbye, stepped into my house, and headed toward the living room. It was only five. The game didn't start until nearly eight, so that left me questioning what I was going to do. Austin and Wilder were at the game, and my sister Heather and her husband, Michael, were still very new parents and not up for going out.

I pulled up the family calendar and saw that basically everyone was working that night or had plans that would leave them unavailable. I sighed as I read through everyone's plans, then my dad's schedule caught my eye. There was an intro night at DASH and it drew my attention. Dad rarely turned down help those nights, though he never came out and asked us for it. Intro nights could get to be a little hectic, especially early in the evening.

Another glance at the dark television screen and my mind was made up. Seth would forgive me for not watching one game; I was recording it anyway. It drove him insane that we often scheduled our lives around his hockey games, but we'd spent so many years following him around the state, country, and world that it was now ingrained in us.

I threw a pizza in the oven before running up the steps to grab a shower. *Shower* might have been the wrong word for jumping into the running water to get my hair wet enough to tame. I hadn't done anything with it after I'd showered at the gym earlier in the afternoon, so no amount of product alone would fix that mess. Even though I kept it cropped close to my head, the length on top had a tendency to have a mind of its own if I didn't do something with it. Something that included gel or mousse or something to tame it into some degree of submission.

I was in and out of the shower within five minutes and wearing a pair of red boxer briefs while doing my hair in the mirror. It only took a few minutes to run some mousse through it and call it good enough. It wasn't like I was going to DASH for a scene, just as more of a moderator in case it was busy.

Shimmying into a pair of black leather pants with my black leather lace-up dress boots made an anxious part of me settle into place. I'd never felt the need to wear motorcycle or combat-looking boots to the club. My style had always been more on the formal side. I added a thin white dress shirt that was light enough that the tattoo covering my chest and upper arm was clearly visible through it but not so thin as to be see-through. Another glance in the mirror and I was grabbing my wallet, keys, and phone.

If I rushed out the door, I'd get to the club before it opened, so I forced myself to eat my pizza and have a bottle of water. I killed an extra twenty minutes scrolling through social media, trying to figure out lines for the night's game, and found myself laughing at a picture of the guys in the locker room posing with their good luck teddy bears. The team captain had bought them the year before and a few of them looked a little more loved than others. Then I wrinkled my nose at how disgusting those things had to be by now. They'd been to every practice and game since they'd gotten them. *Damn superstitious athletes.*

My skillful ability to look casually late had eaten up more than an hour, meaning I'd get to DASH over half an hour after doors opened. I definitely wouldn't look like I'd been bored out of my mind with nothing to do, which was exactly what I'd been. But no one needed to know that.

After living in New York City for years, even the typical downtown traffic jams we got didn't seem all that daunting, but I'd also spent over a decade of my life living in noisy neighborhoods with street noise filtering in at all hours of the day and night. When I'd moved back to Tennessee, I could have easily gotten a nice place in or near downtown, but I'd chosen a place on the outskirts of Nashville a few miles from Zander's house.

It took longer to get to work in the mornings, and it was a farther drive to the club when I went, but the quiet days and nights made it worth it. At least the days and nights I was home. I spent too many nights at the office—much to my mom's dismay—to say I took full advantage of my house, which sat on a double lot in a quiet neighborhood. I'd worked my ass off in New York, and I'd managed to save enough money that I was able to enjoy myself now that I didn't live in the middle of one of the most expensive cities in America.

The parking lot at DASH was busy when I arrived, meaning the turnout had been good. I'd noticed that the intro nights continued to gather larger crowds each time Dad hosted one. It had been refreshing to know that new members were still being drawn to the club.

When DASH first opened, it had drawn in a lot of older men. After nearly two decades, the membership was balanced nicely across age groups, but I was noticing a rapid uptick in the twenty-to-thirty crowd.

I found a spot near the back of the building, then headed around to the front entrance. The front door handle was still in my hand when I heard my gram's voice ring out. "Nathan! What are you doing here tonight? I thought you were watching the game?"

I gave her a casual lift of the shoulder in hopes of conveying that my plans changed. "Seth asked Zan for help, so I decided to record the game and see if Dad needs some help."

Gram gave me a weird look that didn't go away as she stood up to give me a hug. "Oh. I see." She barely came up to my chest, but there was a part of me that still remembered the feel of the wooden spoon she'd whack me with when I got in trouble as a child. Even through jeans, those swats stung, and it never escaped my notice that she still had a wooden spoon hanging from the cabinet in her kitchen. It wasn't the *same* spoon, as she'd broken that one on Austin a few years earlier when he'd swiped the cookies she was making for a community bake sale. The story was still told, and Austin wore the badge with pride, happily bragging that he was the one that finally broke Gram's spoon.

She'd replaced it shortly afterward but had never swatted us since then, though she still threatened to from time to time.

I gave the top of her head a kiss. "Gram, a couple is coming in."

She stepped back, scurrying to her spot at the desk, then held out her hand to me once she was seated. "Card."

I handed over my membership card, waiting for her to scan it into the computer. An octogenarian woman in control of the front desk at the gay BDSM club hadn't been planned, but Gram was now an essential member of DASH. Dad had originally hired a guy to be the front desk person, but on the night of the soft opening, he'd been a no-call, no-show. With all the adult kids at college and Mom home with the youngest boys, Dad's back was against the wall. What was supposed to be a one-night gig for Gram turned into her retirement job. She loved the members, the members loved Gram, and she'd been the person who had greeted every new member since that day.

After being checked in, I headed through the door to see what people were getting up to. I could see a group of about fifteen in the conference room and Dad's voice filtered out as he talked. From the sound of it, he was discussing different striking implements... and lo and behold, I heard him talking about a wooden spoon.

The main floor was quieter than I'd expected it to be. I made my rounds of a few people I'd seen around before, and I answered several questions for a couple of new members, and then I bumped into Zander along the far wall.

I knew my brother's look of shock had to rival my own because we were both blinking dumbly at one another for much longer than would be considered polite. Zander's mouth flapped open and closed a few times before he pulled himself together. "Hey. I wasn't expecting to see you here."

I narrowed my eyes at Zander before beginning to whisper-hiss at him. "The fuck? You told me you were helping Seth out. And where's your boy?" Worst-case scenarios ran through my head and caused my temper to flare.

Zander held up his hands in a placating gesture. "Down, tiger. I *am* helping Seth out. He asked me to come keep an eye on someone new. Someone he was worried about because he was going to be here alone. That's exactly what I'm doing. My boyfriend *is* at work and very aware of where I am and why I'm here without him."

My anger dissipated almost instantly, and Zander snorted his discontent. "You need to learn to trust. Listen, I told Seth I would keep it confidential, and I really didn't expect you to show up here unannounced."

"Sorry, Zan. You shocked the hell out of me." I took a few steps away, trying to regain my footing after the shock of his appearance.

Whoever he was here to watch over, he was doing a great job not looking at them. Hell, who knew if the guy had even shown up. I wasn't going to press or distract my brother any longer than absolutely necessary, so I clapped him on the shoulder. "I'll make myself scarce." I shot him a playful wink and turned away, only for my eyes to land directly on the last person I'd ever expected to see at DASH.

I swung back around to face Zander, who had dropped the cool-as-a-cucumber Deputy Johnson vibe and was staring back at me with deer-in-the-headlight eyes. "My *attorney*?" I couldn't help the way my hiss had risen in pitch. I was too shocked to keep it inside.

Zander gave me the patented big brother look. The one that told me he meant business no matter what I thought.

"He doesn't even know I'm here. So make yourself scarce like you said you would."

That would be a hell of a lot easier if I could take my eyes off Elliot.

He hadn't noticed me, of that I was sure. He was in a dimly lit area of the club, and his eyes were focused intently on a man kneeling at a Dom's feet. I forced myself to look away from Elliot long enough to see who he was watching. I didn't know the couple well, I'd only seen them around a few times in the past, but they were quiet and had always been kind. They were definitely still newer to the lifestyle, so I wasn't surprised to see them. Then again, the Kool-Aid Man could have bust through the wall and I probably wouldn't have been as surprised as I had been to see Elliot standing across the room from me at DASH.

And he was nervous. I'd seen him the first day at the office, tentative and unsure. I'd witnessed it firsthand when I'd thrown my plans on him a few hours after he'd walked in the door for the first time. He didn't hide his nervousness well. From the way he gnawed on his lower lip to the way he kept fidgeting with his hands, he was so far out of his comfort zone it was hard to watch.

My protective instinct went on high alert. "What's he doing here?"

"All I know is that Seth asked me to come and keep an eye on him." Zander's voice was level. I was pretty sure that if I looked at him, he'd have his shoulders lifted in a shrug.

But I wasn't looking at him—I couldn't take my eyes off Elliot.

As I watched, Elliot's eyes occasionally moved from the couple he was watching but always quickly found them again. I couldn't help but wonder what he was so drawn to, but by the way he tilted his head as he studied them, some of the tension leaving his shoulders each time his eyes found them, told me he saw something he liked.

"Why not me?"

My brother scoffed. "I'm sure there are plenty of reasons, not the least of which is your quick dismissal of everything and everyone. But you know, he works with you, and from what I've heard, you've been cold, distant, and were a total ass to him... at least in the beginning."

"I've toned it down."

"And I'm sure you've extended that olive branch along the way." The eyebrow cocked upward at me told me he knew very well that I hadn't.

Brutal honesty at the kink club. Had to love my brother.

I didn't have an excuse or a retort available, so Zander took it as permission to continue. "You're not really as big of an asshole as you portray. You bend over backward to help us out when you can, but you have this need to be in control of every aspect of your life that is getting in your way. I see the way you're looking at him, like you're mad that he didn't tell you he was coming here. He's not your submissive and from where I stand, this doesn't look like his cup of tea."

From where I stood, this looked exactly like what Elliot wanted. Even from across the room, I saw the way his eyes softened when he looked at the man kneeling for his Dom. And each time the Dom touched his sub, Elliot leaned toward them. What Zander saw as... well, I wasn't exactly sure what Zander saw in Elliot's gaze. I saw an intense longing.

Then his eyes would drift away for a moment. That time, his eyes fell on the only impact play scene happening. I suspected my dad had something to do with it since the Dom and sub were regular members who normally gravitated toward more extreme impact play. Them doing a scene with just a flogger and a leather paddle was out of place for a normal night. It was a good way for people interested in impact play to dip their toes into the water while not overwhelming them with whips and crops.

Elliot's eyes widened, then he winced like someone had hit him when the suede flogger came down on the sub's ass cheeks. All the peace he'd found watching the first couple was gone in an instant. His finger went to his mouth and he chewed at his nail, his other hand balling into a fist, and I swore he sank in on himself.

I definitely had the asshole vibe down well, but I was also a Dom who hated seeing someone visibly uncomfortable. BDSM was supposed to bring release, not cause stress. Though, looking back on what I knew about Elliot, I was pretty sure everything brought him stress.

My feet were reacting before my brain. To the point that I only barely recognized Zander's displeased hiss of my name as I stepped away from him and began to close the distance to Elliot. I was officially flying by the seat of my pants, something I rarely did.

"JesusFuckingChrist," I heard Zander hiss at me as I headed toward the other side of the room.

This was an epically bad idea, but I couldn't seem to make myself stop.

CHAPTER 10

ELLIOT

I COULDN'T BELIEVE I'd actually talked myself into going to DASH. Thirty minutes after arriving, I still hadn't decided why I'd really shown up. Was it for research? Was it for personal knowledge? Was it curiosity? Maybe it was a little of all of the above.

I'd been thankful for the quiet, dark corner I'd found shortly after arriving. No one seemed to know I was there, no one had spoken to me, and I was free to just watch. And watch was all I wanted to do. I'd been totally content to people watch and listen to the guy in the room beside me talk about kink, BDSM, and how it related to life in general. He was passionate about the discussion and had been answering every single question thrown his way. He sounded nice, and I didn't know why that surprised me.

From what I knew of my brother's boyfriend, he was a genuinely nice guy, and he was a Dom too. But he was a Daddy Dom, not just a Dom. I knew there was a difference, but I didn't fully understand what the differences were. Why did I associate Daddies with nice and not-Daddy Doms with mean? Maybe it was because I'd quickly figured out that Nathan was a Dom and he always had a scowl on his face. Until I'd met Nathan, I'd never been intimidated by a coworker. Nathan intimidated me like no one else before, yet he was also intriguing and my body reacted to him anytime he was near.

I wasn't sure how long I'd zoned out for, simply observing my surroundings and listening to the discussion in the room next to me, but I was pretty sure I had. At some point, a man had taken a seat and the guy next to him had gone to his knees beside him. My attention was immediately drawn to them. It was like the pictures on the Internet but different at the same time. The Dom was seated, the sub resting his head on the guy's thigh.

They looked peaceful.

And the Dom was always touching the other guy. His fingers in his hair, touching his cheek, resting his hand on his shoulder. Even when people came to talk, they spoke to the guy sitting in the chair, not the one on the floor, but the Dom never took his hand off his partner.

I reached up and rubbed at my chest, trying to make the tightness go away. It wasn't until my lip came free from my teeth that I realized I'd been chewing on it. It was a nervous habit I'd always had, but I hadn't known how hard I'd been biting it until that moment.

The pain in my lip distracted me briefly and I looked

away from the two in front of me. That was a mistake. My eyes fell on a man with a flogger. The guy in front of him was wearing nothing but a jockstrap and was holding onto a wooden cross. His skin was pink, and now that my attention had landed on them, I was unable to pull it away. The flogger struck the guy's ass and I swore I could feel it on my skin. I recoiled slightly.

This was too much.

I didn't want that.

I shook my head at myself when I felt my teeth dig into my cuticle. Nope, too much. Much too much. This wasn't for me.

A little voice in the back of my head asked what exactly wasn't for me? Did I not want to be that person kneeling? Or did I not want to be the person being flogged? Or was it a no-go in terms of work? What was I even reacting to? All I knew was now that I'd seen and heard the sound of leather, or whatever material that was, making contact with skin, my own skin felt hot and tight.

Before I made a spectacle of myself, I needed to get out of there. I thrust my hand in my pocket, the hard plastic of my key fob helping ground me. For the first time, I understood security items. That piece of plastic kept reminding me that I would be fine.

I'd made it a grand total of two steps toward the door when a hand landed on my shoulder.

"Elliot."

No. No, no, no, no, no, no, no. I knew that voice. I'd

known coming to DASH was a risk, but I'd played the odds and hoped I'd been right. I didn't want to talk to Nathan about this... about any of it: submission, work, the club.

He'd have questions. And where would I start? The research, why I was there, my motives? Fuck. I might have come out to Austin and Seth, but I'd felt safe with them. I felt anything but on even ground when it came to Nathan. Whether he was gay or not hadn't entered into my equation about telling him about myself.

"Breathe for me."

I knew that voice, but I didn't know that tone. Nathan sounded genuinely concerned.

Remembering the morning in my car when I'd been talking to Emma before work came to mind. I'd worried that he'd overheard our conversation, but he'd never even glanced my way, so I was pretty sure he hadn't. But now he was standing in front of me at a gay BDSM club and I had nothing to say for myself. The only thing pinging around in my brain was *no*.

"You're not breathing yet. In." His voice was deep and commanding, leaving no room to question his instruction. Even if my head wanted to ignore him, my body could not, and I inhaled sharply.

And damn, Nathan was wearing a pair of skintight leather pants and a white shirt only buttoned up about halfway, with a silver hooped earring in his ear. I couldn't get over how sexy that piercing was.

Something I'd never noticed before was the bold tattoo

on his chest and shoulder. He must have worn heavier shirts or undershirts to work because there was no way the thick black lines could have been hidden beneath a normal white dress shirt.

My eyes were initially drawn to the tattoo, but with his shirt opened, there was no mistaking his smooth chest as well. Did he shave? Was he naturally hairless? I didn't know if it mattered when all I could think about was how his skin would feel against my hands. I could so easily bury my face in his chest and lick his skin.

When my logical brain caught up with me, I stopped breathing again. I was standing in front of Nathan, thinking about what his skin would feel like and taste like, and my cock had been reacting accordingly. It reminded me of the reason I'd been avoiding him like the plague for the last week and a half.

His eyes widened subtly, and I wasn't sure if I was seeing amusement or concern in them. "In. Now. You stopped breathing again."

Why had my body forgotten how to do the most basic functions? My eyes were beginning to dry out from staring at him, my mouth had already gone dry, and my chest was starting to ache from not breathing.

Nathan repeated the command, his voice more forceful that time. "In." He reached out and grabbed my hand, putting it on his chest as he took a deep breath.

I didn't know if it was from the shock of his touch or his no-nonsense tone, but I finally pulled in a lungful of air.

My breathing came faster than his slow breaths, but at least I was breathing again.

Or so I thought.

"Slower. You're going to pass out or hyperventilate. After the disaster with Noah, I don't think we can take another guy knocking himself out here."

The statement was so surprising I found myself following his lead. Did I want to know who Noah was? Or why he'd knocked himself out here? Or hell, *how* he'd managed to do so?

With my hand still on his chest, I felt the relief wash through Nathan's body even before he spoke. "Better."

Yeah, I was breathing again but was that really better? I'd been spotted at DASH by the one guy I'd wanted to avoid, and my body had reacted to him in inappropriate ways. I had no idea what to do or say. At least the worry about what Nathan would say next had the situation in my pants calming down rapidly.

Was he going to be upset that he'd found me here? Was my reaction going to be enough that he'd think I wouldn't work out? It had been a constant worry since my third day at work when I'd overheard a phone call where he'd told the person on the other end of the line that he'd been close to hiring someone before his mom hired me. He hadn't wanted me at the office. That much had been clear from the moment I'd stepped in the door. Wouldn't it figure the one time I did something without my parents' approval, I would fuck it up without trying?

My eyes stung, and my chest was tight again. I needed to get out of there.

A rumble beneath my hand had my attention focusing back on the man in front of me. "Jesus, you're a mess."

That time the flogger striking the guy behind us hadn't been what made me wince. Nathan gripped my elbow. "Come on, let's get you off the main floor."

A big guy came toward us, his arms crossed in front of his chest, and stared Nathan down. "What are you doing?"

"Taking him to the office."

I watched the bigger guy's eyebrows rise high on his forehead. "The office?"

"Not *that* office, Z. Mom's office. He clearly doesn't belong here, and he is in no condition to drive."

The words stung and I pulled my hand away from Nathan's grasp as I glanced back at the couple sitting near us. The older guy had his hand resting on the younger one's head and they both appeared to be at peace. I wanted to feel that.

I wanted to belong somewhere.

I hadn't belonged at home in Chicago. My parents had all but pushed me out the door to college. Not that I would have stayed local anyway, I'd been ready to leave. I'd wanted to figure out who I was, wanted to explore my own sexuality. But as it turned out, I hadn't belonged in New York, either.

I'd been overwhelmed at first, and living in the closet was a lot easier than coming out of it. So I'd stayed there.

Besides, my parents had always had my next move planned out for me. It got worse when Kyle left for college. He'd told them he wasn't following their dreams and left. The guy had more courage in his little finger than I had in my body. But that left me taking the brunt of their energy, even living half a country away.

When it finally got to be too much and I was about to break, Emma and I had happened to find something that worked for us. In the end, I'd spent over fifteen years in New York City, and I'd never put down roots there. I'd never made my own friends, pouring everything I had into my work and making partner.

All I had to show for that hard work were two parents that were disappointed in me, a brother who hated my existence, anxiety, and a rented guest house in Tennessee.

My life was truly pathetic.

I was thirty-five and I'd never done anything for myself. Not until Emma started to push me to find my happiness. Not until I took a job against my parents' wishes. Not until I'd discovered that there was something incredibly appealing about being the guy on his knees handing over control.

But I didn't belong here either.

Maybe it was time to admit that I would never find a place I belonged.

The bigger guy, Z—who I could only assume was Nathan's oldest brother, Zander—looked worried. "Hey, are you okay?" He'd come to my side, effectively blocking me from the rest of the room and leaving me boxed in by two big guys.

I nodded, not trusting what would come out of my mouth with my head such a mess. All I wanted to do was get out of there, head back to my place, and regroup. Maybe Emma would have some advice for me.

It was all overwhelming and I hadn't noticed the tears leaking from my eyes until the big guy's hand gently turned my head toward him and used a thumb to brush the tears from my cheek. "You don't look okay."

My smile was forced and wobbly, but all I could do was hope it looked more convincing than it felt. "I'm fine. Got lost in my head."

Nathan growled, a deep, low rumble that did funny things to my insides. That sound definitely shouldn't have made me want to curl up in his lap and beg for all of his attention, yet that was exactly what it did.

And what did it say about me that I was so attention-starved that a sound of annoyance made me needy?

Nathan continued like he hadn't noticed my reaction, so maybe I'd kept it to myself better than I'd thought. "He needs out of here. Mom's office is quiet and neutral."

His brother didn't look as convinced as Nathan appeared to. "Do you really think that's a good idea?"

"Want him to stay out here and gain more attention?"

What happened to the BDSM community being accepting? DASH was welcoming—that was what Seth had told me.

Was it that clear that I didn't belong here? A big part of me just wanted to scream that I wanted someone to tell me where I belonged, because I was ready to belong. I was ready to find a boyfriend. I was ready to have a kiss that felt more than platonic. I wanted to know what sex felt like when I wasn't faking it. I wanted to find a group of friends that would actually miss me when I moved away after fifteen years.

Zander narrowed his eyes at his brother. "If anyone should be taking him to Mom's office, it's me."

Nathan visibly bristled. "I work with him."

"He's new to everything. We can step outside and talk, then let him decide if he wants to go home or stay."

The two continued their back-and-forth like I wasn't there. I waited a little while to see if they would stop, but when it was clear they wouldn't, I finally cleared my throat. I was feeling better and the two had clearly forgotten I was standing there, despite talking about me. "I'm just going to get going."

My hand went back into my pocket and I took a step back. The sooner I could get out of here, the better.

"Wait!" The two had chorused the word and my traitorous feet stopped before my brain could tell them to ignore the men and keep walking.

Zander and Nathan had a silent conversation. In any other situation, it would have been funny; right now it just pissed me off. Everywhere I looked, there were couples who were in tune with each other. Very little conversation was happening in the center of the room, and even the quiet conversations along the edges of the room were hushed and brief. Aside from a few times with Emma, I'd never shared that connection with anyone.

Anxiety, annoyance, and anger at the entire situation made me snap. "Why?" I kept my voice to a hiss, aware enough of those around us to keep my voice down. "So you two can continue talking about me like I'm not here? To point out a little more that I shouldn't be here? Or do you just want to get it over now and tell me not to come to work on Monday?" I snapped my mouth shut, horrified that I'd said everything in my head out loud.

I shouldn't have been surprised at myself. I got frustrated and spouted off before I had a chance to think my thoughts through. It had gotten me into trouble more than once.

The loud smack in the room didn't faze anyone around us, but Nathan rubbed at the back of his head and shot his brother a look. "What the fuck was that for?"

Zander shook his hand out, and it was then I figured out the sound had been Zander's hand making contact with the back of Nathan's head. "I know you like to pretend that you're an asshole, but I didn't think you really were an asshole."

Nathan glowered at his brother. "I'm not an asshole."

Zander's scoff was so exaggerated it was nearly comical. "Keep telling yourself that. Typically, I'd tell you you'd be an idiot to take him to Mom's office, but in this case, I think it's best. You need to talk this out, whatever *this* is. I can't even venture a guess as to what you've gotten yourself into, but I'm pretty damn sure that you've opened your mouth one too many times."

I didn't know Zander, but I liked him. Despite the racing thoughts in my head, I found myself smiling at the way he was scolding his brother.

Nathan made to say something, but Zander let out a growl that was far more menacing than the sound Nathan had made a few minutes before. "Go. And I'm waiting outside the door." He was mumbling about his brother being a bigger moron than he'd given him credit for as he turned to me. His expression softened when his eyes met mine. "My brother's an idiot sometimes. He takes himself way too seriously, and he's a Johnson... we're all stubborn as mules. But he understands limits. If you tell him no, he's going to listen."

I had no idea what he was talking about in terms of limits and the conversation we were going to have. Limits sounded a lot like we were moving toward BDSM and not having a talk about my job.

Nathan grumbled something I couldn't make out but stopped as soon as Zander turned an icy glare his way. "You're not going to be an asshole, Nate. Go talk to him."

Nathan glanced my direction, sighed, then inclined his head toward a dark hallway. "Z's right. We need to talk. We haven't gotten off on the right foot and this is not where or how we should be having this conversation."

CHAPTER 11

NATHAN

IT FELT a lot like heading to the gallows as Zander, Elliot, and I walked toward my mom's office. Seeing Elliot standing along the wall looking like he wanted to shrink into the background had done something to me. The problem was I couldn't figure out what it was. Part of me had felt like he was invading my space, which I knew was ridiculous. Part of me had wanted to do something incredibly atypical and comfort him.

I didn't know what had happened when I'd stood there and watched him, but a nontrivial part of me ached to go over and comfort him. Though Zander might have been right. I came across as harsh, and the two of us didn't have enough of a relationship for him to trust me. Hell, we didn't *have* a relationship. I'd spent two weeks pouting like child and pushing him away.

Seth knew enough about him to know that he was

coming to DASH and had thought to call Zander to make sure he wasn't totally alone. Austin and Elliot had become close since he'd started work too. To the point that Austin spent most of his time bugging Elliot instead of me. I still hadn't figured out why that bothered me so much, just knew it did.

But seeing Elliot standing in the shadows that night, my heart had constricted painfully. He looked lost and out of his element. I knew he wasn't familiar with kink from the way he'd reacted when I spoke about my plans, so I didn't figure he was here for pleasure. The way he'd reacted when he'd heard the flogging spoke volumes about his discomfort at the entire scene.

Zander staring me down hadn't helped me get my head on straight. Now I was questioning every move I made. The uncertainty didn't go away when I reached for the office handle and Zander grumbled about not liking this at all. The words didn't help Elliot's overall nervousness either. He bristled noticeably and it looked like he was going to step away.

"You aren't Dad."

Zander sighed and closed his eyes. "You're right. But there's definitely a voice in my head that sounds an awful lot like him, telling me that I am an idiot." Zander's normally warm expression turned frigid as he leaned forward to speak quietly in my ear. "That door stays unlocked. You will not force him to talk about anything he doesn't want to. And so help me, Nathan, if you get in over your head, just knock on the door. He looks somewhere between a spooked horse and a scared kid, and I don't know how that's going to play out."

I nodded once in acknowledgement and stepped back from his grip. Alarm bells were ringing in my head too.

I should have sent Zander over to check on him, not me. Zander was the nurturer of the family. He was the open ear that Mom and Dad always were, but he didn't have that parent vibe to him. He was our big brother, the fixer, the caretaker, and we all leaned heavily on him.

I was the cold, detached one in the family. My siblings didn't come to me if they had problems. I wasn't the sounding board for complicated issues. My house wasn't filled with family members, and my door wasn't always open. I was the wrong person to be comforting anyone, especially Elliot; he needed someone like Zander, not me.

Shit.

It was going to take me longer than I had to truly gather my thoughts, so I was officially winging it. I pressed the lock code slower than normal, though it only bought me a couple seconds. And since I had to think more about each number instead of using muscle memory to just press in rapid succession, I had only succeeded in delaying the inevitable.

With the door open, I flicked on the light and gestured for Elliot to come in. For the first time in I couldn't remember how long, I felt off-kilter. I wasn't sure how this was going to go or even where to take it. I gently shut the door behind him and, remembering Zander's words, didn't lock it.

I gestured to the comfortable couch Mom kept in the office. It had been used for more than one nap over the years, and I could honestly say it was more comfortable than the couch in my house. "Take a seat."

Some long dormant, possibly never-before-surfaced part of me wanted to sit next to Elliot on the couch and provide comfort, but I knew that was a terrible idea. We didn't have that relationship, even on a coworker level, so I stepped back and leaned against the desk, gripping the top with my hands and crossing my legs at the ankle in an attempt to look casual.

Elliot looked between the couch and me a number of times, questions in his eyes, but when I didn't say anything else, he eventually took a seat. I knew he'd wanted to bolt by the way he had eyed the door a number of times. I could see the wheels turning in his head as he worked out just how quickly he could get out of the office.

If that was what he wanted, I wasn't going to stop him. No. I was not planning to leave this spot. Besides, I needed to know why he was at DASH. I needed to remind him that he didn't have to be involved in my plans. He had an attention to detail that I couldn't deny, and I could see why my mom had been so excited about hiring him. He also had a work ethic like mine, except Mom didn't let him take files home.

If he didn't take files home at night, what did he do with himself in the evenings?

"Are you okay?" The question seemed like a reasonable place to start. He'd looked upset from the moment my eyes had fallen on him, but since then, he'd cried, he'd gotten angry, and he'd nearly had multiple panic attacks. I wasn't wholly convinced he wasn't still in the midst of one.

Elliot blinked a few times, the familiar pink blush spreading on his face. "Yeah. I'm fine. Be better if I could go home."

I lifted my shoulder casually. "I'm not stopping you."

He scoffed. "Could have fooled me. You and your brother both told me not to leave. Now I'm in this office with you while he guards the door."

Okay, he had me there. "It wasn't quite like that exactly. Neither of us want you to get hurt if you're not okay to drive."

Elliot crossed his arms over his chest. He'd spent way too much time sitting behind a desk because his arms were thin compared to mine. Hell, they were thinner than Austin's, and Austin hated the gym. He swore there were better ways to burn calories than lifting weights and suffering through gym locker rooms.

"I'd be fine to drive."

The dried tear tracks on his cheeks and the way he'd stopped breathing on me twice said differently, but I wasn't going to argue that now. "I told you already that I'm not expecting you to be involved in the kinkier side of the firm. Mom's office is on the other side of the building, so you won't even need to see all that once I go over there. I can't figure out why you'd come here when it's something that bothers you so much."

Over the last two weeks, I'd seen Elliot shy, flustered, embarrassed, confused, and on more than one occasion, laughing and smiling while he chatted with my mom or brother. I'd also witnessed a kind, compassionate man as he'd spoken to Maxwell. Maybe that was what was throwing me off so much. He hadn't seemed to be turned off by Maxwell and Matt and had seemed to bond with Maxwell to a degree.

The Elliot I was looking at now, the one with a cold look of disgust—his head cocked to the side, his eyes hard—and the throaty scoff he let out was new to me. "God, don't be so fucking full of yourself. Yeah, part of me wanted to know how I felt for work reasons, but after talking with Maxwell, I'd already known I could handle that."

I couldn't parse the information he was giving me. "So you came here for what?"

Elliot's sigh told me I was missing something obvious, but his words were pained. "It doesn't matter, does it? I don't belong here." He stood up from his spot on the couch, avoiding my gaze completely. He was only a few inches shorter than me, but right then he looked tiny, almost deflated.

Then his words jarred something in my brain. "Wait, what do you mean you don't belong here?"

An eyebrow rose on his forehead. "Your words. Not mine. So you tell me. All I really want to know is if I should show up on Monday or not. Don't dick me around and not give me a chance to pack my stuff up from your brother's place this weekend."

His words were bouncing around in my brain and I was struggling to keep up. When had I told him he didn't belong here? And why wouldn't he be coming back to work? And why did the idea of not having Elliot in the office bother me more than my mom hiring him in the first place had? That was a weird feeling that I hadn't expected and I was unable to take the time to process it with Elliot across from me.

Elliot's jaw was set like carved granite, but just behind the cold exterior, I could see pain. I was mentally kicking myself for not seeing it earlier. The false bravado had been clear in every interaction from the minute he'd seen me the first time until now. I had to give him that he had a great poker face, but if I'd taken the time to really see him, I'd have noticed it earlier.

The man in front of me was almost always on the verge of breaking down. Fear and uncertainty lurked just behind the stiff shoulders and square jaw. With the realization, a deep, unexpected sadness hit me low in my stomach.

I'd picked up enough to know that Elliot was intelligent, but it hadn't hit until then that—between the conversations I'd overheard and the things his old boss had said—his self-confidence was nearly nonexistent. I'd heard him on the phone enough with his friend Emma to know that she was his go-to person. She'd talked him off more than one ledge in the last two weeks. He'd called her for everything from coming out to my brother to trying to contact his own brother. The last topic had almost made me curious enough to ask him about it, but the way he'd so resolutely insisted that it was pointless made me withhold the question.

There was a lot I could pick apart from every interaction we'd had for nearly two weeks, but going back to the beginning wasn't going to happen tonight. I needed to make sure to focus on the conversation we were having now, but even that left a lot to discuss. I chose the one thing that I thought might be easiest. "I honestly don't remember telling you that you don't belong here."

"Well, because you didn't tell me. You told your brother. But the meaning was clear."

Yeah, I'd said he hadn't belonged here. What I hadn't meant was in the club in general, but I could see why Elliot would think that.

Truthfully, I'd been nothing but an asshole to him and had gone out of my way to rub it in that I was kinky. *Shit, I was an asshole.* My face screwed up, but there was no point in trying to hide it. I'd been wrong. "Please, don't leave." I sounded defeated and maybe that was what I was. "I did say that, but I hadn't meant it the way it came out. It definitely isn't an excuse, but it's the truth."

Elliot hesitated with his hand outstretched toward the doorknob.

I was going to take the hesitation as a win, or at least a very short reprieve, so I spoke quickly. "I wanted to get you off the main floor. You looked genuinely terrified and you'd stopped breathing."

Elliot let out a laugh that was anything but humorous. "Maybe because you suddenly showed up? I know that your parents own the club, but Seth said you watch the games, so I thought it would be safe and I wouldn't see you here."

I really hadn't made a good impression on Elliot if he was actively trying to avoid me. I had no idea how to make that better, and it didn't look like he was going to give me a chance. He'd built up a head of steam by this point, but I'd be lying if I said I didn't find it refreshing to see him with his guard down.

He threw his hands in the air and nearly yelled at me. "Counting that damned application I filled out for tonight, I've told precisely four people I'm gay. I'm so fucking far out of my comfort zone tonight that I'm pretty sure I left it in a different time zone. But I didn't do this for you or your career plans; I did this for me. For once in my goddamned life, I wanted to do something for myself. I thought I found something I understood, even if it was just a basic understanding. So yeah, I was interested. Okay? *I* was interested.

Apparently, I was wrong about that too." He didn't bother hiding the tears that welled in his eyes. He simply ducked his head and reached for the door again.

My mouth was faster than my brain and words spilled from my mouth.

"Wait. Please don't go."

He swung around so fast I was pretty sure he was going to punch me. Not that I didn't deserve it at that point. "Why? Why should I stay someplace I'm not wanted?" His hands flew upward in frustration. "It's the story of my life. Don't belong in Chicago, or New York, or Tennessee. Don't belong at DASH or the straight clubs."

He flung the door open before I could process everything he'd said to me, but he ran straight into Zander before he made it all the way out.

Zander caught him by the shoulders. "Whoa, there. Slow down." His voice was calm and steady, and Elliot didn't try to push back. There was something about Zander that made people relax, even me. And I couldn't deny I was glad to see my big brother entering the room.

Elliot didn't fight as Zander guided him gently back into the room and sat him down on the couch. "First, are you two okay?"

I nodded my head while I watched in awe as Elliot's mask slid right back into place and he followed my lead. "I'm fine."

If I hadn't seen how upset he'd been a moment earlier, I'd have believed him. From Zander's raised eyebrow, I got the impression he felt the same way. "Okay. Care to tell me why you were hauling out of here like your ass was on fire?"

I opened my mouth but Elliot's voice stopped me. "I simply realized what a mistake this had been. And I need to go."

He got up and left the room before Zander or I could stop him. At that point, I figured it was better to not stop him. We'd already cornered him a number of times. There was a fine line between making sure he was okay and holding him against his will.

With Elliot gone, I finally allowed myself to take a seat on the couch. Zander gave me a few moments to gather my thoughts before he looked over. "Care to talk about it?"

I fell back against the couch and rubbed at my forehead. "Fuck if I know. Honestly, I don't have a clue where to go with it. I think I fucked up."

Zander's light scoff told me he wasn't surprised. "That sounds about like you. You're so bullheaded. But what has you tied in knots about him?"

Was that what I was feeling? Was that what that pit in my stomach was? "I wish I knew. I'm only just beginning to figure him out. I've been an ass, and I know that." I held up my hand before Zander could say anything. "You don't have to tell me I've been an ass since the day I met him. Mom threw me for a loop when she hired him. I'd been about to hire someone else. I have a vision and I'd wanted an attorney who would see eye to eye with me. What I hadn't seen at the time was that I didn't need my duplicate. Elliot's great with our current clients. He can totally hold up that end of the business for me and let me focus on other things."

My brother narrowed his eyes. "Do I want to know what you're planning?"

He was overthinking it and I knew it. "I want to take on more clients from alternative lifestyles. I'd found a person I thought would be a great fit and I'd been about to offer them a job. I knew nothing about Elliot—hell, I still don't know much about him. I immediately pegged him as straight, without a kinky bone in his body."

Zander's narrowed eyes told me I was an idiot, not that I could blame him. I probably was. "I'm guessing you've learned differently."

I rolled my head so I was looking at my brother. "He definitely surprised me tonight. We could say it was quite eye-opening."

"So what are you going to do about it?"

That wasn't what I'd expected Zander to say to me. My initial reaction was to tell him nothing, but even I knew that would be the wrong thing for me to do. "What I'm going to do and what I should do are not in sync with one another."

Zander tried to suppress his laughter but air still escaped his nose. "You don't say? When has what you should do and what you did ever been the same thing?"

I stuck my middle finger up at my brother, but even that was halfhearted at best. "He's gay."

"Figured as much... what with him being *here* instead of at Cuffed."

"Okay, smart-ass." Cuffed was a few blocks away but catered toward the straight community.

Zander just smiled at me, letting me know he was going to wait for me to talk.

"And I fucked up tonight."

That time Zander didn't bother hiding his laughter, though it lacked any humor. "No shit."

"If I'm reading it right, he'd come mostly for himself."

Zander squeezed my knee. "I have to say you're right."

I closed my eyes, replaying the last twenty minutes. *Damn, a lot had happened in a short period of time.* "Yeah. And I said he didn't belong here. I think I meant that he shouldn't have been on the main floor. He'd obviously been panicked."

"You think?" That damned cocked eyebrow spoke volumes.

"Yes, I think... I'm not entirely certain, but I think I'd spoken from sheer surprise. Looking back, I understand why he thought I was telling him that he didn't belong at DASH. And now he thinks that I'm going to fire him because he got in over his head."

"So what should you do about it?"

I thought for a moment before speaking. "I should call

him and let him know that his job is safe and he is welcome at DASH any time, without judgment from me."

The answer pleased Zander and a smile played at his lips. "Yes, that would be reasonable. But you've already told me that you're not going to do what you *should* do. So what exactly are you going to do?"

"Go to his place and talk to him."

Zander's eyebrows shot upward, and I knew immediately that he didn't agree with my plan. "Well, that's a stupid move if I've ever heard one. He tore out of here like his ass was on fire. You could easily call and apologize and be reasonable, but you're going to go invade his personal space?"

When he put it that way, it sounded like an awful idea. Yet there I was, nodding my head. "Yeah. I am. My gut is telling me that I need to go and talk to him."

Zander eyed me suspiciously but eventually gave a single nod. "It doesn't matter what I say—you're going to do it. Your guy screams *scared submissive* to me. Tell me you get that."

I didn't answer right away, wanting Zander to understand that I'd thought about this. "Until tonight, I'd thought socially awkward, but I now see the same thing you do. And I need to talk with him because I think Elliot's got a lot more happening in his head than meets the eye. The way it was left, I don't think he will ever come back here if I just call him."

Zander hummed as he thought. "Then go. You better

figure out a damn good way to grovel because I think you've just about lost yourself a damn good attorney, at the very least."

I jumped up and was halfway to my SUV before Zander's words caught up with me. "What did he mean by 'at the very least'?" It wasn't like the night air was going to answer me, but I wished it could.

CHAPTER 12

ELLIOT

I DIDN'T HEAD STRAIGHT BACK HOME, but there weren't many places I could go to in Nashville. It wasn't like I knew much about the area or anyone around. Even if I had, it wasn't like I was going to end up being good company.

Twenty minutes after I left DASH, I pointed the car toward my temporary home. It probably wouldn't be my place much longer. I'd seen the anger in Nathan's eyes, so it was hard to imagine that he would want me to stay at the firm. I'd made a fool out of myself anyway. It wasn't like me to get emotional like that—lose my cool, yes, emotional, not so much—but being surrounded by Nathan and his brother had made me feel vulnerable in a way I'd never felt before.

And maybe there had been some sadness too. I'd spent my entire life living up to expectations of other people so that at thirty-five I'd never experienced a heartbreak. It would be hard to experience heartbreak without falling in love, something I'd also never done. You couldn't fall in love without dating or kissing a person you were truly attracted to. I'd never had anything like the couples at DASH had.

I'd spent my entire life being the one that held everything together, even when I didn't want to. I'd just begun to discover why it was that I didn't always want to be the one in charge of everything, and the rug had been pulled out from beneath me before I could even talk to anyone.

The guest house was a welcome sight when I finally pulled into the driveway. Seth would be gone for a number of hours yet, and I should have a reprieve from his questions about the night until the next morning at the earliest. Austin's questions too. At least that would give me time to figure out the thoughts in my head and maybe have an answer to something. Hell, an answer to anything would really be welcome at that point.

My phone pinged in the console and it wasn't until I couldn't read the screen that I noticed I was once again crying. I swiped at my eyes and tried to focus on my phone. The name surprised me so much I had to read it three separate times to convince myself I was seeing it right.

Kyle: *I've seen your missed calls and texts, but I haven't known how to respond. Daddy's been telling me to stop ignoring them, and Emma says I need to give you a chance. Except, I don't know what to say to you. So this is me, telling you I don't know what to say at this point, but I'm listening.*

I didn't know how long I'd stared at the phone. For over

six months I'd been calling Kyle's phone and had started texting him from time to time. I'd told him I'd moved and I'd like to talk. I hadn't apologized, nor had I told him where I'd moved to, but I'd been trying. Now I'd found out that he'd been talking to Emma. How long had he been talking to her? And why hadn't she told me? How much did he know? And why did that make me feel so violated?

I swung my car door open and chucked my phone into the dark, not caring if it broke or where it landed. I needed space from everything. I could not handle Kyle suddenly deciding to reach out when the rest of my world was such a disaster.

There were a number of things I'd expected when I'd let go of my phone: a sickening crunch as it collided with the concrete driveway, the rustle of a bush, the splash of the pool. What I hadn't expected was the "Oww! Fuck," followed by a muffled thunk as it landed in what I could only guess was mulch.

Was it better or worse that it probably hadn't broken from the impact? And why was I more concerned about the phone than the voice in the shadows?

I slammed my door, pissed off enough that the featureless voice didn't bother me. If anything, I was pretty sure I'd be able to take the guy out if he came toward me. At least I had been, until the figure stepped from the shadows and I couldn't miss the designer boots or the skintight leather pants. I knew exactly who was standing there before my eyes made it up to his face.

Anger, resentment, and frustration boiled over and I yelled into the darkness. "Why? Why the fuck are you here? I think you said enough earlier tonight."

He held my phone out. "That's a hell of an arm you've got on you."

"Fuck you." I turned away, ignoring the phone in his hand, and stalked toward my front door. My frustration was so high that my hands shook as I tried to line the key up with the lock.

Nathan's voice came again, that time right behind me. "I deserve that. I do."

I shook my head, finding myself frustrated at the man for not leaving. For trying to hand me my phone. For being behind me, close enough that I could feel his body heat on my back. For my body responding in the most inconvenient ways.

"Just leave. You might as well take the damned phone with you." I finally got the key in the lock and managed to turn it so the doorknob twisted open.

Nathan didn't move. He didn't come closer, didn't step away. He didn't even respond to my outburst. He just stood there as I stepped into the house.

When I didn't slam the door immediately, he tilted his head to the side and studied me. "Do you always throw a fit when things don't go right?"

My eyes narrowed at him. "Are you always so cocky?"

He smirked. "It's a Johnson thing."

I couldn't help it, my mind went to something that

wasn't his last name, and I started to laugh. It was a moment of laugh or cry—again—and I chose to laugh. I laughed so hard my sides hurt and Nathan went from confused to concerned. "Yeah. Time to get you inside."

Nathan didn't wait for me to argue; he stepped in and gently shut the door. Part of me wanted to feel alarmed or threatened to have him in my space uninvited, but nothing about his presence felt threatening.

He didn't hesitate as he walked me toward the couch. "Take a seat while I get you a glass of water. You've clearly had quite a night. I'm just going to put your phone on the table here. You might want it at some point."

Doubtful, but I kept my mouth shut. What I really wanted right then was space from everything. Then again, how much space did I really need? "You know what sucks?" I wasn't sure if I was talking to Nathan or if I was simply thinking out loud. Nathan didn't answer, so I continued, happy to be able to fill the quiet. "Never being good enough. That was my brother." I gestured vaguely toward my phone as Nathan returned with the water glass.

He looked at my phone with narrowed eyes. "You threw your phone because your brother called?"

"Texted. For the first time in nearly seven months. I was an asshole the last time we saw each other." I shook my head because that wasn't right. "Not just the last time. Every time we've seen each other since he was about eleven, I've been an asshole."

Nathan hummed as he handed over the glass. "I know a thing or two about being an asshole."

His self-deprecation would have been welcome if I hadn't been so in my head. "But Austin still talks to you, so do Zander and Seth. Jesus, I've been around the office long enough to know that you all basically share a life."

To my surprise, Nathan laughed. "That's a good way to put it. We can definitely be in each other's pockets, as Gram would put it. It's the way we were raised, though. Family comes first."

I dropped my elbows to my knees as I leaned forward, letting my head hang down. "Yeah. Not in my family. Conformity matters. How much can you fit in and keep up with the Joneses. Actually, we *were* the Joneses. Biggest house on the block, Mom and Dad had successful careers. We weren't supposed to make waves. Private school kids with trust funds. The whole nine. But my brother never fell in step. He was always a few steps in the other direction from us. From an early age I learned that if I did that, my life would be hell. The guy was grounded all the time, but he never seemed to care. He just kept doing what he wanted. Going to my grandparents' farm, coming out and openly dating guys. Went to a college my parents didn't approve of to get a degree my parents didn't agree with. All the while I was in the closet, keeping my head down, and doing exactly what they told me to do."

Nathan pushed the glass into my hand. "Drink."

I adjusted so I could take a sip, then set it on the coaster in front of me.

"So why did you stay in the closet and keep doing what they wanted after you graduated?"

"Habit? Fear? They were paying for college. I saw what happened when Kyle went against the grain. College was on him. Housing was on him. They held everything over our heads. I was scared."

Nathan sat down on the other side of the couch from me. "Sounds rough."

I bit my lip. "I think I'd always known that, but at the same time, I hadn't thought about it until it was too late."

"So why did you try to knock me out with your phone?" Nathan was cautious, but I appreciated having someone there at the moment. I didn't even feel like I could call Emma at this point.

I rolled my eyes at the statement. "I didn't try to knock you out."

"Okay, maybe not knock me out, but I can tell you I'm going to have a cell phone-shaped bruise on my chest."

"I didn't even know you were there. I just wanted the damn thing away from me. Yet, just like the rest of this shit night, it's walked right back." I winced when the words left my mouth. That sounded awful and while I didn't mean it exactly as it had come out, it was the truth.

I'd left DASH, but it had followed me home. I'd thrown my phone, but it had found me. I'd run from myself, but damn, here I was. There was no escape. I rubbed at the tight muscle between my neck and shoulder, inclining my head to try to stretch it out. Stress liked to settle there and tension headaches had been my best friend for years.

"I could see why you feel that way. It isn't how I meant it, showing up here tonight."

My fingers found the tight muscle and I squeezed, my face contorting as pain radiated from my shoulder to my temple. "It's definitely not just you."

"Come here."

My head shot over to where Nathan was sitting, the sudden movement not helping the knotted muscle. "Wh-what?"

Nathan spread his legs slightly. "Grab a pillow and take a seat. I'm actually really good at giving massages. I spent most of my teen years giving Seth massages after games and practices." His smile was fond as he spoke of his brother, and I started realizing there was more to Nathan than just the gruff asshole that my dick really liked. There was a sweet side of him lurking somewhere there.

The fond smile on his face turned slightly cocky. "Actually, I ended up enjoying it so much, I took a few massage therapy classes and even an anatomy class in college. Kind of weird with pre-law courses."

I had nothing to say about that. He was a complex guy that had made me feel a bit off-kilter since I'd seen him barreling down the hallway toward Austin the first day. I could either argue that I wasn't in pain or give in and let him, hopefully, take some of it away.

The fight had left me sometime between seeing Nathan at DASH and Kyle telling me that Emma had been texting him. I didn't have it in me to tell him no. Maybe something about this night could be saved, and maybe I could finally sleep without pain. Choosing to not overthink my actions, I stood up.

Nathan didn't hesitate to reach beside him and grab one of the big cushions off the couch. He threw it on the ground between his feet then gestured toward it. "I promise I'll make you feel good."

I somehow managed to keep a snarky remark to myself as I sank down. The cushion was thick enough that it didn't feel much different than sitting on the couch. Then Nathan's thumb found my neck. He'd barely touched it, but the knot rolled and my eye twitched.

"Jesus, Elliot. That's one hell of a knot."

I opened my mouth to tell him I knew that, but all that came out was a long moan.

"Keep making noises like that and we're not going to be talking about what's got you so upset."

It took a moment for the words to fully sink in. Why would a moan keep us from talking? Why were we talking, anyway?

Nathan didn't say anything else while he rubbed at the sore muscle, leaving my brain to turn the sentence over a few times. When I finally figured out what he'd meant, my eyes widened. My cheeks were hot from embarrassment, but not because of what he'd said, more that it had taken me so long to process what he'd meant.

I turned so quickly I surprised us both, but found myself on my knees between his legs. His crotch was at eye level in this position, and it would have been impossible to miss the erection straining in his pants. Not like I had much firsthand knowledge of these things, but it looked impressive from where I was.

Forcing my eyes from his crotch, I looked up. "Did I do that?" Not what I'd meant to say when I turned around. I couldn't even remember what I had been so shocked about that it had made me want to turn around like that.

His gray eyes were intense, his nostrils flaring as he took me in. He could have laughed at me, he could have brushed my surprise off like it was nothing, but instead a soft finger came down and caressed the line of my jaw. "Yeah, you did. And seeing you in that position isn't helping any."

I looked down at myself, feeling like I was two steps behind. I was between his legs, looking up at him, and... oh. Ohh. I was kneeling at Nathan's feet. My blush hurt and I ducked my head.

"Hey, none of that. Tell me what's going through that head of yours. You keep a lot inside, which seems to be how we ended up here in the first place." His hands tangled into my hair and I sucked in a deep breath. It was ridiculous that his hand in my hair was the most intimate touch I could remember having in my life. My dick wasn't the only one who liked it.

Nathan cleared his throat, bringing my eyes back to focus on his. "What made you blush so hard?"

His voice sounded different, rougher, a little more commanding than a moment before, but also kind and gentle. Was that combination even possible?

Fuck if I knew why, but words flowed from my mouth in a totally uninhibited way, unlike my normal thought process that made me overthink everything. "That I didn't understand why you'd find me attractive. Or think of me in that way. Not just because you haven't wanted anything to do with me from the moment I was hired, but because you know yourself and who you are. I've got a toe out of the closet and I'm not even sure if I'm submissive or not. I'm not desirable in any way. I'm an asshole who's spent too much time working."

My words made me drop my head, disgusted with myself. I was going to remain single for the rest of my life if this was what I said when someone took any interest in me.

To my surprise, Nathan's voice was thick with emotion when he spoke. "I was wrong from the beginning. I had wanted to make you uncomfortable."

"You wanted to hire someone else. Someone who knew more about the community and shared your goals."

That time, Nathan winced. "You heard that?"

I nodded slowly. "Yeah. Your voice carries."

He heaved a sigh. "So I've been told. I'm sorry you

heard that. I was having a bit of a temper tantrum myself. Not my finest moment. At the time, I'd been upset that my mom had felt the need to butt in. I know that she was trying to help, and that she really was worried about me. I can also say that I'm glad she found you. You're smart and the clients love you, and over the last few weeks, you've grown on me."

I glanced up, not believing the words I was hearing, and his finger ran down my cheek again. "And you turn adorable shades of red each time someone compliments you."

I allowed myself to lean into his touch. Fully expecting him to pull back, I didn't press hard, but when his hand remained, something inside me snapped. Confusion, frustration, self-doubt, it all seemed to clear as he continued to hold my head. For the first time in months—if not years—I felt some of the constant stress and anxiety I carried around ease.

"You're beautiful kneeling there." Nathan's words felt far away, but his voice was strong and confident. "Having you in that position, there's no way my body wouldn't react to you, Elliot. And I like to see that you're reacting to me."

I looked down at my crotch. My dick hadn't gotten any softer while we talked and was now pressing uncomfortably at my fly. Not for the first time, I had no idea what to do.

CHAPTER 13

NATHAN

If thoughts could be heard, I heard every one of the thoughts running through Elliot's head. He'd been truly shocked that I'd been turned on; he was shocked he was turned on. It was his shock at turning me on that had my heart doing funny things.

I'd grown up in a family that was open about sex and sexuality. We'd been taught that what we wanted, no matter how outside the box, wasn't something to shy away from. Even Larson had accepted that he was a little, despite being convinced he'd never find a Daddy who would understand how the firefighter who looked more like a lumberjack could want to be Daddy's little boy.

Elliot had grown up in a family that sounded less than understanding about anything and everything that might be different than their ideas. And the fact that the man between my legs honestly had no idea that he was attractive did something to me. I wasn't even sure that he knew what to do about his own arousal at that point.

And the fact that he didn't know if he was submissive? I was pretty sure that alone had made some of my grouchy, hard-nosed Dom soften just a bit. He was thirty-five years old and just beginning to figure out that he was submissive. The way his face was leaning against my hand, the hand of the man who'd been an asshole to him for the better part of two weeks, told me just how attention-starved he was.

I let my thumb caress his cheek a few times and he nearly melted into a puddle on the floor in front of me. He'd gone pliant under my touch, and yes, my dick wanted attention badly, but I also knew I couldn't take advantage. Tonight he'd found himself kneeling in front of me and showing me a side of himself that he'd left completely unexplored.

Since I'd met him, Elliot had been stiff as a board: back straight, posture tense, muscles ticking in his jaw. But the longer he knelt in front of me, the farther his shoulders dropped and the looser his muscles became. He would be fun to send flying, but that wouldn't, and couldn't, be the goal tonight.

The scene at the club pinged back to my memory. Elliot hadn't been watching the flogging when I'd first seen him. He'd been looking at a different couple. "You were watching Theo and Shane."

Sleepy brown eyes blinked up at me. The tension had to be exhausting to carry around. Now that he was relaxing, I could see he was fading fast. He suppressed a yawn before speaking. "Who are Theo and Shane?"

"Theo was the guy sitting in the chair. Shane is his boyfriend. Shane was kneeling beside Theo."

Elliot was silent for a beat longer than I'd expected before he finally nodded against my palm. The man wasn't willing to break contact and I wasn't ready to analyze why I wasn't going to make the first move to do so. When he finally spoke, I could hear the wistfulness in his voice. "They looked so peaceful. There's something so freeing about putting myself in the submissive's shoes. It's beautiful. I was standing there thinking about how I couldn't see anyone ever looking at me like that."

He must have been more exhausted than I'd thought because he didn't even flush as he spoke. "Why would you think that?"

Elliot gave me a sad smile. "I'm a thirty-five-year-old who's never even kissed another man. I don't know the first thing about dating because the few women I've been with were casual at best, and my relationship with Emma was never romantic. I'm close enough to forty and just discovering that I'm drawn to submission. Who's going to want to take that on?"

He picked his head up from my hand and forced an uncomfortable chuckle. "I still can't believe that your dick would take an interest in anything about me even for a few seconds. Hell, my body doesn't usually react the way it has around you, and it made me realize how fucked I am. No one wants the shit I've got going on in my life... me included." His lips turned downward. "Listen, if things are going to be too awkward at work now, I'll give you my key Monday. I've got a few things in my office I need to get out."

The man bounced around like a kid strung out on sugar... but his sugar high was the most morose in history. One depressing thought to the next, always expecting the worst. I took his hand and helped him to stand. I ducked my head a bit so that we were eye to eye, but the sadness and uncertainty that followed him around made him seem smaller. I wished we were at the point that I could hold him. It would be too presumptuous for me to take him to his room and get him into bed before I left.

The only thing I could do was smile at him. "You are not giving me the keys back. You need them to get in and out of work every day. And I can assure that it won't be awkward."

At his disbelieving stare, I groped at the front of my pants. My dick was still hard and the damned leather was not very forgiving. "Don't look at me like that. The last ten minutes are going to play on repeat in my brain for the rest of the weekend. I'd love nothing more than to take you to your room, lay you out on the bed, and discover everything that makes your body react. But you have a lot to think about, and I'm not about to rush you."

Watching Elliot go slack-jawed could be addicting. "I'm going to block out my lunch hour on Monday and we're going to go to lunch and talk. If you are still interested in submission, if you want to see where it goes between you and me, then we'll talk about it. If you want me to help you find another Dom, then I'll help you with that too."

I really hoped it didn't come to needing to help him find another Dom. There was something intriguing about Elliot. I just hoped he felt the same way about me.

It took a few seconds for my words to process, but when they did, I found Elliot nodding his head as he struggled to find words. "Oh. Yeah. Um, okay. That works. Yeah."

I couldn't hide my smile at his shock, but I turned serious for a moment. "Will you be okay, Elliot? I don't want to leave you alone if you're too out of sorts."

The statement made Elliot laugh. "I'm going to be fine. Yes, I'm out of sorts but not in a bad way. I just need to work through some thoughts. I'll be okay." He pulled his lower lip between his teeth and shoved his hands awkwardly into his pockets, but he didn't break eye contact.

I studied him closely, trying to decide if he was displaying false bravado. All I saw was genuine honesty, meaning there was no reason for me to stay any longer. I wished I could tug his lip free. He was going to need ChapStick if he kept biting at it as hard as he was. And that overwhelming urge to lean in to kiss him was almost unstoppable. I managed to hold back by reminding myself that he'd never been kissed by a man, and I didn't want to rob him of that first kiss if he wasn't completely ready.

Asshole that I was, I was also respectful. There was no way I was going to push him beyond what he was ready for, no matter how much my libido and hormones demanded attention.

We made our way to the front door, and I paused before I let myself out. "If you need something this weekend, please call."

Elliot released his lip and as expected, it was red, swollen, and I was pretty sure I could already detect a crack in it. "Yeah. Okay. Um." His words trailed off as he scratched at the back of his head nervously. "Um, drive safely."

"Thank you." I needed to get out of there anyway. If I didn't, one of us was going to do something we'd regret, and I didn't want that to weigh on either of us. "I'll see you on Monday."

Elliot watched me leave, and I slipped into my SUV just as the door shut to his house. My phone buzzing in the center console drew my attention and I was surprised to see I'd left the phone in my car.

Zander: *How's it going?*

Zander: *Is Elliot okay?*

Zander: *Are you okay?*

Zander: *Nate, I'm getting worried. Do I need to come by Seth's place?*

Zander: *Five minutes, Nate.*

Zander: *Two minutes. I'm going to tell Gram goodbye now.*

Zander: *I'm in my car. I'll be there in fifteen minutes or less.*

How fast could my fingers tap a message out on the screen? It was time to find out.

Me: *Sorry. Left my phone in the car. No need to come over, I'm leaving now.*

With the initial message sent, I tried to anticipate what Zander would want to know and began tapping out another reply.

Me: *Elliot is fine. I'm fine. I left before anything could happen that wouldn't be able to be taken back. Didn't even kiss him... Though I wanted to. I told him we'll talk on Monday. I think my new attorney has a kinky side.*

Zander: *That doesn't surprise me in the least. I saw the way he was looking at Shane and Theo.*

Me: *Yeah. I behaved. It was hard. He's so unsure of himself.*

Zander: *Probably better if you stay away from him.*

I hit the call button, knowing full well that it was a bad idea to continue sitting in the driveway Elliot shared with Seth. Seth would be home sooner rather than later at this point, and I didn't want to make Elliot nervous with my car sitting in the driveway.

The phone didn't even ring once before Zander's voice filled my car. I was already heading down Seth's driveway, so I eased onto the road and listened as my big brother went, well, big brother on me.

"If he's that confused, then you need to stay away from him."

If I were parked, I'd have pinched the bridge of my nose, but I was driving, so I settled on letting out a sigh. "He's not a kid."

"And you're not known for your patience."

He had me there, but there was something telling me to pursue Elliot. "I know that. I do. But he's different."

Zander's scoff told me he didn't believe me.

"No, seriously, Z. I walked out of there without coming, hard as a fucking rock, after I checked to make sure he was okay. Hell, I didn't even kiss him, even after he ended up kneeling between my legs!" This was enough that I deserved that proverbial cookie. Hell, I didn't need a proverbial cookie—I was going to stop at the all-night cookie store and pick up a few real cookies. Maybe one of them would make it home with me. I'd earned them.

There was silence for a moment before Zander let out a huff that told me he had no clue what to make of me or the situation. "I'm sorry. I think I misunderstood what you said, Bubby."

I growled into the line. Zander knew I hated being called Bubby, but Seth had called me Bubby from the time he could speak until he was nearly ten. By that point, Zander had figured out how much it drove me nuts and still threw it into conversations from time to time.

The thing about growling to another Dom was that it never had the same effect as it did with a sub, even within our family. If anything, Zander sounded a little more annoyed with me. "How the hell did he end up kneeling for you?"

"It wasn't like I *asked* him to! It was mostly accidental. But I'm telling you, he turned to a puddle of goo before my eyes. I hated to leave him, but I'm not an ass. Mom and Dad's lectures over the years have sunk in, believe it or not. I made sure he was doing okay, told him to call me if he started to overthink, then hightailed it out of there before one of us did something we'd regret. Oh, and I told him I was going to take him to lunch on Monday. I must be stupid because I told him that I'll help him find a Dom if he doesn't think it will work with us."

Zander whistled low. "Okay, I'm willing to say that I misjudged your motives here. I'm here for either of you if you need me." He muttered something about putting his foot in his mouth.

I wasn't dumb enough to think I wouldn't need my brother's help along the way. Compassion and sensitivity weren't my strong suits, but watching Elliot melt into my touch and listening to his worries had me wanting to try for him. It wasn't going to be easy and I was sure to fuck it up, but if Zander was on my side, I had a chance of actually making it work.

"I have your number and I'll use it. I'm going to need it at some point. We both know that. But for now, I just pulled into the cookie place, and I've earned a giant fucking cookie after walking away from Elliot with massive blue balls."

Zander's laugh was rich as it filled my speakers. "Yeah, go get yourself some cookies. You've earned them."

I sighed as I turned off the ignition. "Later, Z."

"Night, Nate."

First cookies, then home to take care of the issue in my pants.

CHAPTER 14

ELLIOT

I THREW my phone into the passenger seat before stepping out of the car. Emma had been blowing up my phone since Saturday evening, but aside from a proof-of-life text I'd sent when she threatened to have the police do a welfare check on me, I hadn't said anything to her since then. I couldn't help it—I still felt a bit raw knowing that she'd been talking with my brother.

Part of me didn't know what was worse, that she was talking to him or that he was talking to her when he wouldn't talk to me. I headed toward the front of the office, cursing myself and my stupidity. Kyle didn't have a reason to talk to me. We'd never been friends, and I wasn't going to pretend that we had been. There was just enough of an age gap between us that I'd been able to actively choose to not spend time with him while growing up.

My fault. Not his. Because looking back, I'd seen how frustrated our parents got when I played with toys, so when he wanted to play, I found reasons not to. That extended to video games when we got older or really spending any time with him at all.

Spending time with Kyle had meant that I got yelled at. It was self-preservation to a degree, but I should have said something or done something differently.

Hindsight was twenty-twenty and all that. I'd been a shit brother and was living with that now. It was time to admit that it might be too little too late. At least my musings kept me from thinking about Nathan inside the building somewhere. I knew he was there because his SUV was parked in his spot.

Between the Emma and Kyle drama over the weekend and the constant thoughts of what had—and hadn't—happened with Nathan on Saturday night, I was a mess. "Stop being an idiot."

"Stop being mean to yourself."

I jumped, the squeak that came out of me anything but masculine. It was Nathan's voice, but looking around, he was nowhere to be seen. His laughter filtered out an open window in his office. "No one ever thinks about how much their voices travel when they walk by this office."

When he paused, I busied myself with my key, but the door beside his office popped open before I made it to the front door. "Come in. I want to know what has you so out of sorts so early this morning."

Could he have maybe not dressed like a fucking sex god for Monday morning? A slim-fit navy suit, the top two buttons of his shirt unbuttoned, exposing just enough of his chest to see a hint of the tattoo I now knew was there. A black tie draped around his neck but not tied. The earring he had on in the club was still in place. This was a different side of Nathan than I'd seen at work. He was sexy and self-assured, but he didn't wear the same unapproachable mask that he'd always worn so well.

As I slid in between the door frame and Nathan's body, he placed his hand at the small of my back. I fought to hide the shiver that radiated from the point of contact. Even though I was wearing a shirt and coat, it still caused my skin to tingle and goosebumps to rise.

He didn't pull his hand away when I was through the door, instead guiding me gently toward his office. I could have pulled away and told him I was heading to my own office, but the contact felt too good and the urge to argue with him was gone.

Connie had told us that she and her husband were getting away for a few days, and Austin had texted me on my way in to tell me he was going to be late. That meant that Nathan and I were going to be alone in the office for the next few hours. The thought of being alone with Nathan should have scared me more than it did.

He didn't bother shutting his door as he led us directly to the couch along one wall. Once seated on opposite sides of the couch, Nathan angled his body so that he could see me better. "What's going on? You sounded genuinely annoyed with yourself as you walked up."

"It's been a long few days."

Concern creased his features. "About what?"

My laugh was forced and my voice came out strained as I tried to speak. "It's hard to explain. First, everything that I saw at the club. Now my go-to person to vent to is not currently my go-to."

A smile was tugging at the corner of Nathan's mouth, but I didn't understand why. Whatever the reason, the softening facial features helped me relax some. I liked the less-intense Nathan. "Let's start from the beginning. How are you feeling about DASH and what happened between us on Saturday night? You've had some time to think about it and process it."

Instinctively, I pulled my lip between my teeth as I thought. It was only there for a second before Nathan reached over and used his thumb to gently free it. "Don't get me wrong. I love how red and swollen that lip gets when you've been abusing it, but I don't like to see that you've chewed on it so much that it's cracked."

I ducked my head as my tongue ran over my lip to feel the damage. I'd already known that it was cracked and battered. I'd been coating it in ChapStick since Sunday morning. "I don't regret it. Any of it."

Nathan made a sound of contentment but didn't speak while I worked through the things I'd been planning on telling him when we had a chance to talk. "My brain had been all over the place, overthinking every minute of the night, but when I found myself kneeling, it was easier to think."

The only sign that Nathan liked my response was the way he exhaled slowly. For reasons I wasn't ready to analyze, it made me feel better that he wasn't as confident as he always seemed. It made it a lot easier to continue with my thoughts. "I haven't spoken to Emma but for a text or two since Saturday night. I'm struggling with that."

My voice caught in my throat as I thought about her. "I must be an asshole because she's my best friend. She was the only one who knew I wasn't straight for years and years, and she never told anyone. I don't think she meant to hurt me, but she did and I can't figure out a way to move past that." Words had spilled from me so fast that I had to take a deep breath in when I finally paused.

Nathan studied me closely for a moment before nodding his head like he'd made a decision. "Can we try something?"

"Huh?" The question had been so out of left field that I didn't have a better response.

"Will you kneel for me?"

My eyes widened and I could feel my eyebrows creeping higher on my forehead. We were at work. Sure, we were alone, but we weren't totally secluded from anything or anyone.

Nathan spoke again before I could work out the myriad of reasons this was a bad idea. "You just told me that it was easier to think when you were kneeling on Saturday night. I witnessed firsthand just how much you relaxed for those few minutes. And beyond all that, I saw the way you looked at Theo and Shane at DASH. I hadn't realized it at the time, but now I see it for what it is. You're drawn to it."

My lip got pulled into my mouth again, but I released it before Nathan could say something about it. "I. Yeah. I, well..." I sighed. He wasn't wrong.

Nathan chuckled. "Come here, Elliot." He adjusted himself so that he could spread his legs apart, then grabbed one of the cushions from the couch and dropped it between his feet. It was the same thing he'd done on Saturday night. It was a small gesture that showed me he was thinking about me and it also made me feel cared for.

I had to stop thinking so much. I knew that somewhere along the line I'd become my own worst enemy. But to willingly submit to Nathan, was that crossing a line I wasn't ready for? I had no idea. As it turned out, the pull to let some of the stress go was far stronger than my desire to hold everything in and repeat the same behaviors that had been making me miserable for years.

I stood up and walked over to him, sinking to my knees on the cushion before I could talk myself out of it. From there, I had no idea what to do. Thankfully, Nathan knew he needed to take control. *That was probably why he was a Dom and I wasn't.* "For now, saying stop will stop everything." He smirked, and while it held a hint of the wicked ideas running through his head, it looked genuinely sincere. "I can't promise you that stop will always stop everything, but until we've got things figured out, it's enough. And, Elliot?"

My eyes focused on his and all I could see was sincerity reflected in them.

"I like you being there."

Shock had to be evident in my features. It only made his light smirk turn downright devilish, yet his soft words belied the expression he was wearing. "Can I touch you? You seemed to like being touched on Saturday night, and it's hard to sit here with you so close to me and not touch you at all."

How could the asshole I'd known since I started my job be the same man who was quietly asking me if he could touch me? It was like I'd met two different people, and my brain didn't know how to reconcile the knowledge that they were both, in fact, Nathan. "I like touch." Not that I'd had much of it, but I knew I'd liked when Nathan's big hands were touching my face on Saturday night.

The smirk was replaced with a soft smile, and he wasted no time reaching out to place his hand on my cheek. Just like Saturday night, I felt myself lean into the touch. I felt like a starving man being offered a steak dinner.

"Good boy."

Was it possible for a human to preen? Because those two small words did something to me that I'd never known was possible. Pride, peace, and a deep sense of relaxation that I'd never felt before.

He caressed my cheek with his thumb as he watched me carefully. "What happened with you and Emma? I want to know if there is something I can do to help you."

I let my eyes drift shut as I gathered my thoughts. They weren't racing anymore, so it made it easier to put them in some semblance of order before I spoke. "She's the one that told me about the intro night at DASH. I think she might have known that it was something that I'd like. Not just because I knew that you were looking for someone kinky for the office, but because it would actually appeal to me. I was nervous but she told me I should go."

Nathan hummed quietly, though it filled the entire room. "She sounds smart."

I found myself smiling. Emma was smart, and a ruthless attorney who could bend opponents to her will with a look. It was almost like she was a female version of Nathan. Did that say something about me? "She is. We've been friends for years. We worked in the same building, and she's my old boss's daughter. After the wedding, when we were working out how things were going to go with us, she made me promise that I would follow my heart for once."

Now Nathan looked confused. "What wedding?"

That morning, it was easier to smile at the disaster the last two years of my life had been. "It's truly a long story, but we got married to appease other people in our lives. Hell, we weren't even dating for more than appearance's sake. Our engagement had been a misunderstanding that snowballed from there. One day, I won't have to keep explaining this. It's awkward every time I do."

Nathan's laugh was genuine and I found myself relaxing. "One day, I want to hear this story. But today, I just want to know why you're not speaking to your friend."

"She's been talking to my brother."

That time, Nathan's eyes went distant as he worked something out. When he spoke, it was measured and cautious. "Okay. What happened with you and your brother?"

When my back bristled, he moved his hand so he was cupping the back of my neck, his fingers rubbing at the tense muscles there. I leaned forward slightly to give him a better angle, but the new position put my head near his thigh. It looked comfortable and holding my weight up was harder than it should have been. I found myself leaning my head against his inner thigh as I tried to figure out what I needed to tell him to get him to understand.

"You've tensed up on me. What's going through that pretty head of yours?"

My sigh came from nothing but frustration at not being able to find the right place to begin. "I'm mostly confused because I don't know where I need to start in order for you to understand what happened and why it hurt so much that they are talking."

Nathan didn't say anything right away, but I could tell

he was thinking. "How about you start talking and I'll let you know if I need more information."

I liked that idea. "We're about three years apart. We've never been close. He bucked every convention our parents had, and at some point, it got more dangerous to spend time with him than to distance myself. Not that my parents were abusive, but they never approved of a thing he did. I was going into college when he came out. They refused to acknowledge it and my mom has been aghast every time he's brought a guy home. Not that Kyle does anything to make her not freak out about it. He kind of throws everything in her face."

Nathan continued to work the muscles of my neck, and I scooted forward a bit so that he could reach me better. Of course, the position put my face only a few inches from his crotch and the bulge that I'd been watching grow slowly for the last few minutes. He hadn't said anything about it, but it couldn't have been comfortable in the snug pants.

"The older we got, the more he pulled away. The more I tried to conform, the more I pulled away from him. It's gotten to the point that I honestly don't know how to interact with him without being a total asshole. I wanted to spend time with him during the week of the wedding, but he showed up with his Daddy. His Daddy is also his boss, his best friend, and his boyfriend. You can imagine how well that went over with my parents."

Nathan chuckled. "I don't know your parents, but I'm already sensing that this wouldn't have gone over well."

Nathan had stopped moving his hand and I glanced up tentatively. His gray eyes were dull, but he didn't seem upset, just deep in thought. I didn't like the Nathan that thought every word through and carefully spoke in a near monotone. "I could imagine that didn't go very far in repairing your relationship."

I allowed my eyes to flutter closed. "No. I know that I did way more harm than good. And by the time the disaster was over, he and Rand had flown back to Tennessee before I'd had a chance to talk to him, and he hasn't answered a call or text from me since then."

When Nathan didn't immediately respond, I rushed forward. "When I pulled up to the house on Saturday night, Kyle texted me. I should have been relieved, but then he said that Emma has been pressuring him to reach out to me. So now I know that Emma's been talking to Kyle and I have no idea about what, but she never once told me she'd spoken to him."

Nathan's hand tangled in my hair. Until he did it, I'd been planning on going to get my hair cut, but with his fingers gripping my hair and moving my head so that I had no choice but to look up at him, I quickly decided that there was no way I was going to cut it now. I liked that feeling so much, my dick responded to the tug against my scalp.

When I finally forced myself to open my eyes, Nathan's expression was tender. "That's a lot to take on by yourself. Your parents have been wrong from the beginning. Your behavior wasn't something I'd ever condone, but I think there was a bit of survival instinct going on there too. If you're not ready to talk to Emma, that's fine. You've said a few times in the last couple of weeks that you're finally doing something for yourself. You need to make these decisions on your own now. But don't cut Emma out. From everything you've said and everything I've heard, she really does care about you. She just might be a bit of a force of nature."

I laughed at his description of Emma. A force of nature she was. And I didn't want her to change, but I was hurt. I let my eyes drift shut again, and that time, Nathan didn't force me to open them.

CHAPTER 15

NATHAN

Elliot drifted off to sleep. I suspected that the stress of the weekend had kept him from sleeping well. I'd already crossed so many lines that I didn't think it mattered that he was sleeping on the job.

As he'd drifted off, his head had slumped forward. By the time his breathing had totally evened out, his nose was buried in my crotch and warm air continued to engulf my cock through my thin dress pants. At some point, his hand reached up and found the silk lining of my coat. My initial reaction was to pull it free and worry about damage to the fabric, but one glance down at his face had me willing to give him the coat for keeps.

I'd known that he was inexperienced, but I hadn't fully appreciated just how little experience he'd had until he'd started to open up. I debated with myself if I should wake him or let him sleep, and the part of me that liked seeing him relaxed told me to let him sleep. He'd adjusted himself so he was no longer on his knees, allowing me to worry less about his circulation, and I was pretty sure that we were free from Austin until at least after lunch.

Wilder had let it slip that they'd been out drinking with the Grizzlies the night before and neither of them were fit to be seen in public. It was a damn good thing the man was my brother and that we had absolutely nothing pressing going on at the office that week.

Nearly thirty minutes later, Elliot jolted upright and looked around my office, his unfocused eyes filled with confusion. "Shh. You're fine."

My voice pulled a yelp from him and he fell backward, nearly hitting his head on the leg of the chair in front of my desk. "Whoa, there."

I slid to the floor and helped him sit up again.

"I'm so sorry. So, so sorry. Shit." He ran his fingers through his hair, then wiped at his mouth like he thought he might have been drooling. "I didn't mean to. Fuck. I don't even remember—"

Before he could continue, I placed my index finger over his lips to silence his rambling. When he stopped speaking, I smiled and let my pride be heard in my voice. "Good boy." And damn if those words didn't have him sitting up just a little straighter. "If I needed or wanted you to get up, I would have woken you. Let me worry about where you should be and when."

Elliot stared at me for a number of seconds, his mouth

parted slightly as the panic in his eyes gradually dissipated. "I don't know if I can do that."

His honesty caused me to smile. Hell, everything about the man in front of me was causing that reaction. As foreign as letting someone else take his worries was for Elliot, having someone make me smile was just as foreign.

Going with my gut, I ran my hands up his arms. "Well, we're going to have to figure out how to help you with that."

Elliot's pupils dilated, but he kept looking. When he found his voice again, his words came out flirty and husky. "Yeah? And how do you plan on helping?"

I dropped my hands to his waist and pulled him closer to me. It was an awkward position—me on the floor, legs spread open, and Elliot between my legs, his knees nearly in my crotch—but I wanted him closer. I thought about what I knew about Elliot, what would turn him on and what would turn him off. When I spoke, my voice came out deeper than normal and even as I thought the words, my dick began to lengthen again. I should have known its good behavior wasn't going to last.

"You're very tactile." I ran my hands up his sides and watched as he squirmed, but the way his body relaxed was confirmation enough. "So I think lots of cuddles."

Who the fuck had I turned into?

When Elliot let out a little moan of contentment, I knew exactly who I was turning into. I was turning into the guy who just wanted to make the man in front of me happy.

"A lot of kisses."

A blush flared to life on his cheeks, but he leaned in closer to me, his tongue poking out to wet his lips. His voice was barely more than air when he spoke. "Yeah?"

I nodded confirmation. "Of course. Good boys get lots of kisses." For good measure, I added, "All over."

Elliot's entire body shook like he'd just orgasmed, but the desperate whimper told me he was still holding on... if just barely. Though it also told me I needed to pull back, because Elliot wasn't going to be very happy to have cum in his suit pants.

I stilled my hands. "We'll have plenty of time to explore just how good touch can make you feel later." A thought hit me. "Unless, of course, you want to explore this with another Dom. I did tell you that I'd help you find a different Dom if you weren't—"

My words got cut off before I could finish my thought. Elliot nearly bowled me over as he crashed his mouth against mine. It wasn't what I'd expected from the shy, timid guy I'd come to know. I'd fried his brain enough that he'd let his inhibitions down some.

The kiss was clumsy with little finesse, but there was enough passion and desperation behind it that I knew he'd improve with practice. There was something intoxicating about knowing I was going to be the first man to touch him and show him what it felt like to fly. Because there was no doubt in my mind I'd be able to get him there. He was so responsive to touch it would be impossible not to.

Baby steps were going to be key with him, but I was certain he was going to take to submission like a duck to water.

The kiss slowed and Elliot pulled back, his lips swollen and cheeks flushed from something entirely different than embarrassment. It was going to take a hell of a lot of willpower to keep my hands off him at work. Then again, this was my family's law firm and my kinky clients were already beginning to fill my schedule. Maybe I wouldn't have to keep my hands off of him altogether.

I took a cleansing breath in order to remind myself not to overwhelm Elliot. This was new to him. I was going to have to take my time with him.

Elliot touched his lips and his heavy-lidded eyes searched mine. "I'm sorry. That was a bit presumptuous of me."

The damned smile was back on my face. "Don't be sorry. It might have been a little unexpected, but it was more than okay. I liked knowing you wanted that. I especially liked knowing that you wanted me." Because I had already known that I would have been a jealous beast if I'd had to help him find another Dom.

"Your lips are softer than I imagined."

A startled laugh escaped me. "Thanks? I think?"

He ducked his head as he tried to hide his own laughter. "That wasn't what I meant. It's just... I've never kissed another guy. I just thought your lips would feel different." He covered his face with his hands. "I sound like an idiot."

My heart went out to him. I couldn't imagine being my age and just discovering another man's body. "Hey. I'm not going to have you talking about yourself like that. You've got a different set of experiences. That doesn't make you an idiot. It just means we've got a lot to explore." And damn, my list of things I wanted to explore with Elliot was probably far longer than he thought possible.

I patted his hip. "Come on, let's get you to your office so that we might actually get some work done today."

Elliot groaned, trying to subtly adjust his dick in his pants. I fought the urge to tease him and instead made a show of adjusting my own erection. The motion caused Elliot's eyes to drop to my crotch and I watched with satisfaction as he gawked at the bulge in my pants. He pressed the heel of his palm to his dick and I cleared my throat.

I could be about to overstep a number of boundaries, but if I was reading the signs right, this was exactly what Elliot wanted. "Hands off. You need permission to touch."

He automatically dropped his hands to his sides and balled them into fists. Then the implications of my words caught up to him. "Wait. What? Permission?"

I waited until I'd stood up to respond. "Oh yes. Good subs don't touch their dicks without permission from their Doms. Now, if you want to be a naughty sub and see where that lands you... well, far be it from me to stop you. Either way, I'm getting a reward."

Elliot's mouth hung open. I now knew exactly what he looked like totally confused and it made me smile. "Come on, Elliot. Let's go get you settled into your office for the morning." We still had more to talk about, but it could wait until we weren't at work. The last thing I wanted to do was overwhelm him in the first hour of Monday morning.

Dammit, I was going to have to practice patience, something I'd never been good at.

As we headed out of my office, I placed my hand on the small of his back. It was a gesture I'd done with just about every past lover I'd ever had, but never had another person nearly swooned at the contact. I was known as a fairly cold and standoffish man and Dom. I was nowhere near as open with my affection as Zander or Austin were, but I wasn't opposed to it either.

Most of the men I'd been with didn't particularly need or even want a lot of touch. Elliot was going to be different and I was more than willing to adapt. If a hand on his back affected him this way, I could only imagine what my hand or mouth on his cock would do to him. Hopefully, we'd have a chance to explore that sooner rather than later.

We were in his office all too soon and not for the first time, I cursed his office being so close to mine. Although this time I was cursing the distance for a very different reason. With no excuse to continue touching him, I pulled my hand away and forced it into my pocket. "Lunch at noon. If you need something before then, you know where to find me."

Elliot bobbed his head, though he didn't say anything. At some point I'd make him find words, but I figured his head was too much of a mess to force them at the moment. Wanting to see that beautiful blush stain his cheeks again, I leaned in and whispered into his ear, despite knowing we were totally alone in the building. "No touching that dick."

And there it was. The blush appeared before the words had fully left my mouth and it left Elliot stammering and stuttering. "I—Yes—I-I—no." He shook his head, clearly frustrated in his inability to form a full sentence, then tried again. "No, I wo-won't touch it."

I wasn't going to have to touch myself to come in my pants at this rate. I needed to make my exit quickly, so I brushed my lips across his cheek, surprised at the smoothness of his jawline. "Good boy."

He fell back into his chair, a contented smile on his face.

I backed out of his office and headed straight for the bathroom near my mom's office. I needed to be as far away from Elliot Mitchell as possible, both to take care of the issue pressing persistently at my fly and to get some space from the wicked ideas that were bouncing around in my head.

The door had barely shut behind me and I was working frantically at my belt. My dick had been painfully hard and awkwardly pinched in my pants before I'd had to walk to the other side of the building. Now it was aching and needed to be released from the snug confines immediately.

I cursed the complicated buckle on the expensive

leather belt and had to bite my cheek to not groan in relief as I finally unhooked it and eased the zipper of my pants down. Thank fuck for the hook and eye closure. I wasn't convinced I would've managed to open a physical button without ripping the material.

My cock sprang out with enthusiasm, very ready to play and done with confinement. It wasn't like I made a habit of jacking off at work, so I didn't have lube handy, but the bathroom did have a bottle of lotion on the counter. I grabbed it and flipped it around to read the label, sighing in relief when I read the word *Unscented.* There was nothing wrong with scented lotion, but the last thing I needed was for my dick to smell like vanilla or lavender for the rest of the day.

I pumped two squirts into my hand and didn't bother to warm it up before wrapping my hand around my dick. My head fell back against the door and I sighed in relief. Part of my brain told me to go to the toilet or sink to minimize the cleanup required, but my dick refused to wait, insisting it had been too desperate for too long.

That time, I let my dick win and began to jack myself slowly. Just because I had to be relatively quick and mostly quiet didn't mean that I needed to jerk it like a teenager trying not to get caught. I'd been there and done that a few too many times as an actual teenager to find it fun as an adult.

Instead, I found a pace and grip that I knew would get me off quickly but not frantically and stroked myself as I let my mind wander to far more interesting scenes than standing in a bathroom at work. Wrapping my hand around Elliot's cock for the first time was the first image that popped into my mind. I could easily see the look of pure bliss on his face as I touched and explored him. He was going to go off like a rocket the first few times—there was no doubt in my mind.

The scene morphed into him touching me for the first time. Imagining the blushes and tentative looks he'd give as he explored my body was enough to have my orgasm just out of reach. I wanted to be the one to make him come out of his shell, to let him explore just how amazing sex could be with someone you clicked with.

I needed to move the fantasy along. I was pushing my luck being in the bathroom as long as I had been. The last thing I needed was Elliot or the receptionist, who should be arriving right about now, knocking on the door. Elliot kneeling between my legs came to mind once again. He'd been there twice already, and his breath through my pants was what had started the sequence of events that led me to the place I was at now.

The scene changed again. That time, Elliot was still on his knees, but my cock was in his mouth. And the way he looked up at me, his golden brown eyes barely visible around the pupils that had dilated with his desire, his cheeks flushed from arousal. *"That's it. That's a good boy. Just like that. A little more tongue on the underside and watch your teeth."* Elliot's earnest expression and desire to please were so vivid in my mind that I could hear his hum as my cock swelled in his mouth. With a little adjustment to my grip, it was just as easy to imagine my hand being the back of his throat as he worked my cock.

And that was what I'd needed to send me over the edge. With a fist blocking my gasp, I spilled over my hand and onto the bathroom tiles. My knees were weak, my breathing ragged, but my dick was finally sated and going soft in my grip. I squeezed it a few more times, milking all I could out of it in hopes that I wouldn't leak more into my underwear as I went fully soft. There was nothing worse than drying cum against my dick.

Awkwardly, I made my way to the sink, my pants pushed down below my balls, my dick still hanging out, to clean myself off and wash my hands. When I was put back together, I turned my attention to the puddle of cum I'd left near the door and set to work cleaning it up. This was not going to be something I made a habit of doing because cleaning cum off a bathroom floor was absolutely disgusting. Then again, the relief and the ability to think clearly for the first time in an hour had made the cleanup well worth it.

I ran a dry paper towel over the spot one last time to ensure any evidence of my escapades were removed, washed my hands again, double-checked my outfit, then opened the door. Darcy was at the front desk just like I'd expected her to be, though she was just getting settled, so I guessed she'd recently arrived.

"Morning, Mr. Johnson."

"Good morning, Darcy." I hoped my smile and voice were genuine enough that she didn't notice my cheeks were still a little flushed or my legs were just a little wobbly as I made my way back down the hallway toward my office.

I couldn't help but poke my head into Elliot's office, even though it had taken me a few extra steps to do so. He had his head bent as he read over a document. The scene was completely normal, but I could see his feet beneath the privacy panel of his desk. They were spread farther apart than was normal, and he was gripping the paper with both hands.

Pride radiated through me. He was definitely going to earn a reward.

CHAPTER 16

ELLIOT

Nathan's head popped around the doorway Thursday evening as I was finishing up for the day. "Want to come to my place for dinner?"

I looked up from the filing I'd been doing—something I'd never done before I started here. There weren't enough files to warrant a bunch of clerks to do the work for us, but to my surprise, I found I enjoyed it. Nathan was standing in the doorway wearing another expensive black suit and white dress shirt. Though I could admit I missed the buttoned-up look he'd been sporting earlier on his way to court, he'd shed the tie and unbuttoned the top few buttons of his dress shirt, and I could definitely admit he was sexy.

"Your place?" That was different. Monday evening he'd brought dinner over to my house. Tuesday he'd taken me out to a quiet restaurant on the outskirts of Nashville. Wednesday night we'd made dinner together at my place. We hadn't done anything more than talk. Each evening he'd left me with a sweet kiss, but we hadn't gone further. He hadn't even seen my bedroom.

We'd spent a lot of time together over the week, but we hadn't broached anything kinkier than we'd done so far. The previous evening had felt domestic in a way that made my heart ache. It had felt right and exciting and I found myself feeling things way more complex than a few short days warranted.

Nathan's eyes sparkled with mischief. What he was thinking, I couldn't tell yet, but I could see he had something planned. "You haven't been over yet. I thought you'd like to see my place."

"Yeah. I'd like that. I don't know where you live, though."

His laugh was rich and warm and it made my dick shift in my pants. "Yeah, I forget that you don't just know where I live. You can follow me home." He paused for a second. "Alternatively, we can swing by your place and you could get a change of clothes for tomorrow."

It was pointless to hide the surprise in my eyes. "A-are you asking me to spend the night?"

The only way I could describe the look on his face was bashful. "Yeah. I think I am. I'd like to have you all to myself tonight."

Wicked thoughts went through my head. We really needed to talk more about sexy things, because we hadn't talked about those things yet. I knew it was because

Nathan didn't want to rush me, but I was starting to get antsy. I was ready to be pushed.

I found myself nodding eagerly. I liked the idea. Even if we didn't do more than kiss, it gave me a reason to spend more time with him. Grouchy Nathan still made my dick twitch and my brain turn to mush, but his scowls and growls were no longer turned on me. They were reserved for Austin or one of his equally dramatic siblings. Of course, there had been that lawyer the day before who had accompanied his client for a deposition and had pushed Nathan just a bit too far. I'd seen it coming as soon as the guy asked for spousal support from the man his client had been cheating on. The client also had a lengthy domestic abuse record to go with the cheating.

As soon as Nathan had set the file down, I'd seen the storm brewing in his eyes, and I knew it was over. It had actually ended faster than I'd expected, but during his icy listing of all the pain and suffering the attorney's client had caused as well as the other various grievances, I'd gone hard as a rock in my pants.

For all the grouch he had in him, I was learning about a much sweeter side and I was pretty sure I liked it just as much. He helped set the table, he cleaned the dishes, and he also liked to give me gentle orders. They were so subtle I hadn't noticed until the night before. It was when he'd told me to clean the last pot before bringing our water glasses to the table that I'd figured out he'd been giving me easy commands for days. I'd followed every one of them without thought. He'd always told me I was a good boy when I did them and I would do just about anything for those compliments.

Until that week, I wouldn't have ever guessed I'd have a thing for being called a boy. Hell, I was older than Nathan by a year and change, yet I still found my heart speeding up each time he said the words.

Spending the night with him would hopefully give me plenty of opportunities to earn praise from him. "I'd like that, yeah."

"Great. Stop by my office when you're ready to leave and I'll follow you to your place."

I was pretty sure I blushed like a boy who'd just been asked out for the first time as I nodded my head. "Sounds good."

Nathan leaned forward and kissed my lips. "Don't take long."

I managed to withhold the squeak that threatened to burst out from me, but I found myself turning my attention back to my work. "Yes, sir."

The words had come out of my mouth without thought, but Nathan gave a low groan and it made me pause.

"Those words are beautiful coming out of your mouth."

The blush was back, and so was the bashful dip of my head. This was going to be a good night. Nathan turned and left, and I found myself filing quickly as I wished there was someone I could talk to about these developments. As it was, I still hadn't spoken to Emma about more than just letting her know that I was fine but needed some time. She hadn't liked that answer, but it was the best I could give her. I started leaving my phone in the car throughout the day, so it wasn't like her texts were bothering me.

And Nathan was keeping me busy enough that I was hardly checking my phone anyway. The only other people that tried to get in contact with me were Austin and Seth, but Seth had just begun popping up at my house when he saw that Nathan's car wasn't there.

The two of us had had numerous conversations over the last few days. We'd sit at the pool—me with a beer, Seth with a sparkling water—and talk about anything and everything that came to mind. Since he already knew that Nathan was a Dom, it had been easier to open up to him a bit. It wasn't like I could hide that I was exploring submission when he already knew his brother's interests. We hadn't talked about anything in depth, but I was comfortable enough talking with him about it when he was around.

That night, Austin was already gone and Seth was on a road trip, so the two of them weren't available. While I didn't know if Austin and Seth were submissive, I couldn't imagine either of them as Doms. I just knew that both were easy to talk to.

I'd met another one of Nathan's older brothers earlier in the afternoon when he came to drop off Nathan's SUV. Nathan had introduced Larson to me and from that brief interaction, I suspected he would have been able to easily understand the submissive side of me. It would have required obtaining his phone number, though, and since I didn't know him, that would have been all sorts of awkward.

Despite looking like a lumberjack, Larson had spoken quietly and blushed easily at Nathan's teasing. He definitely didn't have the same vibe about him as Nathan or Zander. I hadn't asked, but I suspected if I did, I'd find out that Larson was submissive as well.

No matter how I cut it, talking with his family about what we were planning to do behind closed doors was overwhelming. Maybe it was time to join some of the munches that DASH sponsored. At least I could meet someone to talk with about the things I was only just beginning to understand about myself. And those meetups would give me a way to talk to people not related to Nathan.

My thoughts had carried me through to finishing my filing. A quick glance at the clock told me it had only taken a few minutes. There were technically five minutes left on the work clock, but Connie had never been strict about our work hours as long as we got our jobs done.

As it was, my work was done. I locked my computer, turned out the light, and headed toward Nathan's office.

He was at the window when I walked in and I could hear a voice filtering in from outside. From the sounds of it, the person outside the window was having a heated phone conversation. I was pretty sure that person was Austin, but I wasn't able to see through Nathan to confirm the suspicion.

"No! Last night was not a mistake." The closer I got to the window, the more convinced I was that it was Austin, but his voice had come out in a growl I wouldn't have thought possible from him.

There was a pause before Austin spoke again. "W—we've been dancing around this for way too long to decide it's a mistake now!" That time his voice had risen high and I winced.

Nathan's head dropped back and it looked like he was praying for patience. "Austin can be so damn dramatic."

He tapped on the window. "Austin, take your drama elsewhere." To me, he sighed. "Why does no one realize this is my office? The number of phone calls and conversations I overhear from that window is staggering."

I couldn't say much to that. I had definitely been guilty of having conversations in front of that window over the last few weeks. What had he overheard? Well, he definitely hadn't overheard anything from Emma and me over the week, but the previous weeks could have been a very different story.

Sensing my thoughts, he leaned into me. "Yeah, you too, though not so much on the phone. You just have a tendency to talk to yourself. However, your thoughts are very enlightening."

All I could do was groan in response.

Nathan didn't let me stew in my thoughts too long. "Come on, it's time to get out of here."

I didn't think anything of him shutting the window before he ushered me out the office door and closed it behind us. He had just shut the side door of the building when Austin turned, forgetting all about his phone conversation.

His eyes widened in shock and turned as purple as the shirt he was wearing. At first, I'd thought it was because Nathan's hand was resting on the small of my back, but as it turned out, it was something else completely. "You don't have a briefcase with you?"

I glanced over at Nathan and was shocked to see pink staining his cheeks. A blush?

Nathan cleared his throat. "I've got other plans tonight."

Austin looked between the two of us and grinned. "I don't know what's going on with you two, but seriously, Elliot, keep it up. This asshole hasn't left the office without a pile of folders with him since he started."

I was too shocked to say anything until we made it to our cars. "Your mom yells at me every time I try to take files home in the evenings, but you take them?"

Nathan looked sheepish as he responded. "Mom tries to tell me I can't take them home."

His voice traveled more than we'd realized because Austin called over from the sidewalk. "No, Mom used to tell you that, then you started sleeping in the office. She'd rather you sleep in your bed than on a couch, so she stopped trying to get you to leave work at work."

He held his middle finger over his head as he muttered to his youngest brother. "Menace."

My laughter surprised me. Since I'd started here, I'd come to love the relationships they all had. They were warm and affectionate, no matter how insane they drove each other. And by the way Nathan's voice didn't hold any malice when he responded to Austin, I knew he didn't actually mind the prodding.

He gave me a roll of the eyes, trying to convey annoyance with his brother, but it failed to convince me. "I'll follow you to your place. If you want, you can leave your car there and ride home with me?"

I didn't know if he'd meant it to sound like a question, but that little bit of uncertainty had my nerves relaxing a bit. "Yeah. That would be nice."

And if it was that easy to make Nathan smile like that, I'd do it more often.

It didn't take long to get to my place. Seth's house was dark, but that wasn't surprising since he'd mentioned something about weird practice schedules for the coming weeks. He ate, slept, and breathed hockey, but I guessed that was par for the course with any professional athlete. It wasn't like I'd know firsthand. I hadn't played a sport since soccer in high school, and I'd been terrible at it. I was pretty sure that if colleges could give out scholarships for *not* being part of the team, I'd have been awarded a full ride.

Nathan was already standing outside of his SUV tapping away at his phone when I stepped out of my car. "Do you need me to come in with you?"

I shook my head. "I'll be quick. Is it okay if I change into something more comfortable?" The question was already out before I thought about how strange it was that I was asking permission to change my clothes.

Nathan didn't blink an eye at my question. "Change. I want you comfortable this evening."

My dick twitched in my pants, though I couldn't figure out what it was about the statement that had it taking notice. If I analyzed everything going on in my head and in my pants, I was never going to get ready for the evening. So I did something uncharacteristic and pushed the thoughts out of my head, going only with my gut. My gut was telling me to hurry up and get ready for the evening, so that was exactly what I did.

As I headed toward the door, Nathan spoke up. "I'm going to just double-check the house for Seth. He left for an away game today, and he gets nervous."

I began to nod but then stopped. "If he's nervous about the house being unattended, should we just stay here tonight?"

Nathan sighed. "No, we're fine. He had some reporters hounding him a while back. Nothing about him but something that happened with a teammate. When people show up here, it makes him nervous, and then it takes him a few months to relax again. I'm just going to check the doors and we'll double-check that the gate is locked when we leave. He can see the security cameras on his phone and Zander has a link to his phone too."

His words helped ease some of my concerns as I headed into the house. If I let myself stop, I'd talk myself out of whatever I was about to do. For once, I was determined to follow my heart and not my head. My heart was telling me to see where this went. So I quickly changed and threw a hastily packed overnight bag together, then picked out a clean suit for the morning.

I was locking the door just as Nathan returned. "All clear. Seth's place is locked up tight and I've let him know. Zander also promised that he and Noah will stop by once a day just to double-check. That's got him relaxing some. For being a professional athlete, one of the first out professional athletes at that, the man *hates* both being away from home and publicity."

While I wasn't a professional athlete, I could understand being a homebody. I liked routines and didn't do well when things arose unexpectedly. At least Seth had his brothers to look after him and his house.

Nathan nodded toward the back seat. "Go ahead and put your bag back there and we can get out of here. I'm getting hungry and I really want to get you to my house."

The way his eyes raked over my body had my pulse picking up. I had no idea how or why, but Nathan seemed to really want me. That was enough to have me opening the door to deposit my stuff in the back.

A blanket that looked like it had been through a few war zones was on the seat as I tossed my stuff in. If it weren't for the fact that Nathan's car was immaculate, I would have thought it was just a random blanket to move things in. I didn't know what to make of the discovery, so I went with a joking tone. "Didn't want to leave your blankie at home today?"

Nathan's eyebrows turned downward at the question. "Huh?"

Now I was really confused. "There's a blanket back here that appears very well loved."

He didn't even look in the back before he groaned. "Shit. We've got to make a stop on the way back to my place. Thankfully, it's not too far out of our way. Climb in."

Weird. I didn't question him as I climbed into the front seat. Nathan got in and was already tapping at his phone when he hit the button for the ignition.

A few seconds later, his phone rang through the speakers. Nathan was pulling through the gate when the person he was calling answered.

I glanced at the display just in time to see Larson's name appear when a deep voice filtered through. "Hello?"

"Hey, Lars. You home?" Nathan's voice was softer as he spoke to Larson than it was when he spoke to his other siblings. Honestly, it was probably softer than when he talked with me.

"Just walked in the door. What's up? Everything okay at Seth's?"

Nathan watched the gate shut behind us before he spoke again, that time chuckling lightly. "Yeah, everything's fine. How'd you know I was there?"

"He's gone on a trip and Elliot's staying there. I figured you'd go over to see him."

Nathan's smile grew. "No keeping anything from you all. Yeah, I went over to see him. He's coming back to my place tonight."

Larson's chuckle was warm. "Good for you... and him."

Nathan glanced over at me and winked. "Thanks. But hey, there's a reason I called. Elliot was putting his stuff in the back seat and Blankie's back there."

I blinked, trying hard not to show my surprise. I'd thought Larson was single, and out of the entire family, only a few of them had kids. Most of his brothers and sisters had actively rejected the idea of having kids while good-naturedly ribbing the ones who did. And, for whatever reason, I could not see the lumberjack as a dad.

"Shit." I could almost see him chewing on his lip as silence filled the car. "I'm sorry. Want me to stop by your place and get it?"

"That's silly and a waste of time." Nathan's response had come instantly and was no-nonsense. "Your place is not far off the highway. We'll swing by and drop him off to you."

To you? Was the blanket Larson's? I couldn't imagine the big, burly firefighter having a blanket.

"You sure?" For all of Nathan's insistence, Larson was equally unconvinced. "I don't want to impose."

Nathan scoffed, though it wasn't mean. "It's not an imposition. Besides, you've had a busy day. We'll be there in fifteen minutes or so. Need anything while we're heading that way?"

"No. I'm good. Thank you. And seriously, it's fine to pick him up at your house."

Nathan growled, legitimately growled, like a wild animal. "Lars, we'll be there in a few minutes."

Larson actually laughed at the growl and I found myself smiling. "Okay, thank you. Drive safe."

"We will. Love you."

"Love you too."

The line went dead and I sat there staring at the dashboard, trying to figure out what had happened.

Nathan reached over and squeezed my leg. "You've got questions, but unless you use words, I don't know what I should be answering."

I barked out a surprised laugh. "Um, yeah. I don't even know where to begin. That's Larson's blanket?"

Nathan relaxed into his seat and flicked the blinker on to change lanes. He merged into the other lane and reached a comfortable speed before he spoke. "Larson's always had a blanket. That one is probably the fourth or fifth Mom's made him over the years. I think his refusal to give up his blanket as he got older was our first clue that he's a little."

My eyes popped open. I knew enough to know that my brother was one as well; I'd just thought they were more uncommon. And he was so big, I was struggling to see him wanting to play with toys or have a blanket.

"He's self-conscious about that side of him, but we've always been accepting. It would kind of be shitty of us to not be. He's so certain he'll never find a Daddy that I think we've all kinda started going out of our way for him." He chuckled to himself. "Okay, that's a lie. We spoil the man rotten, but he would never do it for himself and totally deserves it. But our attention is not a very good substitute for a real Daddy."

I took advantage of Nathan's driving to bite on my lip. My brother had always been confident and always gone after what he'd wanted, but when I'd seen him in New York over the fall, he'd been at peace in a way I'd never seen. Even with my poor behavior and attitude, he'd remained happy. A little smug, but mostly calm and happy.

What if that peace and happiness was because of Rand... because of his Daddy? If that was what Larson needed, it sucked that he didn't have it.

"Yeah. I can see that."

I realized then that I needed to apologize to my brother again, with more than just a texted *I'm sorry*.

CHAPTER 17

NATHAN

Elliot was silent as we made our way to Larson's house. I knew he was working through something, so I let him think for a while. Nothing about his body language told me he was upset or angry, and sometimes we all needed a good think.

He finally blinked back to the present when I pulled into Larson's driveway. His house was set back from the road a long way. He'd been buying houses, remodeling them, then selling them for years. It was just something he loved doing as a hobby. While I wouldn't say it out loud, Larson was talented enough to make it a profession. He loved working with his hands, so once he had a house to the point that there weren't any more projects, he sold it and bought another. The housing market had changed after he'd bought this house, so he'd stayed longer than he'd intended.

Elliot let out a little gasp of surprise when Larson's house came into view. With the irises in bloom in the front flower beds and leaves filling out the bushes next to the porch, it was a quaint little Craftsman-style home. Well, *little* wasn't exactly the right word for it, but from the outside it looked small. With the interior walls removed and a gleaming white-and-gray kitchen, the inside was downright spacious.

"Larson likes to work with his hands. This is a project. He's always got something going on—I think he's building a deck out back right now."

"It's beautiful. I don't know what I'd expected, but it wasn't this."

Larson would have loved to hear the compliments that Elliot was paying his work—but maybe not while I was delivering his blanket to him. The house had looked nothing like this when he'd bought it. I'd called him nuts the first time he showed me the house, but Larson had seen the potential. He was also more than ready to move, but real estate in the Nashville area had gone insane. He didn't want to overpay for another fixer-upper, so he was doing more renovations to keep himself occupied.

I pointed over to the detached garage. "That's his workshop. I honestly don't know where he finds the time, but he loves getting out there and making things. He's incredibly talented. We'll come over sometime and he can show you some stuff he's made."

Elliot was still wide-eyed when Larson stepped out onto his porch in a pair of old sweats and a baggy T-shirt. I squeezed his leg and watched as he pulled his attention from the house back to me. "Let me take him his blanket and we'll be on our way."

Elliot just nodded, so I grabbed Larson's blanket and headed toward the porch. "Figured you'd miss this guy."

He rolled his eyes at me, but his smile was barely hidden. "Thanks."

"You doing alright? I haven't been around much."

Larson took his blanket from me and gave me a look like I was insane. "Seriously? You're hardly ever around. And now you've got someone to keep you from working yourself to death, I'd be shocked if I saw you often." He glanced over at my SUV. "Things going well?"

I lifted a shoulder but found myself nodding. "He's discovering a lot about himself, but we're getting to a good place."

"You're taking him to your house. Given that I've only been there a handful of times since you moved back, I'd say things are going well."

"Speaking of, I should get going. Glad we found Blankie before it got too late."

Larson's cheeks turned a bright shade of pink but he nodded as he pulled his blanket closer. "Me too. Thanks for bringing him over."

"Anytime." I went in for a hug and Larson wrapped his arms around me in return.

"Have a good night, Nate."

If my plans went anywhere near how I hoped, it would definitely be a good night.

When I returned to the car, Elliot seemed to be out of his funk. "That was nice of you to stop by and bring that to him."

"You've never seen my brother when he can't find his blanket. I swear, we need a tracking device on that thing." I was only half-joking. If there was a way to chip it, I was pretty sure Larson would jump at the chance. Usually, it just got lost somewhere around the house and turned up pretty quickly, especially since his house was neat and tidy. But sometimes it got left in a car or truck and Larson would be nearly panicked before it was found.

Elliot gave a fond smile. "It's awesome he's got a supportive family."

While I tried to figure out how to respond, Elliot changed the subject, effectively shutting the topic down. "So, what's for dinner?"

His stomach rumbled, telling me that whatever it was, it was going to have to be quick.

"I'm not known for my cooking skills. But I make a mean pasta."

Elliot's laughter was genuine and worth my self-deprecation. Besides, I did make a good pasta, and if I used the rigatoni noodles, it would be easy to feed him. My dick was going hard just thinking about feeding Elliot his dinner while he knelt beside me. I thought tonight would be a great chance to ease him into submission and hopefully let him find that happy place he was so desperately searching for.

"I have something for you before that."

Elliot eyed me suspiciously. My tone must not have been as casual as I'd hoped. "Oh yeah? What's that?"

"Let's get home. We're almost there."

And we were. Larson only lived a few minutes from my house, so we were already pulling off the highway again. My neighborhood was half a mile from the highway, and we were turning into the development quickly.

The corner of Elliot's mouth turned up in a smile. "This neighborhood is nice."

My house wasn't as big as Zander's or my parents', but it was still more house than I needed. Elliot's grin was contagious, though, and I couldn't help but be thankful he let me in on his thoughts. "I always wanted to live in an area like this. Growing up, we had this huge brownstone in Chicago. There was never any space to go out and play when we were little. There was no soccer in the front yard or a place to ride our bikes. Then I moved to New York and it was a bunch of shoebox-sized apartments with neighbors everywhere and I found myself longing for a house somewhere with a yard."

That would have been a sad childhood. My siblings and I spent countless hours running wild outside. The neighbors all knew us; the shop owners downtown knew us. It hadn't been until I was a teenager that my parents had moved to a gated community, but even then, the yards were huge. We had a basketball court in the back of Mom and Dad's house that was still a regular hangout for us.

The melancholy lifted as we pulled into my driveway. Elliot wiggled in his seat and the sweatpants he'd put on didn't hide his growing excitement. Even without knowing what had his dick taking interest, I liked that he was excited. I could only hope he'd still be that excited when we got to my room.

Glancing down at his crotch, I let desire bleed through my words. "Someone's excited about tonight."

Elliot turned red but didn't deny it. To my surprise, he ran his hand up the length of his dick. "Yeah, he kind of has a mind of his own, and he is pretty sure that interesting things are going to happen tonight."

I hummed, not disputing his assumption. "Well, let's grab your stuff and we can go see just how interesting tonight turns out." Then I raised an eyebrow at the man sitting next to me. "But do good boys touch themselves?"

When he stopped moving completely, I had to admit there was a chance I'd overwhelmed him. I cleared my throat and watched as his head slowly turned to face me. His blown pupils belied any hesitancy he might have been experiencing. "How about I grab your stuff and we'll go upstairs."

His head bobbed, but a squeak was all he could muster by way of sound. At least he was reaching for the door handle at that point. I really hoped he didn't fall out of my SUV. If my brother's experience had taught me anything in the last few months, it was that a nervous sub was not always the steadiest on his feet. Thankfully, Elliot seemed to be more sure-footed in the face of nervousness than Zander's boyfriend had been.

Noah had definitely not been graceful for the first month he'd known Zander, and when he'd ended up with a concussion at DASH after the two met unexpectedly, I wasn't sure they were going to move past it. Thankfully, they had worked things out and I'd never seen Zander happier. However, I could do without a boyfriend with a concussion.

Elliot might have been sure-footed, but he was also absentminded. He completely forgot about the stuff in the back seat, so I reached in and grabbed it before directing him toward my door. I had no intentions of showing Elliot around while his brain was not firing on all cylinders. Instead, I placed my free hand at the small of his back and led him directly toward the steps.

If I hadn't known better, I'd think the blush that wouldn't leave his cheeks was makeup.

In my room, I set his bag by the door and hung his suit bag on the back of my closet door. I looked at it hanging there and smiled to myself. I didn't bring men home with me, and I definitely didn't invite them to stay over. With Elliot, it was different. I still didn't know exactly what was driving me to invite him over to spend the night, but it was a pull I wasn't fighting.

"Take a seat on the bed. Let me get changed."

Elliot complied with little thought and I began to get myself into more comfortable clothing. A pair of jeans worn soft from years of wear and a comfortable Henley were calling my name.

I shrugged out of my jacket and hung it on a hanger, then reached for the bottom of my shirt and pulled it free from my pants.

With each layer that came off, the tension in my body released more. I liked a well-tailored suit, but taking it off always felt heavenly. I got so lost in removing the items that I totally forgot Elliot was on my bed until I had my shirt halfway unbuttoned and I heard a quiet, strangled moan.

When I glanced over to the bed, Elliot's face was red and the bulge in his sweats had gone from a swell to a full-blown tent. "Like what you see?"

He tried to find words but all that came out was a squeak I was becoming familiar with. He tried again and when he only managed another squeak, he finally nodded his head.

He was good for my ego, but I really hoped he found a way to relax soon. Yes, I wanted a submissive partner, but I also wanted an equal. I'd seen more than a few glances into the sharp-tongued, confident man that Elliot was, but my job now was going to be to get him to that point with me. Hopefully, my plans for the evening would go a long way toward helping him relax.

I finished taking my shirt off a little slower than was

necessary but enjoying the way Elliot's eyes tracked my every movement. By the time I reached for my belt and the hook and eye closure on my pants, I'd managed to mostly forget about his intense scrutiny. If I continued to let his eyes distract me, the odds were I was going to come in my pants before I finished undressing.

There was no reason to hide my erection from him and part of me hoped that my showing him just how turned on I was would help him calm down. Instead, as my pants dropped and the gray cotton of my briefs did little to hide my arousal, Elliot made a low moan that drew my attention toward him. He was still on my bed, his eyes so wide I could see white all the way around, biting the knuckle of his thumb so hard I worried he'd break the skin.

Then it dawned on me that Elliot had never gotten to enjoy watching a man undress. It was easy to forget that he was still new to everything, despite having understood he was gay from a young age and being well into his thirties by now.

I managed to get my pants and dress socks off before I couldn't resist going over to him. Elliot didn't blink as I stalked toward the bed, his eyes never straying from the erection tenting my briefs. I stopped between his legs and he finally looked up at me. His pupils were dilated, but nervousness was clear in his eyes and in the way his fingers were twitching in his lap.

Towering over him, I gave an easy grin before I spoke. My voice was thick, and I was sure it was simply from the way Elliot had been eyeing me for the last few minutes. "Have you ever touched a man's dick before?"

"N-n-no." He shook his head for emphasis, though the stutters had been enough.

"Do you want to?"

Elliot's pupils dilated and his breath caught in his chest. "I... can?" He cleared his throat and tried again. "Can I?"

The stammering was oddly endearing and I found myself nodding. "Of course."

I didn't know if that was the right answer or not, because now Elliot's fingers were twitching desperately against his thigh, but he didn't seem to be able to do anything about it. We were going about this out of order, and we hadn't talked about limits. I was flying by the seat of my pants—or lack thereof at the moment—and didn't have a playbook for this situation.

Realizing that Elliot wasn't going to make a move, I decided to turn the tables. "Can I touch you?" I was standing directly in front of him now and could see just how hard he was.

Elliot gave me a nod but never opened his mouth.

"We're going to have to have a talk later, but for now you say stop and I'll stop."

He swallowed hard before he forced a single word from his mouth. "O-okay."

I pushed gently at his shoulders and he took the hint, leaning back against the mattress but staying propped up on his elbows. That was fine because all I needed was a way to access his dick and balls, and maybe his hole. I gripped at the sweatpants and began to work them down, watching his eyes for any sign of discomfort or hesitation. All I saw was desire and need, and it fueled my confidence.

Elliot's cock was straining against his surprisingly skimpy black boxer briefs. To say I hadn't expected the buttoned-up attorney from work to be wearing a pair of underwear that barely covered his dick and framed a body I'd had no idea he'd been hiding under his suits would be an understatement.

My dick pulsed in my underwear and I tossed his pants to the side, then checked in with the man lying in front of me. "Still good?"

The pink in his cheeks had faded, the embarrassment replaced by lust in his eyes. "More than."

Thank fuck. I tried not to sigh in relief as I reached out to trace the line of his erection. To my relief, he didn't flinch away. Instead, he arched into the touch and let out a desperate moan. I suspected that he wasn't going to last, no matter how much he wanted to, but after thirty-five years, I'd be like a pressure cooker too.

I worked the briefs down and was greeted with a beautiful thick cock that quickly settled along his stomach. Elliot sighed at being released, and I sighed at the thought of finally getting to touch him. His underwear had already had a wet spot on it, and precum continued to bead at his tip.

I glanced over at the nightstand drawer, debating with myself if it was too soon, but I was curious. I ran my finger over his tip and pulled the sticky liquid down his length, over his balls, then trailed my finger past his hole. Far from flinching at the contact, Elliot relaxed into the bed and his hips rocked downward as he chased my finger.

"Do you play with yourself?"

Elliot groaned but shocked the hell out of me when he quickly recovered and gave me a downright naughty wink. "I'm inexperienced with men, Nathan, but I'm well acquainted with my ass." When he saw the surprise on my face, he actually laughed. "I have toys. I'm a gay man who's been single my entire adult life. I'm not in denial about who I am or what I like. I just haven't had the courage to pursue it outside of my bedroom."

I really shouldn't have laughed but I did. It was partly from surprise at his words, partly relief that he had explored his body already. Mostly, it was for selfish reasons alone. "In that case, I have something that I think is going to be perfect for tonight."

It was hard to ignore his whimper as I stepped back and headed toward my nightstand drawer, but the prostate massager would do a great job of keeping him just crazy enough to hopefully not overthink every interaction tonight.

His eyes tracked me closely and I didn't miss the way they widened momentarily when he saw what I pulled out. "Want me to put it back?" The slightest hesitation from him would have had me putting it away, but the way his cock jumped and his breath quickened told me he didn't want me to.

I wondered if I'd broken him but he finally shook his head. "You're good."

Just what I'd hoped he'd say. I swiped the bottle of lube off the top of the nightstand and headed back to where he was lying. "I have to admit I like knowing that you know what you like." I poured a generous amount of lube onto my hand, placed the bottle beside him, then brought my fingers to his entrance at the same time I used my free hand to reach for his erection.

Simultaneous attention to both his hole and his cock had Elliot nearly coming off the bed, and a guttural moan escaped him that I was pretty sure could wake the dead. I had barely touched his hole and I could already feel his cock thickening in my fist.

He fell back, his arms on either side of him. "Holy shit. It feels so different."

His needy noises spurred me on and after tracing his hole a few times, I slid my index finger inside him. He was tight, his body closing around my finger quickly, but not so tight that I worried about him. Judging by the sounds he was making, he'd relax quickly.

Within a minute, his body was doing just that and I felt comfortable enough to add a second. The massager wasn't thick, so I wouldn't need to stretch him beyond two fingers. His body relaxed faster after the addition of the second finger than it had with just my index finger, and he was quickly rocking down into my hand.

He was ready for the plug, but I wanted to torment him just a bit more, so I crooked my finger and pegged his prostate. I was rewarded with a keening sound and his cock spasming in my hand as cum spilled over my fist. I was going to need to wash his shirt and the bedspread, but it was worth it to see the blissful expression on his face.

Elliot's chest heaved as he gulped in lungfuls of air, and I took the moment of distraction to slide my fingers from his ass and quickly replace them with the plug. He made a startled noise as the plug fully seated in his ass, but he didn't complain. "We're going to have fun working on your control."

Elliot cracked an eye open. "I never once heard you say I couldn't come."

The blanket was a goner, so I wiped my hand on it and headed to the bathroom to grab a washcloth to clean him up. "You're right—I didn't. We haven't had that talk yet. We'll get there, though."

Elliot groaned in frustration, but I found myself smiling. "Come on, let me wipe you down. Then I need to put your shirt in the washer. At least you don't have cum in your underwear or pants."

He threw his forearm over his eyes. "Ugh, so embarrassing. I came in, like, three seconds."

I ran the washcloth over Elliot's stomach, my erection still hard and persistent but much less important than taking care of the man on the bed in front of me. "I was giving you a lot of stimulation. You're not used to it. I would have been more surprised if you hadn't come quickly."

He didn't respond, but I wasn't sure if that was because he didn't have anything to say or if he'd started to fall asleep, wrung out from the orgasm.

I finished cleaning him in silence, then tossed the cloth into the hamper. "Come on, up you get. Time to go make some dinner and I need to wash your shirt."

He blinked his eyes open. "You might want to get dressed first?"

I looked down and chuckled to myself. I was standing there in just my underwear. My erection had gone down while I'd been cleaning Elliot up, but it wasn't going to remain that way if he kept staring at me like that. Before I could overwhelm him by getting hard again and causing him to wonder what to do about it, I headed to the closet to get dressed.

Bathroom jerk-off sessions were becoming normal for me and I saw one in the near future.

CHAPTER 18

ELLIOT

I HAD no idea what was worse: Nathan in a suit, in just his underwear, or the worn pair of jeans and faded green Henley he was currently wearing. So far, I'd decided they were all equally dangerous for very different reasons. And the plug in my ass wasn't helping my brain focus on anything.

There was part of me that understood Nathan was trying to keep me distracted and from overthinking every move we made that night. Yet the only thing I was thinking about was how amazing it was to come with his fingers in my ass and his hand wrapped around my cock. And now I was in his kitchen, wearing my sweats and one of his T-shirts that smelled like him.

"Elliot." The amusement in Nathan's voice told me he'd tried to get my attention more than once.

Trying to look calm, I glanced at him. "Hmm?"

He took one look at me and burst out laughing, a full-body laugh that surprised me to my core. I'd never heard him laugh like that and I honestly hadn't thought I ever would. He was bent over, his hands resting on his knees as he caught his breath. "Sorry. Sorry." He gasped a few more times and pulled himself together. "Your face caught me off guard. It was like Austin trying to look sweet and innocent and I just hadn't expected it from you."

I put my hand on my hip in mock offense, popping it to the side for emphasis, then moaning as the plug nailed my prostate.

That had Nathan laughing again.

When he finally pulled himself together, Nathan stood up. "You're going to kill me. Please grab a plate from the cabinet. Dinner is almost done."

He pointed toward the cabinet on the other side of the stove. My stomach had been rumbling for twenty minutes by that point. A mind-blowing orgasm made me ravenous... who knew?

I went over and grabbed a plate like he'd instructed and handed it back to him. I was more focused on pasta covered in a creamy white sauce, steamed broccoli, and the smell of the garlic bread baking in the oven than wondering why I'd only grabbed one plate. He'd jokingly told me that he made a killer spaghetti, and this really did smell heavenly. It wasn't necessarily complicated but nicer than any meal a date had ever made me before. Though not like I'd had a lot of experience to draw from.

Nathan put a large serving of pasta on the plate,

followed by an equally large portion of the broccoli, then reached into the oven, pulled the garlic bread out, and precariously balanced two slices on the edge. He glanced over the kitchen. I'd been cleaning as he cooked, so aside from the pots he was actively using, everything was clean.

He gestured to a drawer. "Grab a fork, please."

Now my curiosity was piqued. He had one overflowing plate and wanted "a" fork. I narrowed my eyes, but his slightly inclined head and raised eyebrows told me I needed to follow directions. Since common sense had left the moment I'd met Nathan, I grabbed a fork and followed him... past the breakfast nook and the dining room, and directly to the living room.

Nathan set the plate on the end table and plucked a pillow from the end of the couch, dropping it between his legs. This was familiar. We'd done this already. The underlying uncertainty I'd been feeling disappeared as I sank to my knees between his legs. Even the movement of the plug hadn't been enough to distract me.

Nathan reached out and stroked my hair, and I leaned into the contact. I couldn't get enough of his touches. We sat there like that for quite a few minutes before he finally sat back. "Let's get you fed."

As Nathan reached for it, the single plate made sense. *Holy shit, the man planned on feeding me my dinner.*

He stirred the pasta with the fork, then placed a bite in his mouth. "Ah, good, it's cool enough." Nathan's smile was tender as he looked down at me.

What had I ever done to have anyone look at me like that?

He stabbed another bite and brought it to my lips. I opened instinctively and closed my mouth around the tines. With my mouth full of the rich pasta, Nathan began to speak.

"I've been watching you closely the last week. There's a lot I think I have figured out." He produced a napkin I didn't remember seeing him grab and dabbed at the corner of my mouth. "I know you like to kneel."

There wasn't a question in there, so I continued to chew.

"And you really didn't like the flogger."

I wasn't going to argue that one.

"What are your feelings on impact play as a whole?"

Dammit, there was a question I had to answer. I swallowed the bite of food in my mouth and worked on gathering my thoughts. Nathan didn't rush me and eventually I had them in order. "Um, I don't think I like it? I don't know for sure, but the flogger hurt."

Questions ran through Nathan's eyes and I could see him fighting to give me time to work through my thoughts before he asked for clarification. "Every time the flogger made contact with the guy's skin, my body ached. Not in a good way either." I sighed. "I couldn't see that being comfortable, but I've never experienced anything else." Not like that should have come as a surprise to him. My experiences were limited at best.

He rewarded me with a bite of broccoli. I must have been zoned out when he'd added butter and garlic to it, but it tasted amazing. "I think I understand that. I'll be honest. I've always been a pretty strict Dom. Impact play has always been part of my relationships—even casual—but it's also always been a two-way street. My subs got a lot out of it and so did I."

Tension built in my stomach. Was this going to be the end of whatever it was we were building?

Nathan took a bite of the pasta and I could tell he was gathering his thoughts. Logically, I knew he was making sure he didn't misspeak, but it didn't help my nerves settle. He glanced down at me after he swallowed. "I don't think impact play is a must for me. I'm going to sound like an asshole when I say this, but I thrive on control. I like knowing that I'm giving my submissive what he needs. I enjoy impact play because I know my sub does. I know it helps them work out whatever it is that they're dealing with, be it stress, anxiety, or emotions. But I get just as much pleasure and enjoyment out of rules and routines as I do impact play. It will be different, but I don't think I need the impact play as much as I do the ability to know that I'm giving you what you need."

One ball of tension loosened and another formed. *What did I need?* Did I know?

Nathan held a bite of pasta out to me and I took it, not really tasting it as I chewed.

"You're a pleaser, Elliot. I know that. You want to

please me; you want to please my mom. You want to please your friend... what's her name? Emma?" I found myself nodding in agreement. "You want to please your parents and everyone around you. But when do you get to please yourself? Did you ever stop to think about where Elliot comes into play?"

I swallowed the bite of food in my mouth. "I'm happy when I make other people happy."

Nathan's smile turned soft. "You definitely have a praise kink. I see the way you light up when anyone gives you a compliment. Especially when it's for something you've done for them. The question is, though, are *you* happy? Do you actually find pleasure and happiness in making everyone around you happy? Or are you just finding pleasure in the praise?"

The question drew me up short. I had no idea how to answer, even after Nathan took another bite of his dinner in order to give me more time to process. When it was clear that I wasn't going to respond, Nathan nodded slowly. "That's what I thought. And that's what I am going to thrive on: helping you figure out how to make yourself happy, and making you happy. It's fine to like praise and I'll praise the shit out of you, especially knowing that you thrive on it. But you shouldn't have to do things you genuinely don't want to do to get praise from someone who only cares about themselves... like your parents."

I opened for the bite of food he offered me. There was no point in trying to come up with something to say.

"When Emma drives you nuts and you need space, I want to be the one you come to. I can help you figure out what to say. When someone tries to pile more work on you, I want you to talk to me first. When you're stressed and you don't know why, I want to be able to help you with that. All that stress you feel and don't know how to make go away? I thrive on taking it on myself and helping you figure it out."

He offered the last bite of pasta to me and I was surprised to see the plate empty. I had no idea when we'd eaten all the pasta and broccoli, but it was gone and only the bread remained. When I had the bite in my mouth, Nathan gave me a smirk. "I have rules, as well. I already told you that I like control. You're new to submission, so we're going to have to figure out what will work best for you. He glanced down at my dick and grinned. "First and foremost, I want to control that."

My eyes widened. I forced myself to swallow the bite of food in my mouth. "You want to control it how?" I kept seeing cages and chastity and pain, and I was so not into that.

Nathan's chuckle wasn't demeaning, though I could tell he knew exactly what I'd been thinking. "I want you to tell me if you want to play with yourself or come when I'm not around."

I couldn't find words and found myself just staring at him—most specifically at his crotch, where his erection had grown noticeably over the last few minutes—as he waited me out. "So you're not going to, like, cage it?" I glanced down at my cock. It had deflated quickly at the thought of being locked up.

Nathan threw his head back as he laughed. "Not unless we talk about it first. And given that reaction, I'm going to guess we're a long way off from you being that comfortable."

I wasn't going to deny that. "I hope you don't ever expect me to be *that* comfortable."

Nathan grinned and I honestly had no idea why his smile was so wide, but he looked genuinely happy at the moment. "I love that you're not afraid to tell me what you don't like. I can't help you if you don't tell me what's wrong."

I was going to blame my full stomach and fuzzy head for voicing my thoughts. "But what if you don't like what I say?"

Nathan broke off a piece of bread, ran it through the leftover sauce, and held it out to me. "Then we talk about it. I'm not a petulant child, despite what Zander might tell you. I can understand limits and when enough is enough." He held out another piece of bread and I took it, thankful for the distraction. "This isn't a traditional conversation about limits, but it gets our feet wet and lets us know what we like or not. Zander had a contract with Noah to begin their relationship, but the most important thing is that we talk—a lot. If a contract makes you feel better, I'm happy to have one."

I'd done enough reading to know what a contract was and I couldn't imagine having one. It felt impersonal to me and very formal. "Right now, would it be wrong for me to just ask for us to talk and use safewords? Like that stoplight system I've read about? Red means stop, yellow to slow down, and green is good?"

Nathan popped a piece of bread in his mouth as he thought, then slowly nodded. "If that makes you feel better, we can do that. But if it ever feels too much, know that a contract in BDSM isn't like a contract in law. It is a fluid document that changes with us."

I nodded. I liked the way he explained that, but my brain was getting tired of talking. I'd been fantasizing about finally being with a man for most of my adult life and I was finally here... yet we were talking instead of doing something more exciting.

While my erection might have flagged over the course of our conversation, Nathan's hadn't, and I was ready to do more than look at the bulge in his jeans. I flexed my fingers, debating for a moment if I should take the first step. While a contract might have helped me navigate this situation a little better, I still couldn't imagine sitting there and spelling everything out in painful detail, so I went with what felt right.

"Can I touch you?" It wasn't quite a *Sir*, but the look on Nathan's face said that the question had been close enough for him. I doubted that would last, but for now, I wasn't ready.

Nathan nodded slowly, then laced his fingers behind his head. "My body is yours."

That was overwhelming, but the way that Nathan was so confident had my own confidence higher than normal. That didn't translate into knowledge, but his easy, laid-back demeanor made it feel like he trusted me, and to an extent, I guessed he did.

I reached for his button and Nathan hummed his approval. I popped it open and the zipper worked itself down without my prompting. I was pretty sure his erection actually sighed with relief as it lost the layer of well-fit denim around it.

Impulse said to tug his underwear down so that I could see all of him, but logic told me that would be uncomfortable. I'd had enough experience with seated jerk sessions to know that it was a hell of a lot more comfortable to pull my pants down. I reached out and took the waist of his jeans, tugging gently to let him know what I was trying to do. Nathan quickly took the hint and lifted so his pants came down.

I was in an awkward enough position that leaving his jeans around his knees wasn't an option, so I tugged them free and placed them beside him on the couch. As soon as I returned my attention to Nathan's crotch, he moaned before I could touch him. My eyes flicked up to find his lips turned upward. "I have never had anyone look at my dick the way you are looking at my underwear right now."

While I wanted to be embarrassed, the heat I was

expecting in my cheeks never came. There was a thin piece of fabric separating Nathan's dick from me, and I'd been fantasizing about the moment I could actually explore another man's body for so long that the fabric felt more like Fort Knox. I wanted... scratch that, I needed to see, touch, and experience Nathan without barriers. Yes, I'd waited a long time for this moment, but Nathan had been the first person who had actually *seen* me and taken time to get to know me. And from everything he'd said and done to this point, I was confident that he didn't care that I was inexperienced and he was willing to push me to an extent, but not to the point I was uncomfortable.

The uncertain guy I'd always been left me, replaced with a man who had more confidence than I'd ever had. I reached up and gripped at the waistband of Nathan's briefs and worked them off the same way I had his pants. And now I was left staring at his gorgeous uncut dick.

Relief washed over me when I finally took him in. He wasn't huge, more like proportionate to the rest of his body —still large, but not unreasonable. I was pretty sure there were a few dildos in my nightstand that were the size he was.

Now was not the time to be slow and tentative or thinking about my dildos when I had the real thing in front of me. I reached out and wrapped my hand around his cock. It was warm and weighty in my grip but familiar at the same time. He had a pronounced vein that ran along the underside, just like I did. His girth was similar to mine as well. The only real differences were that he was longer and uncut, which I had to admit made it more interesting to move my hand up and down.

Nathan hadn't stopped making pleasured noises since I'd touched him, so I knew I wasn't doing all that badly and it spurred my desire even more. When I saw the head of his dick peek out from the foreskin, covered in a layer of precum, I couldn't resist leaning forward and licking the slit.

Nathan's entire body tensed and the moan he let out went directly to my dick. I instinctively clenched my ass, pressing the plug against my prostate again. My moan joined his and I wasn't about to wait any longer. I wrapped my lips around his tip, the taste of his precum filling my mouth. Tangy and a little salty, it wasn't as off-putting as I'd expected it to be.

There was no way I was going to be able to take all of him into my mouth at once, so I used one hand to wrap around the base of his cock and began to work him in time with my sucks.

Nathan's body trembled and I could feel his balls tighten up below my hand. Curiosity got the better of me and I reached out to feel them with the hand that had been resting in my lap. They were heavier and larger than my own and I rolled them gently in my grasp as I explored.

Above me, Nathan grunted into the room and another spurt of precum filled my mouth. "E. E, baby, I'm going to come."

I loved the way he'd shortened my name. No one but Emma had ever called me anything but Elliot. I knew he was trying to get me to pull off when he began to tug my hair, but I found myself shaking my head and redoubling my efforts. I'd come this far, and I wasn't going to back off now.

A few more sucks and Nathan roared into the living room as his cock swelled inside my mouth. He grit out a frantic "Coming," one last-ditch effort to warn me to move away before his release filled my mouth.

I discovered quickly that I had taken too much of him inside me and couldn't swallow, so I pulled back to give my tongue and throat room to work as he continued to shoot volley after volley into my mouth. I swallowed as fast as I could, but some still dribbled out of the side of my mouth.

In the end, I couldn't say it was something I'd do every time, but it wasn't something I'd hated either. With the look on Nathan's face—totally blissed out, head leaning on the back of the couch, eyes closed—I'd absolutely do it again and again.

It wasn't like I'd come, but I felt exhaustion pulling me under as well. His cock was still softening in my mouth as my eyes closed. It had been a long day, filled with conversations and emotions, and I was feeling as wrung out as Nathan looked.

I must have fallen asleep because the next thing I knew, Nathan was chuckling as he roused me. "Come on, sleepyhead. You've been warming my cock long enough.

It's time to get us cleaned up, that plug out of your ass, and to bed."

The world was fuzzy, but I followed his directions, standing slowly to find my knees sore from kneeling for however long it had been. My feet were a little tingly, but the real pins and needles didn't start until I was laid out on his bed and mostly back asleep. I'd been so out of it I didn't remember him removing the plug or crawling into bed and wrapping me in his arms.

What I could say, without a doubt, was that I slept better than I ever had before.

CHAPTER 19

NATHAN

"YOU KNOW, just because you've finally found a guy who will tolerate your grumpy ass, doesn't mean that you're able to ignore the rest of us." Wilder sank down into the chair across from my desk. He hadn't bothered knocking and I'd only discovered his presence when he'd started talking.

I looked over, unamused, from my computer screen. My heart was pounding from the surprise, but I wasn't going to let him have the satisfaction of knowing he'd scared me, so I made my voice sound as disinterested as I could. "What the hell are you talking about?"

Wilder rolled his eyes at me, then shook his head like I was an idiot. "You didn't come to family dinner on Wednesday."

"Your point?" I'd gone out to dinner with Elliot that night, and then we'd fallen asleep on his couch watching a movie. Things were frighteningly easy with him, to the point that we'd fallen into an effortless routine of spending most evenings together.

We'd spent Wednesday evening discussing expectations over dinner at the local Chinese restaurant. Elliot had liked the idea of checking in with me regularly throughout the day and before making decisions. I'd noticed a lightness about him on Thursday that hadn't been there before. He'd texted frequently and had popped his head into my office more than once over the course of the day to let me know what he was doing or where he was off to.

Just this morning he'd poked his head into my office and asked if I minded if he went to the coffee shop with Austin. Actually, that had been twenty minutes ago and they hadn't returned. Which probably explained why Wilder was bugging the shit out of me instead of Austin.

Wilder's sigh reminded me that he was in my office. "Nate, you're becoming a recluse!"

He was so dramatic. "I'm not a recluse. Elliot is going to be overwhelmed by our family. Give him some time. And I'm certain that very few people actually missed me."

"Well, Austin definitely didn't miss you. I don't know how the hell he works with you every day. Zander was wondering where you were, though. Mom said that you've finally learned that honey is better than vinegar."

I threw my hands in the air. "You nosy assholes need to get lives. Seth wasn't there and you're not hounding him."

"Seth was in Florida."

I'd known that, but I had hoped my brother wouldn't remember it.

"I'm sorry I have a life that doesn't revolve around the family."

The side door opened and Austin's and Elliot's voices filtered down the hallway. I made a shooing motion with my hand. "Begone. Go bug Austin. I'm guessing that's why you're here in the first place. God knows the man needs another distraction." I'd said the words with love and affection, but the truth was, for as detail oriented as the guy was when it came to legal documents, he spent just as much energy avoiding work.

Wilder flipped me off but stood to go track down our brother. "We were going to go out to lunch today."

I looked at my watch. "It's quarter to eleven. It's a little early for lunch."

Wilder lifted a shoulder. "It's Friday. Want to join us?"

I shook my head. "Again, it's not even eleven. I'm still primed to be subsisting fully on coffee for another hour at least."

"Your loss." He'd barely left my office before Elliot appeared with a cup of coffee in his hand. "Coffee, Good Sir."

That was a new one over the last few days. He'd begun calling me Sir, but usually in a joking tone. I guessed he was trying the word on for size. I liked the show of respect from my submissives, so I wasn't going to discourage it, but I wasn't going to force something unnatural either.

"Thank you. I appreciate your thinking of me before you went."

Elliot beamed with delight at the praise. It was a different swell of pride than he'd had in the past when I'd told him he'd done a good job. When my mom told him he'd done a good job with something, Elliot would sit up a little straighter and give a big smile, but when I thanked him for doing something for me or complimented him on something he'd done, I swore he grew two inches and nearly floated away.

He gestured with his head to his office. "I need to get to work."

"Sounds good. I should get back to work. Wilder showed up a few minutes before you got back and was bugging me." Before he could leave, I got up and pulled him into my arms. I wasn't going to get tired of the way he always melted into my touches or the way his lips became totally pliant under my kisses. That time he didn't go quite as relaxed as he normally did, his body remaining tense even as we kissed.

"What's up?"

Elliot sighed and leaned into my arms. "Something doesn't feel right. Emma hasn't texted me once today."

The conflict between them had gotten out of hand. Not being directly involved, it felt to me that they'd both been in the wrong. Emma shouldn't have been talking with Elliot's brother behind Elliot's back, but Elliot should have explained to her why he was so upset. Instead, he'd been speaking to her just enough to keep her from hounding him.

"When we get to my place tonight, you're going to call her."

Elliot groaned and in that moment, he gave me a pout that Larson would have been proud of.

I booped his nose. "No pouting. You're going to talk this out because it's gotten out of hand."

He huffed and narrowed his eyes, but the resignation was already there. He knew he wasn't going to get out of it that easily. "Fine." He blew a raspberry in the air that made me laugh.

"Drama queen. Go back to work." I leaned in for a quick, chaste kiss, then pulled back. "Have a good rest of your morning. I'll see you for lunch."

Elliot grumbled something about bossy Doms that had me chuckling as he left. Thankfully, after Elliot was gone, I was able to focus back on my work. I quickly got lost in reading a deposition and was nearly halfway through when an argument from outside my window caught my attention.

"For the love of everything." I slid back from my desk and spun my chair around to find a woman on a cell phone arguing with the person on the other end. *Why was this the discussion window? Was there a sign on it that I'd missed?*

I went to tap on the window to tell her to move along when she nearly yelled into her phone. "I have to make this right!"

I sighed and rolled my eyes at the lover's spat outside the window of a divorce attorney's office. Sometimes I wished I could just tell clients to get a divorce instead of trying to make it work.

"I know you're trying to tell me that my perception of him is skewed, but I can tell you right now that I don't care. You want to make this right, fine. He's been nothing but a dick to me since I was born."

It took me way too long to figure out that she'd put the call on speaker as she dug through her purse and that was why I could hear his side of the conversation all of a sudden. Now I was intrigued.

"Jesus, he's been trying to reach out to you for months and you wouldn't respond! Then you tell him that *I* was the one that told you to reach out. Well, you and Rand. You couldn't just say hello?"

My eyes widened. I was starting to put things together and this wasn't good. There were too many coincidences, and I was sure I'd heard this story already and knew the main characters. The person outside my window was Emma and the guy she was talking to was Elliot's brother. With the pieces coming together, I picked up on her New York accent.

Shit. How the hell did I handle this?

"Well, I don't want to mend that fence, Emma. Elliot made his bed. He can lie in it all he wants."

She pushed a button then jammed the phone back to

her ear. "You really should hear him out, Kyle. You don't know what you think you do."

There was a brief pause in which I could only assume Kyle was disputing her claim. I took the momentary quiet on her end and opened the window a little farther to hiss out. "Knock it off!"

She jumped and nearly dropped her phone, juggling it around a few times before catching it in her hand and swinging around to look at my window. At the same time, Elliot's voice came from my doorway. "Ugh, maybe I need to just call Emma. Now I'm hearing her voice in my head! Maybe I shouldn't wait until we get back to your place tonight. Should I call her at lunch?"

I pinched the bridge of my nose. This was a mess.

Emma's eyes were wide as I turned to Elliot and forced a smile I didn't feel. "I don't think that's going to be necessary."

Elliot's eyebrows drew together. "Oh?"

Reaching back with my hand, I gestured for Elliot to come closer. My windows were tinted, so I knew she couldn't see me despite my seeing her clearly. He hadn't reached me when I turned back to my window. "We'll meet you in the lobby."

Elliot joined me by the window. "Who are you talking —" His sentence cut off as he saw her walking away. "Was that..."

When he didn't finish, I simply nodded. "Your friend seems upset that you're not speaking to her."

He rubbed at his eyes. "So she just showed up here?"

I couldn't help but agree with his sentiment. I was struggling to see how traveling halfway across the country without warning was a good idea.

"You don't have to talk with her if you don't want. You're at work and she showed up here unexpectedly. You don't owe her anything."

Elliot was quiet for a long moment. "If I don't talk to her here, it's just going to loom over me, and all I'm doing is putting off the inevitable."

"I'm glad that you're looking at this logically, but I understand this isn't going to be easy." I motioned toward the door. "Let's go get this over with."

Elliot stayed close as we made our way down the hallway and toward the lobby. I could already hear my mom's voice echoing down the hall and I winced.

"You're here to see Elliot?" She sounded genuinely excited. It wasn't a stretch to say that my mom had taken a liking to Elliot from the moment he'd walked in the door. Then again, my mom basically adopted anyone and everyone who came into our lives. "Are you a friend from New York?"

"Elliot and I were roommates. I took a long weekend to surprise him." Emma's voice had been cautious and measured. To the untrained ear, I could believe it sounded genuine, but we were all attorneys here and I heard the hesitation loud and clear.

I cleared my throat and my mom looked over. One look at my face and her head tilted to the side. "You okay, hun?"

"Fine." My jaw ached from clenching it and my lips had barely moved with the word, but I was on high alert at the moment. My only concern was keeping Elliot from bolting. A glance back at him showed his face creased in thought as he looked at Emma.

Mom looked between us again, quickly picking up on Elliot's discomfort. "Do you want her here, Elliot?"

His attempt at a scoff fell flat and came out sounding more like a deflated balloon. "A little late to change it now."

I turned to face Elliot and shook my head. "No, it's really not. I have zero problem telling her to leave right now."

I was greeted with a genuine smile that lit up his eyes. "Thank you, Sir." It had been nearly a whisper, probably too quiet for even my mom's superhuman hearing to pick up. With nine kids, she was the woman that could hear a pin drop in a stampede.

Mom hummed loudly enough that I turned back to her. "I trust that you have this under control, Nathan?"

I gave a curt nod. "Well handled."

She gave a shake of her head. "Remember, you attract more flies with honey than vinegar."

I rolled my eyes but found myself smiling. "I'm going to take over the conference room."

Darcy had been looking between us all since we'd arrived in the lobby but finally spoke up. "You're fine. The conference room is available all day. Can I get you all anything?"

She was clearly uncomfortable with the situation unfolding in front of her but had done a good job remaining polite. Unfortunately, this wasn't the most uncomfortable or tense situation we'd had in the office.

"We're fine. I don't suspect she will be here long." Hopefully, that was a clear enough sign to Emma that she wasn't going to hang around all day. It was going to be a quick conversation and I had no problems telling her to leave if things got heated. I didn't like the fact that she'd shown up at our work and thrown Elliot in a tailspin like she had.

Emma might have been Elliot's best friend, but I didn't know her and Elliot was my top priority. As his boyfriend and Dom... or at least we were getting to that point... his happiness came above hers. I'd be civil as long as the conversation remained civil and Elliot wasn't upset.

More flies with honey and all that.

CHAPTER 20

ELLIOT

I WISHED that Emma's voice had been a figment of my imagination. I wasn't ready to talk with her. I'd just started to figure out my thoughts and she was standing not five feet from me in the conference room.

Nathan came to stand beside me, closer than was strictly friendly. I didn't know what he was thinking but in his eyes, I could see how annoyed he was with Emma's appearance. His shoulders were pulled back and his spine was stiff. He looked more like a bodyguard than the guy who liked to pull me close and snuggle in the evenings.

When no one spoke, I finally cleared my throat. "What are you doing here?"

Emma truly looked taken aback. "You stopped talking to me!"

Subconsciously, I reached behind Nathan's back and placed my hand between his shirt and coat. The cool silk lining brushed against the back of my knuckles and centered me. "I didn't completely stop talking to you. I've been responding."

The way her eyes narrowed told me that hadn't been the right response. "You know what I mean."

Nathan leaned into me slightly, silently urging me to speak up. I hated speaking up to anyone. It was easier to not make waves, which was how I'd found myself not speaking to Emma in the first place. It was easier to ignore it than deal with it. I forced myself to take a breath and focus my thoughts before I spoke.

"I was blindsided and hurt and I've been trying to work through it."

This was not how I had planned on my day going. I sighed and focused back on Emma. "You never told me you were talking to Kyle. Not even a, 'Hey, we've kept in touch.' I've spent how long trying to figure out a way to reconnect with him? All along, you've been talking with him."

A pit formed in my stomach as I spoke. "How much have you told him about me? Did you tell him I'm gay? Did you tell him I went to DASH?" I didn't know why it mattered to me so much, but I wanted to be the one to tell my brother I was gay. I was still holding out hope that one day I'd be able to do that and apologize for my behavior all around.

Emma gaped at me, then shook her head. "What? No! Of course not!" She narrowed her eyes, looking at where Nate and I were pressed together but ignored it for the time being. "“I thought he was nice when I met him at the wedding. Everyone there knew it would be a disaster with the way we were pissed at each other all day. And after the way you behaved to him then, he's still convinced you're an asshole, no matter how many times I tell him otherwise."

She tugged at her ponytail, a sure sign she was frustrated. "I've been trying to get him to reach out to you so that the two of you could actually get to see one another. You live like an hour and a half away from each other and don't even speak!"

"Regardless, around the block or across the world, it doesn't matter if he has no desire to speak with me in the first place."

Nathan maneuvered his arm so that he could squeeze my shoulder and I felt myself lean into him for support. Emma didn't miss the move and her eyes studied the two of us more carefully.

I fought the instinct to pull away. She knew I was gay. She'd pushed me to figure myself out. She was the one who had encouraged me to get out and live life. Though I did feel myself wince slightly when I realized it had been so long since I'd spoken to Emma that I hadn't told her everything that had happened at DASH or afterward.

She sniffed, but I couldn't decide if she was upset or annoyed. "This is new."

Nathan growled a deep, rumbling warning in his chest. "Elliot doesn't have to tell you anything he doesn't want to."

I blinked over at Nathan, too surprised to speak for a moment. He was standing up for me and assuring me that I didn't have to tell her anything I wasn't ready to. I'd never had anyone there for me before. A smile broke across my face and I leaned over to place a gentle kiss to Nathan's cheek. "Thank you." I turned back to Emma and nodded. "It's new, but I'm happy."

There was a crack in Nathan's stony veneer as a small smile twitched at his lips and the corners of his eyes. It was almost imperceptible but it was there, and I swelled with happiness knowing that I'd caused it.

I knew Emma's brown eyes better than I knew my own and when they turned cloudy, my resolve to be mad at my best friend crumbled. She hadn't even sniffled when I left Nathan's side to pull her into a hug.

The scent of her coconut-and-honey shampoo filled my nose, her body pressed against mine in a familiar, comforting way, and her arms wrapped around my body to pull me close. My anger and frustration were gone and the hole they'd left was being filled with all the things I'd wanted to tell her about over the last few weeks.

She sniffed into the shoulder of my suit coat. It was probably stained with her makeup and would need to be dry-cleaned now, but I didn't mind. Emma was truly the closest thing to family I had and I'd missed her like crazy. I'd dry-clean every suit I owned just to be able to talk to her regularly.

Nathan's hand landed between my shoulders and I looked over to him to find him smiling at us. "Take the rest of the day off. You two have a lot to talk about, I think."

"You sure?" There was a pile of files on my desk that I needed to get through and I felt guilty leaving Nathan to do them.

He placed a kiss to my forehead in response. "Austin can look through your files. He's got a keen eye for this stuff and if there is anything pressing, I'll handle it."

I nodded once. "Thanks. Dinner?" I had no idea what Emma's plans were for the night, but I didn't want to miss seeing Nathan tonight either.

"Just text when you're ready to eat. I'll take care of the rest."

He left the conference room, the door clicking quietly behind him. Emma finally pulled back from my shoulder, her eyes red-rimmed and a few tears still showing in them. "He's hot."

The statement took me so much by surprise, I found myself laughing and nodding my head. "Yes. Yes, he is. Let me grab my bag and we can go get lunch. You've got to be starving."

She nodded eagerly. "Starving. But can we take it to go? I have questions that I don't want people overhearing."

Of course she did. With anyone else, I'd have insisted we stay at the restaurant instead of going somewhere private, but with Emma I knew there was no use. She'd pepper me with questions in public or in private, and knowing her as well as I did, the questions she had were going to be things I wanted to keep out of the small deli I planned on taking her to.

It didn't take long to get to the deli and order our lunches. "I'll follow you."

"My place isn't too far from here, maybe ten or fifteen minutes." As I said the words, I remembered how private Seth was about his house and pulled my phone out.

Me: *Hey, I wanted to let you know that my friend is coming back with me today.*

Seth: *It's your place. You don't have to tell me when you bring someone back. Shouldn't you be at work?*

I hadn't expected his answer so quickly. They were in the playoffs, and while they were down a few games and it wasn't looking good for the Grizzlies that season, they still had at least two more games to play. Seth had basically been living at the arena or on a plane the last few weeks.

I shot a quick text back to fill him in on Emma's arrival in Tennessee and my unexpected day off, then wished him luck at the game that night before I pocketed my phone.

As expected, his SUV was gone by the time we pulled into the gated driveway. I drove behind Seth's house to the guest house with Emma following close behind. It had become second nature to watch the gate shut in the rearview mirror, a habit I didn't even think of until I kept seeing a car behind me instead of the closing gate.

Emma was on a mission as she made a beeline toward my couch with the deli bags in her hand. I didn't know if her goal was to eat or pepper me with questions, but I shrugged my suit coat off and inspected the damage to the shoulder. It wasn't as bad as it could have been, but the coat was definitely done for until I got it to the cleaners.

On my way toward the couch, I loosened my tie and popped the top button of my shirt. I didn't bother unbuttoning my vest and sank down beside her like I used to on our couch in New York. Emma never missed a beat as she handed my bag over and curled her feet to the side of her so she could sag against me.

A homesickness I hadn't felt since I left New York settled over me. I'd missed our easy relationship more than I'd realized. It was comforting to know that there weren't expectations on me around her.

She jumped into questions as she unrolled her sandwich from the deli paper. "Okay, what happened at the club? I'm guessing you went?"

The next hour was spent with her peppering me with questions about everything that had happened since the club. It felt good to tell her everything, even the more intimate parts of our relationship. Getting to talk to someone about the feelings I was having was a relief, and knowing she wasn't judging me but was truly happy for me made it easier.

As I finished telling her about the night I'd knelt before him and he'd fed me dinner, ending in my giving him a blowjob, Emma's eyes widened. "Oh, I bet he's very well endowed." She took a bite of her pickle spear and we both started to laugh.

"I am not going there with you, ever, but especially after that!"

Lunch was long gone by the time she shifted her weight and looked up at me. "Honestly, how does submission feel?"

I chewed on the inside of my cheek as I thought of how to answer. "Truthfully? Aside from kneeling for him a few times, and my texting him frequently, we haven't done much. I know he's afraid to push me too far, too fast. Part of me is scared to rock the boat. What if we try it and I hate it?"

Emma was watching me closely, so when I didn't answer right away, she prodded gently. "What if you love it?"

My huff of breath had been unintentional but appropriate for the situation. "Yeah, that's a possibility too. But I feel like I have a lot more to lose if I don't like it."

She hummed as she squeezed my thigh. "I can see that. But it's still new. You know that his being a Dom is part of his self-identity. He's told you that physical punishments aren't a deal breaker for him, but I'm guessing there's only so much the guy can ignore about his natural need for control before he pushes you away. If you continue on as you are, your heart is going to get more involved than it already is, and it's going to be a hell of a lot harder to say goodbye if your interests don't align."

I hated when Emma was right. I really, really hated when she was right. I knew we needed to talk, but I was scared. "I feel like I need that push, yet I'm scared to push for it."

"That sounds like the Elliot I know. Play it safe. Don't rock the boat, even if it's something that directly impacts you. El, you promised me you'd start living for you. If you don't push for what you need, want, or hell, are just curious about, then you're never going to know what does it for you." She was smiling as she said the words, but it didn't help the bite of truth.

I sank back into the couch with a sigh. "I hear you. I get what you're saying. Logically, I know it's the right thing to do. In practice, it's much, much harder."

Emma patted my chest. "You, Elliot Mitchell, are a mess. But you're going to be a bigger mess when you fuck everything up because you refuse to talk to him." She looked at the clock on the wall and sighed. "I hate to say this, but I need to go. I'm supposed to be having dinner with Kyle tonight."

My eyes widened. "You're going to dinner with my brother?"

She had the decency to look uncomfortable. "Um, yeah. I told him I was coming to Tennessee and he asked if we could meet up for dinner. Is that going to be a problem?"

I thought about the question for a moment before finally shaking my head. "No. At this point, he wants nothing to do with me and I've tried. Can you just do me a favor?"

Emma nodded slowly. "Sure. Anything."

"Just tell him I'm happy for him."

She pursed her lips, then nodded. "I can do that." She kissed my cheek. "I've got a hotel in Nashville for the night. I'll talk with you later."

"Talk with you later. Have a good dinner."

She was gone a few minutes later and I found myself standing at the front window watching her leave, my head filled with thoughts and questions about what I was doing and what I was going to tell Nathan that night. Emma was right. I couldn't keep letting us dance around the subject. It was time to put my big boy pants on and really talk with Nathan. I loved what we'd done so far, but I knew that wasn't going to keep him satisfied forever, and if I was truthful with myself, I didn't think it would keep me satisfied either.

CHAPTER 21

NATHAN

IT WAS AMAZING what peace and quiet did for productivity. Not having Elliot a few feet away all day kept my mind from wandering to him and finding excuses to stop by his office. It also kept Austin focused on his work instead of giggling like a teenager every fifteen minutes as the two chatted about anything and everything.

Yet it felt like something was missing the entire second half of the day. Walking by a dark office on my way to the bathroom was downright depressing. And the lack of laughter and noise was driving me insane.

By four, I was convinced that the clock had stopped moving altogether and any and all progress on the case I'd been working on had ground to a halt. It was Friday anyway, so in an uncharacteristic move, I shut down my computer and put my coat on.

Austin's head popped up when my office light clicked off. "Whoa, where are you off to?"

"Home."

There was no way I was going to get anything past him as he narrowed his eyes at me. "Missing your man?"

"Fuck you."

My brother's eyes sparkled with amusement. "I'll take that as a yes. How are things going?"

I found myself leaning against the wall across from his desk as I thought about the question. "I really like him. Spending time with him is effortless." I grinned thinking about the night before. "I can make him light up with the simplest touches. And I love the way that telling him he's done a good job has him nearly floating away. I've never seen anyone respond to praise like an actual kink."

"I sense a *but* in there."

I chuckled. He wasn't wrong. "Yes, there's a *but*. I just don't know how big of one it is. He's so new to the lifestyle. I'm struggling to figure out when to push and when not to."

The laughter bubbling out of my brother did not help any. "Oh, Nate. That guy screams submissive. He hates trying to figure out what to get at the coffee shop, so he gets the same thing every day. Unless, of course, I tell him to try something because it's good. Then he'll try it and he's always liked it, but the next time, he gets a plain coffee because then he doesn't have to choose between the specials."

I'd noticed that myself. "Yes, but does that equate to rules and structure? He keeps talking about needing to find himself. If I push him to submit to me, am I just going to be like everyone else in his life and make him feel like he has to be one way?"

To my surprise, instead of giving me a flippant response, Austin hummed in thought. "You know, it's a damn good question. I think it boils down to it being the first time in his life that he is free to give up the choice. And remember, *communication.* He's got a safeword, and if he doesn't yet, he should. He should know how to use it. You can be the one person in his life that he's finally free to give control to."

Who the hell was the guy sitting at the desk? The man in skintight navy slacks, a white dress shirt with a bright pink bowtie, with spiked hair and dark-framed glasses looked a hell of a lot like my youngest brother. However, he definitely didn't *sound* like the annoying little brother I'd always known.

"Since your mouth is moving but no words are coming out, I have to assume that I've fried your brain. Go home, Nate. Go home, get a shower, and talk to Elliot. Jesus. You'd think Mom and Dad's lectures all these years went in one ear and straight out the other!"

I growled at my brother but ended up nodding my head as I left the office. Though I did throw my middle finger up in the air at him for good measure just before the door shut. Of course, it hadn't shut quickly enough for me to not hear his cackling laugh follow me down the sidewalk. *There* was the pain in the ass I'd always known. At least not everything had turned on its head.

I'd barely pulled from the lot when my music cut off and the car filled with the computerized voice of a notification on my phone.

"Incoming text from Elliot. Would you like me to read it?"

"Yes." Like I was going to say no to that?

"Hey. Emma just left. She's going out to dinner with Kyle. I'm going to jump in the shower. If you're still up for dinner, let me know."

"Text Elliot. I just left the office. I'll pick you up in thirty."

With the text sent, I sent another to Seth letting him know I was going to borrow his shower. I got a phone call in return that involved him teasing me about having my own house to shower at, or showering at Elliot's place. What he hadn't said was that I couldn't use his shower, so after a few minutes of ribbing, I finally told him I needed to go because I was at his house.

I checked Seth's houseplants while I was inside, then showered quickly. It wasn't like I kept a supply of clothes at his house, but we were close enough to the same size that I snagged a pair of his jeans out of the closet to replace my suit pants. Aside from Larson, Zander, and Austin, we were all about the same size and could easily share clothes. However, I always failed to take into account Seth's hockey butt and thighs.

The jeans that fit him like a second skin were a little big on my ass and thighs, but they were still perfectly acceptable to go to dinner in. And they were loose enough that I could easily sit for long periods of time in them. Something I couldn't necessarily say about my suit pants.

I pulled my red dress shirt back on—this time without the undershirt—and left the top few buttons undone. I'd gone from business to casual in just a few minutes and was ready to go pick Elliot up for dinner and a talk.

Elliot had just stepped outside in a pair of comfortable jeans and a baby blue dress shirt when I came around the house in my SUV. He gave me the most confused look I'd ever seen from him as I parked. His brows were pulled downward and his lips pursed as he watched me get out of my car.

He reached up and touched the side of my head, carefully avoiding the bangs I'd styled with whatever product I'd found in Seth's bathroom. "Your hair's still wet."

My lips twitched as I tried to hide my amusement at his utter confusion. "Didn't want to waste time going back to my house, so I showered at Seth's."

Elliot tilted his head to the side and smirked. "That explains why your pants are so baggy."

My laughter was unexpected but welcome. "Have you been checking out my brother's ass?"

"I mean... He plays hockey. I hate to break it to you—I've been looking at your brother's ass longer than I've known you."

The unexpected, random statement had come from so far out of left field that there was nothing else for me to do but double over in laughter even harder. When I finally pulled myself together, I reached out and hooked my fingers into his belt loops and tugged him toward me, kissing him firmly on the lips.

He went pliant against my body, tension leaving him like air from a balloon. I broke the kiss and grinned. "You better not be looking at my brother's ass anymore."

Elliot leaned around and examined my ass. "I mean, could you start playing hockey?"

What had gotten into people in my life today? First Austin was logical, now Elliot was teasing me. I shook my head. "Are you ready for dinner?"

He pursed his lips and looked me up and down. "More than... Oh! You mean going out to eat? Yeah. That too."

"Get in the car." I'd probably have sounded sterner if I hadn't been trying to hide my amusement at him.

I pointed the car toward the highway and headed in the direction of my house. My favorite Italian restaurant was near it and I had every intention of going there.

I'd already pulled off the highway when Elliot spoke up. "You know, we could cook at your place."

"Unfortunately, no, we can't. I haven't been to the grocery store. I'm out of basically everything. Besides, if we go back to one of our houses, we will likely get sidetracked and not talk."

"That sounds ominous."

Mentally replaying my words, I couldn't help but

shake my head at myself. "Yeah, it did. And that isn't how I intended it."

Elliot's resigned huff surprised me as much as his words. "Yeah, we really shouldn't get so caught up in naked time tonight. There is some stuff I want to talk to you about."

I pulled into the parking lot of the restaurant and into a spot near the front door. "Now who sounds ominous?"

"I've heard a lot about communication today."

I couldn't help but chuckle. "As have I. I think we've gotten more wrapped up in right now than talking about some more difficult topics."

Elliot's answering silence said he'd been having the same thoughts. Now I was worried about what he and Emma had talked about today. As we headed into the restaurant, I kept reminding myself that he'd been flirty and happy when I'd picked him up. Whatever he wanted to talk to me about couldn't be as bad as I was making it out to be.

Thanks to leaving work early, we'd beat the dinner rush and were seated immediately. Elliot barely glanced at the menu before selecting a pasta carbonara that I knew he'd gotten at every Italian place we'd been to together. Austin's words replayed in my head as I studied the menu.

"Can I order for you?"

Elliot's eyes widened in surprise and he pulled his lip between his teeth before finally relenting. "Yeah. That's fine." His words and shy smile went straight to my dick.

I was going to owe Austin a bottle of liquor for the wake-up call.

"Anything you don't like or are allergic to?"

"I don't like mushrooms." The little shudder he gave and the way his face scrunched up was adorable. I set to work picking out our meals and had just decided when a waiter appeared with glasses of water.

In just a few minutes, I had ordered two glasses of red wine, two salads, a decadent chicken meal for Elliot, and a pan-seared salmon meal for myself. My favorite meal there was the saltimbocca chicken, but I wanted to let Elliot have some of my meal as well, and I knew he wouldn't think about it with the mushrooms.

The waiter gave a sharp nod, folded his order pad shut, and hurried toward the computer to input our orders.

Elliot ducked his head, but I could see the corners of his eyes pinched in a smile as he spoke quietly. "Thank you."

"You're welcome. I understand that decisions can sometimes be difficult. And if you know you like something, it can be even harder to convince yourself to try something different."

Elliot's shoulders dropped some and his entire body relaxed as I spoke. I didn't know why it had taken Austin pointing out the obvious for me to see what was right in front of me, but I was glad he had. I was going to take the current situation as an in for the conversation we needed to have.

"From here on out, I'd really like to order for you."

As Elliot's head came up to meet my eyes, his eyebrows rose on his forehead. "Seriously?"

I wasn't sure how to take his question, so I pushed forward with confirmation. "I would. I've had your cooking. I know you like a wide variety of things. When we go out, though, you always have the same things. I think you'd enjoy many more dishes than your standard go-tos."

He spoke more to the table than to me and it saddened me to hear the resignation in his voice as he spoke. "I know I do. But I make so many decisions all day that when I go out, I don't want to make another decision. I see something I've had before and I stick with it. I plan meals all week so that when I go to the grocery store, I know exactly what's going to be made each day. That way I don't have to think about it while shopping or while I'm cooking."

His words gave me confidence in our conversation, though I couldn't ignore the pang of guilt I felt for not noticing earlier. "I was honest with you the first night. I like control. I like knowing that I'm giving my partner what he needs. What I've been neglecting is what you need, but with that, I've also been neglecting my needs as well."

I hadn't expected Elliot to snort at my words. At the very least, I'd expected some confusion or nervousness on his part. Not laughter and relief. "That's exactly what Emma and I were talking about today."

My eyebrow rose in surprise. Those two really didn't normally keep much from the other person. "Really?"

His mouth twitched as he fought to keep a neutral expression. "Um, yeah. I've liked what we've done so far, but I've been unsure of how to tell you that I think I'm ready for more." A blush flared in his cheeks that even the dim lighting of the restaurant couldn't hide.

"Well, we can start to rectify this now." I pulled my phone from my pocket and opened the note-taking app. "Let's discuss ways that we can both find what we need."

The sound that came from Elliot was somewhere between a squeak of surprise and a moan of pleasure. He wiggled in his spot for a moment, then his hand disappeared under the table. The conversation was turning him on and that gave me an immense amount of pleasure.

I cleared my throat and shook my head. "Hands above the table, Elliot." I glanced down like I could see his cock through the table. "First rule, that is off limits to you."

His mouth hung open in surprise and I had to fight to keep a wicked grin off my face. "I like knowing you're hard."

His nostrils flared, so I knew I'd hit a hot button, whether he'd been aware of it before or not. "I'm uncomfortable." Elliot's voice had dropped even lower than my own and he squirmed in his seat again. "I need to adjust myself."

I let my voice go deeper, almost challenging him to argue with me when I spoke. "Then you need to ask permission."

Elliot's entire body went rigid for a moment as I

watched thoughts and emotions fly through his eyes and over his face. He was too expressive to hide them, but they were coming so quickly I had a hard time deciphering them.

When his body relaxed again, his expression was blank, though his cheeks had settled at a pink a few shades darker than his normal complexion. "Please, Sir, can I adjust myself in my pants?"

Elliot was no longer the only one who needed to adjust himself. I'd had no idea I could get so hard so fast and said a silent thank you to the loose denim of Seth's jeans. I needed Elliot functioning for the rest of the conversation, so I wasn't going to torment him by telling him to leave it alone. I gave a sharp nod in his direction. "You may adjust yourself."

He sighed and his hand once again disappeared beneath the table. I knew he'd found a comfortable position when his body sagged into the booth and his hand reappeared. I hadn't expected the quiet "Thank you" he managed at the end but found myself beaming with pride.

Elliot was a natural.

"You're welcome." I cleared my throat as an attempt to get my voice to sound more natural before I continued. "You've got the stoplight system. If we talk about or do something that you are uncomfortable with, I expect you to use that. I will never judge you. I will never ignore your safewords. We will stop and talk about it."

Elliot swallowed hard, then cleared his throat. "Red,

yellow, and green." It sounded more like he was trying them out than asking a question or looking for a response, but I found myself nodding.

"Yes, red to stop, yellow to slow down, and green for good. When I do a color check with you, I expect you to tell me the first word that comes to your mind. And I expect you to tell me if I inadvertently cross a line."

Elliot nodded again, but I was proud when he found words. "Yes, Sir."

"You're worried about disappointing people. You push yourself and then get inside your head. It's a vicious cycle."

Our salads arrived and I stopped talking long enough for the waiter to set them and our wine in front of us. He left after I assured him we had everything we needed.

"My goal is to set up a system that helps you mitigate some of those frustrations and worries."

Tension eased in Elliot's body as I spoke. "Yes, please." I didn't know if he'd even realized he'd breathed the words and I didn't intend to draw attention to it.

I tapped my phone back to life. "How do you feel about regular check-in times with me?"

His brow furrowed. "What do you mean?"

"Like a text or simply popping into my office every few hours to let me know how you're doing. It's a lot like what we have been doing, but with a bit more structure to it. Right now, you're texting me to tell me that you're going out, or if I want something to eat or drink while you're gone. I want a more regular schedule—every few hours, not just when you have a decision to make. With this change, I might text you as well and ask or remind you to take a break or eat lunch."

He tilted his head to the side and studied me hard. "You'd want that?"

I ran through what I thought could be running through his head at the moment, in order to answer the question appropriately. "I like that control. One of the things that's held me back is not wanting you to feel as though I'm controlling your decisions. However, by having this discussion tonight, we're able to set boundaries with what we're both comfortable with. I don't want to pressure you into living your life a certain way—like your family has—I want to empower you. I want you to know that I'm here for you whenever you need it and that I'm always an open ear. Yes, I might be more take-charge than other men, but I also thrive on problem-solving and the knowledge that what I'm doing is helping you in some way. My hope is you'll find that by giving me some of the everyday decisions that weigh you down, you will be able to handle the bigger decisions when they come your way. And if you need someone to talk them through with, you'll always know I'm here."

Elliot's eyes had turned watery as I spoke, and his mouth had formed an O of surprise. "Oh. That sounds nice."

"I thought it would."

He nodded again, but he seemed to be lost in his head.

I tapped a quick note in my phone about regular check-ins and began a detailed list of things I wanted texts or calls for, including when he was horny and wanted release if I wasn't there. Elliot hadn't said anything, focusing more on his thoughts and his food than my hands moving across the screen of my phone.

When I was done, I shared the list with his phone, then pocketed mine and turned to my dinner, which was now cool. "We can talk more about the list I just sent you later. And we are always free to amend it."

His fork stopped halfway to his mouth and he nodded sharply. "Oh. Okay. Yeah."

At least we had all weekend to discuss it.

CHAPTER 22

ELLIOT

My phone vibrated in my pocket and I pulled it out, silencing the alarm before opening the texting app.

Me: *I'm thinking about grabbing lunch after I'm done reading this complaint.*

Nathan's return text was nearly immediate.

Nathan: *Do you have plans? I was going to order from the Chinese restaurant down the road.*

Me: *Well, I hadn't had plans, but that sounds really good.*

Nathan: *Great. I'll call in an order.*

I set my phone down, a smile on my face. It hadn't been anywhere near as suffocating as I'd first imagined to start texting Nathan regularly. The first week had been a bit awkward, but it was more or less from working out the kinks, for lack of a better word. I didn't want to bother him by texting too much but didn't want him to think I was ignoring him either.

At first, I'd settled on quick texts to say hi, tell him what I was working on, and let him know I was doing all right. After about a week, the quick FYI texts had naturally progressed to questions about if he minded my going somewhere. It had happened so subtly I hadn't noticed until I'd found myself waiting for a response before going to grab a coffee with Austin. Nathan always had a suggestion for a drink I'd like, and I hadn't wanted to leave without knowing what to get.

Another awkward conversation followed where Nathan assured me that I wasn't being too needy. Since then, I'd been trying not to overthink the texts I sent him.

Well, all but one.

The idea of asking him for permission to jerk off was painfully embarrassing, to the point that I hadn't touched myself for more than going pee or a clinical clean in three weeks. And since we hadn't spent the night together in three nights, my resolve was beginning to be tested.

I swore I'd just put my phone down and Nathan's head popped around the doorframe. "Hey, lunch is here."

Now that he'd said something, I could smell it and my stomach rumbled. I'd gotten lost in thought and hadn't done more work, but thankfully it was a catch-up day for me and there wasn't any reason I needed to be at the courthouse. If something needed to be filed, Austin was the man to run there.

With a few clicks on my keyboard, my lock screen popped up and I was on my way to the break room with

Nathan and Austin. I'd noticed over the last few weeks that Connie had been coming in less and less, so I assumed that her retirement would happen sooner rather than later. Thankfully, Nathan no longer seemed stressed about it. It had gotten to the point that I'd heard multiple siblings of his mention the change in him.

Nathan unceremoniously dropped a container of food in front of Austin before gently placing a carton in front of me.

Austin snorted, his yellow bowtie with red polka dots distracting enough I almost didn't notice the dramatic eye roll he gave Nathan. "I see how it is. You like your boyfriend more than me."

Nathan snorted. "My boyfriend gives me far fewer gray hairs than you do."

Hearing Nathan call me his boyfriend so easily sent warmth through my stomach and caused a smile to spread across my face. Emma had definitely been right—moving to Tennessee where no one knew me or my past had made it easier to be me. Though I wasn't sure I would have made it this far had it not been for the Johnson family.

Nathan chuckled and I couldn't help but wonder what he'd seen on my face. He didn't let me ask as he leaned over and placed a kiss to my cheek. "I got you spicy garlic chicken."

"Oh, that sounds amazing."

"Well, I know who *isn't* having sex tonight."

A few weeks earlier, I'd have crawled under the table

at Austin's joking, but now I just shook my head at him and felt my cheeks heat slightly. He didn't appear to know that we hadn't made it as far as penetrative sex yet. It was on my list of things I wanted to do, but I also knew that Nathan was waiting for me to tell him I was ready.

Just thinking about Nathan inside me had me adjusting in my seat. I was ready; I just had to figure out a way to tell him.

Nathan smacked the back of Austin's head. "You're awful. But, unfortunately, no, no sex tonight." He winced slightly as he looked at me. "Brian called just a bit ago and asked if I could go over for dinner. Something about needing to use me as a sounding board about a work project."

I didn't know much about Brian's work, but it sounded like he did something for the government and it was a lot of private, top-secret stuff. The way Austin and Nathan spoke about it, it sounded horribly boring.

"Eww." Austin turned his nose up as he shoved a bite of egg roll into his mouth.

Nathan shrugged his shoulder. "You're welcome to come with me. Unfortunately, you'd probably have to hang out with Kelly and the kids while Brian and I talk. The odds are he's probably trying to figure out the legality of something. I know you're trustworthy, but Brian shouldn't even be discussing this stuff with me."

"I'm good, thanks." Kids and I didn't mix and spending the night at a house I didn't know, with people I'd never spent time alone with didn't sound like my idea of a good time.

Austin pointed his chopsticks at me. "Wise man. Hell, Seth is probably home. You two could hang out. He's been down since they got knocked out of the playoffs."

Actually, Seth and I had been hanging out every night that we were both home. The Grizzlies had gotten eliminated two weeks earlier and he'd been down about it a few days, but relief had set in shortly afterward. He'd been ready for a break.

So we'd sit and talk and have a beer for a few hours before each going our separate ways. He was nice, though unnaturally quiet compared to the rest of the Johnson kids. Well, everyone but Larson. Thankfully, he seemed to be relaxing around me and I enjoyed our conversations.

Nathan: *Wrap up. It's nearly five.*

I chuckled at the text as it came in. I'd already been closing files on my computer and wrapping up for the day.

Me: *Yes, Sir. Nearly done.*

Nathan appeared in front of my desk seconds after I sent the text. "God, I want to take you home tonight. I miss my koala."

"I'm not that bad."

Nathan snorted a disagreement. "Babe, if I'm not wrapped around you, you're basically on top of me. But I definitely miss it." He came around the desk and bent so he was level with me. With his finger under my chin, he lifted it slightly so our lips were even, then placed a kiss on my lips.

My dick took notice of his tongue teasing the seam of my lips before my lips did, and it began to thicken in my pants. I moaned lightly as I parted both my lips and my legs, hoping to find some relief from the pressure. Nathan chuckled into the kiss but didn't break contact, his hand moving to cup my neck and his thumb caressing my jaw.

It wasn't until we heard Austin in the hallway that we finally pulled apart, both groaning at our erections and Austin's taunting words. "Nathan and Elliot sitting in a tree, K-I-S-S-I-N-G..."

Nathan reached down and adjusted his dick in his pants as he cursed under his breath. "Austin! You best have been keeping up with your cardio, because if I catch you, I'm going to give you a swirly."

I began to laugh at the serious attorney in front of me threatening to dunk his younger brother in the toilet. I stood and made to adjust my erection, but Nathan focused back on me before my hand could make it to my crotch. He cocked an eyebrow high on his forehead and leveled me with a glare that made my knees feel weak.

"Should you be doing that?"

My hand fell to my side as I stammered for words. "I-I, n-no? B-but you..." I sighed, realizing I was only digging my hole deeper as I stuttered. Nathan wasn't going to stop staring me down. "May I adjust my dick, Sir?"

The satisfied smirk that crossed his face made me want to curse him, but the way his eyes heated and his nose flared kept the words in my head. Well, kept everything but the relieved sigh that escaped as my cock found a better position.

"Good job. I know that isn't easy for you, but I'm proud of you."

And there I went, swooning over his words.

Nathan gave a frustrated sigh as he eyed my erection. "I want to take care of that right now, but unfortunately I'm due at Brian and Kelly's house in under half an hour. Call me if you go to bed before I get home."

How long did he expect to be there? "Okay. Have a good night."

He walked me out to the parking lot and kissed me again, but that time it was fast and chaste, though he did grope the front of my pants before he stepped away. "Remember, this belongs to me."

My dick had begun to behave on our way out of the building, but it was once again alert and frustrated. He narrowed his eyes as I squirmed. "No touching without permission."

"Yes, Sir." I hardly recognized my own voice. The words had come out whispered and needy, and I would have done just about anything to get his hand wrapped around my erection. It had been long enough that I didn't think it would take but a few strokes.

He dropped his hand and stepped back, a proud smirk on his lips. "Later, E."

I nodded my head, but there were clouded thoughts getting in the way of my ability to speak a coherent sentence. Lust and desire had combined with want and a growing need to spend time with him. The last few days, I'd found myself thinking about three words I wanted to tell him.

The problem was I wasn't sure if it was my heart or my dick talking, and the last thing I wanted to do was scare him away with a lust-filled, sex-induced proclamation of love when it wasn't actually that.

I finally forced myself to say goodbye and get into my car, finding relief with the separation the door gave us. I needed to spend the evening getting my emotions in order and figuring out where my heart and head stood in contrast to my dick.

By eight, I'd thought myself out and was no closer to figuring out my feelings. I was pretty sure it was safe to say I felt more than an attraction to Nathan, but did that mean I was feeling love? Wasn't it too soon?

Lying on my couch, my hand flung over my head, I thought about all the reasons I was feeling the way I was. He listened to me. He took time to be with me. He genuinely wanted me to be happy. He liked being involved in my life.

I'd never talked to anyone, even Emma, as much as I'd talked to Nathan in the last handful of weeks. Since our dinner where he'd written expectations out, I'd never felt like a burden or like I wasn't an equal to him. Even when he ordered my meals, he did it with my preferences in mind and always asked if there was anything that I really didn't want. He was thoughtful and caring.

My brain kept looping back to the fact that Nathan was the first man—the first person—that I'd ever felt like my thoughts and opinions actually mattered to. But then I was back to the original question: did that make it love?

I cared about him and I knew he cared about me. Everything from his frequent texts to the way he knew exactly how I took my coffee to the way he always knew what I needed, showed that he cared. It didn't matter if it was a kiss, to chat, or a mind-blowing orgasm—he provided it. And thinking about orgasms had my dick coming back to life.

Then again, my dick had been in some stage of arousal since we'd been at work, and thinking about him bringing me to orgasm was just the latest in a string of sexy thoughts I'd had about him.

For the umpteenth time that evening, I reached for my cock, which was covered by a pair of loose pajama pants, only to remember that I wasn't supposed to touch myself without permission.

Part of me said that Nathan would never know if I didn't tell him. Another part of me said that I was an idiot to think that he wouldn't know because I'd spill the beans in an instant. An even bigger part of me knew that I wanted to make Nathan proud of me.

"You can do this. Don't be a chickenshit."

It probably said something that I was having a pep talk with myself about writing a text to my boyfriend. People did this every day. Dick pics were sent to unsuspecting strangers, yet I couldn't figure out how to tell my boyfriend I was horny.

I growled at myself and swiped my phone off the coffee table. My dick wasn't going to go down anytime in the near future and my pajama pants were already wet with precum. I needed release and then maybe to sleep for the next ten or more hours.

Me: *You still at your brother's house?*

I got a notification that said he was driving, but then got a text a moment later.

Nathan: *Nearly home. You okay?*

Me: *Fine. Let me know when you get home.*

Nathan: *When I said nearly home, I meant I was pulling into my driveway. What's up?*

Damn, there went my chance to give myself a few minutes to cool off and hopefully not have to tell him what was on my mind. Now I had no choice.

Me: *I'm really horny. It's been three days since I came and I'm never going to be able to sleep tonight like this.*

My face was burning with embarrassment as I hit send. He was going to think I was a nutcase. When the phone buzzed in my hand, I almost didn't look at it. Knowing I had now made my bed, I cracked one eye open to look at the screen.

Nathan: *Are you trying to ask for permission to play with your dick?*

He knew damn well what I was asking, but my hormones were finally starting to overpower my natural embarrassment and I found myself tapping furiously at the screen.

Me: *Yes. That is exactly what I'm asking.*

For good measure, I quickly added another line.

Me: *Sir, may I please play with myself and come?*

I hit send, satisfied that I hadn't missed anything. If I asked to both play and orgasm, there was no loophole in which he could say I could play but hadn't asked to orgasm. *Ha! Lawyer brain for the win!*

Then my phone rang in my hand and I squeaked in surprise. Flipping it over, I saw it was a call from Nathan.

Dammit. Now I had to talk to him about it too.

My finger hovered over the answer button for a ring and a half before finally biting the bullet and swiping up.

"Hello?"

CHAPTER 23

NATHAN

Me: *Sir, may I please play with myself and come?*

If there were ever a chance I'd spontaneously come in my pants, that text would have done it.

Brian had driven me nuts talking about a contract he was working on for the government. Even as a lawyer, I found the details dry and boring. I had no idea how the man did that shit day in and day out, but somehow, he found it interesting. However, after hours of debate, my brain had felt like mush and I'd just wanted to get home, strip out of the suit I was still wearing, and collapse on the couch.

I'd thought of going to Elliot's, but that was on the opposite side of town from where I'd been and I didn't think I had another twenty-minute drive in me. After a nearly twelve-hour day, I was done.

Or I'd thought I'd been done until Elliot's first text sounded as I pulled onto my street. Driving or not, there was no way in hell I was going to ignore him and I couldn't resist teasing him a bit.

That was until I read the last text as I turned off my car and began to get out. That short sentence had my cock going from soft to rock hard and my mind struggling between teasing Elliot and resisting the urge to climb right back into the car and head to his house. I could easily see the bright red blush on Elliot's cheeks as he'd tapped out the texts.

There was no doubt in my mind he was near the breaking point if he'd worked the nerve up to text me that he was horny. But that last text? It did things to my body that I hadn't known were possible. Every place my clothes touched felt like fire lapping at my skin. The AC that had been keeping me chilly on the way home might as well have been the heater blasting at full force. My body was flushed like I'd run a marathon and all I'd done had been to look at my phone.

And none of that was taking into account what it had done to my dick. There was a very real possibility that I was going to have a permanent zipper mark on my cock if I didn't get these too-tight-for-an-erection pants off me immediately.

I made sure I had everything out of the car, more focused on my phone than anything else, and power walked into the house, barely remembering to shut the garage behind me.

Safely in the confines of my house, I began to strip

layers off my body as I pressed the phone icon by Elliot's text. The slight delay before he answered gave me a chance to kick my shoes off as I shrugged out of my coat. I heard one shoe hit what sounded like a cabinet and the other the tiled floor, but I had no desire to figure out where in the kitchen they'd landed.

I'd gotten my coat off as I made my way toward the steps, and I tossed it carelessly toward what I hoped was the couch. The hand holding the phone to my ear was getting in the way of my removing the rest of my clothes.

The phone stopped ringing just as I stepped out of one of my dress socks and I left it right there on the steps.

A brief pause and then Elliot's tentative voice filled my ear. "Hello?"

I didn't bother with pleasantries as I stepped out of my other sock in the hallway. "Has someone been naughty tonight?"

Elliot's answering groan was frustration mixed with embarrassment, but his words were clear. "If I had been, I'd have just taken care of this myself and not told you."

A laugh threatened to escape, but I knew it would only serve to embarrass Elliot and that wasn't what I wanted. The effort it took to keep it in had my voice coming out deeper than normal as I spoke. "And what were you doing to get yourself so horny?"

"Thinking." The word had come out quickly, but I could hear annoyance in his voice and it made me wonder what he'd been thinking about to make him both horny and annoyed. I'd press that subject later. For now, I wanted to focus on his arousal. I needed to find a way to make his embarrassment at telling me he wanted to jerk off well worth it.

In my bedroom, I needed the rest of my clothes off quickly, but getting them off while talking on the phone wasn't an easy task. A button popped off my shirt as I fumbled to undo it one-handed, though I couldn't be bothered to care about the button. All I wanted was the shirt off my body.

I forced myself to keep my voice light and teasing, hoping I didn't step on a land mine when I asked the next question. "Were you thinking about me?"

A frustrated huff filled my ear and it didn't help my worry. "Of *course* I was thinking about you." There was something he wasn't telling me, but I focused more on his obvious arousal. It couldn't have been bad if he was so desperate to come.

"What were you thinking about?"

That time, there was no frustration or annoyance to his words as he spoke. "You blowing me under the desk last week."

Ah, yes. I'd had more than a few orgasms thinking about that encounter. We'd gotten carried away after lunch, and I'd ended up under his desk, his cock in my mouth, when Austin had walked in. Listening to Elliot try to focus on Austin's questions while I teased, sucked, and licked at him had brought me far more pleasure than it should have. Somehow, he'd managed to have a somewhat intelligent conversation with my brother, and Austin had barely left when Elliot let out a soft sigh and came down my throat.

I'd refused to be embarrassed when I headed back to my office and Austin asked how my knees felt.

"That was fun. You make the best noises when you're turned on."

I was pretty sure the groan Elliot let out was supposed to be embarrassed, but it definitely came out sounding needy.

Finally, I freed myself from my shirt and fought my own groan of relief as my fingers found the fly of my dress pants and worked it open. The tailored pants made my legs and ass look amazing, but they were uncomfortable to get hard in and a bear to get down quickly. I wiggled and shimmied and finally left both my pants and underwear crumpled on the floor before I collapsed onto my bed.

Looking down at my body, my cock was hard and already beginning to leak onto my stomach.

"Do you wish I was there to make you feel good right now?"

Elliot didn't bother to hide his whimper. "God, yes. So much. I-I want you inside me."

My breath caught in my throat. We'd talked about it before, but Elliot had seemed hesitant. I was willing to take things at his pace, so I hadn't pushed too hard, but to hear that it was what he wanted made my resolve to stay home waver slightly. Then again I'd have to get dressed in order to go there and after finally getting naked, that was the last thing I wanted to do.

"I'd make sure to prep you well." I glanced over to the side of my bed and found the bottle of lube I kept there. "Where's your lube?"

Elliot squeaked and I heard him moving around. Then he groaned, that time genuinely frustrated. "In my bedroom."

I chuckled. "Go get it. I want to make you feel good tonight."

Movement from his end filled my ear as he headed to his room, and I took the opportunity to grab my own bottle of lube and slick my hand and cock with it. I'd already put my phone on speaker and propped it up next to me when I heard his bed squeak slightly as he got into it. Then I heard the telltale snick of the lube bottle being opened. "Got it."

"Are you naked yet?"

It was Elliot's turn to chuckle. "I am now. I did that as I was getting into bed."

"Good. Get yourself lubed up and start stretching yourself... slowly. One finger to start."

Elliot was silent for a moment but I could hear him moving, then the unmistakable gasp as his finger entered his ass. Fuck, I wanted that to be my finger stretching him. I wanted to see firsthand what he looked like as he writhed under my touch. "Fuuuuck." The word had been nothing more than a whisper, but it had gone straight to my balls and I felt them tighten.

Maybe it was a good thing this was over the phone because there was no way this would have lasted more than a few seconds if we were together. There was a very real chance I would've come just from stretching him. Hell, there was a good chance I was going to come just hearing him stretch himself.

I ran a finger along the length of my cock. "You're so needy."

The answering moan was enough of a confirmation for me. "Yeah? I bet you can already take another finger in there."

"Fuck, yes. More. I can take it. Yes."

I'd had no idea this man had been hidden behind the blushes and awkwardness, but I wished I'd pushed him sooner. "One more finger. I want you stretched and ready."

Unlike the hiss he'd made with the insertion of his first finger, Elliot let out a breathy whimper as his second finger entered him. "Oh. Shit. So good. So, so good. Want you here. Want you inside me." The quiet sound of the bed shifting and the squelch of well-lubed fingers working his hole filled my room.

I was close and hadn't wrapped my hand around my cock yet. Another low moan from Elliot and my resolve broke. I pressed the camera icon and waited for the video chat to connect.

Elliot gave a startled gasp that quickly transformed into

a groan when the video call rang through. "Seriously? Video chat? My fingers are in my ass!"

"The noises you're making over there are damn near making me come without touching myself. I need to see you right now."

Video of Elliot's flushed face filled my phone screen and I found myself smiling at him. "Hey, beautiful."

The flush turned into a full-on blush at my words. "I cannot believe I have my fingers in my ass and I'm on video chat."

"Believe it, because I really want to see your fingers in your ass right now."

His voice rose an octave. "Seriously?"

"Yes. The noises you are making are driving me insane. I want to see that ass stretching wide and how much your cock likes it. I bet you've already left a puddle of precum on your stomach."

Elliot let out a surprised laugh, then gasped as his pupils dilated. "Oh, shit. That feels weird. I just laughed with my fingers in my ass."

"E, you're stalling."

The hesitation in his eyes was noticeable, so I decided to give him something as motivation. I tapped on the screen and turned the camera around, focusing it from my belly button down, my erection and the string of precum easily visible in the frame.

Elliot sucked in a sharp breath and I watched as he licked his lips. "Jesus, I'm going to be mortified later."

I was pushing him hard and I didn't want to push too far. "What color are you?"

The question took him by surprise at first, but I watched his eyes as he thought about it. "Chartreuse?"

I barked out a laugh. "I don't even know what to make of that."

He chuckled, some of the tension leaving his eyes. "I'm still green but pushing yellow. I've just never done anything like this before."

I flipped the camera back around so he could see my face. "We can stop right now and you can get yourself off just like this. No judgment at all."

Elliot shook his head, sighing at himself. "I don't want to stop. It's so fucking hot to see your cock like that. I need to be pushed. Please. Get me out of my head."

Elliot had been nothing but honest with me until that point. Telling me that he was pushing yellow couldn't have been easy, yet he'd done it. So I had to trust that he meant his words. I gave him a reassuring smile before flipping my camera back around so he could see my dick. Even during our serious discussion, my erection hadn't eased any and I hoped like hell his hadn't either.

"Let me see your fingers stretching you."

The blush came back, but the uncertainty in his eyes was no longer there. It took him a beat, but eventually he moved. It was awkward and clumsy to the point I almost told him to remove his fingers for a moment, but I didn't want to pull him out of whatever space he'd found that was allowing him to get out of his head for the time being.

After a few fumbled attempts, Elliot managed to get the phone and himself positioned so that I could see his ass, balls, dick, and most of his face. I had no idea if he could see me from that position, but I was going to pretend that he could.

His fingers were still in his ass and his mouth had parted slightly.

Seeing him in that position, I said the first thing that came to mind. "Fuck, you're gorgeous."

I couldn't see his eyes, but I watched as his lip got pulled between his teeth and his cheeks moved to approximate a smile. "Yeah?"

His uncertainty still surprised me. I didn't know how it was that he could possibly think I didn't mean what I'd said, but I'd spend forever convincing him that I meant it. The thought had come out of nowhere. Thinking in terms of forever wasn't something I'd ever done and hadn't ever considered with anyone before. However, in the middle of phone sex was not the time to start contemplating the meaning of that thought, so I forced myself to focus back on the here and now.

"Yeah. Stretch yourself for me. I want you nice and loose. I want to know that when we do this in person, you'll be able to handle me."

I was treated to the most beautiful view as Elliot scissored his fingers in his ass. I could hear the pleasured sounds he made and I watched the way his head fell back as he worked to stretch himself. His cock was just as angry red as mine, if not more so, when I finally told him to add a third finger.

Elliot complied with the order without hesitation and I felt a surge of pride rush through me. I'd gotten him out of his head and he was clearly enjoying himself.

With Elliot lost in his own pleasure, I finally wrapped my hand around my cock and pulled the foreskin back to expose my glistening tip. Elliot must have been able to see the screen because he moaned at my movement and I looked at the phone in time to see his tongue dart out and lick his lips. "I want to taste you."

The words had come out reverently, and damn did I want to be with him so he could, though I wouldn't have traded this view for anything... well, anything but the real thing. "Next time. Right now, I want you to wrap your hand around your dick for me."

Relief washed through Elliot's body as he moved the hand that had been fisted at his side toward his erection. He let out an erotic moan as his fist closed around the shaft. His legs fell farther apart to give just enough light to the picture that I could now see all his features clearly.

Cheeks flushed, lips parted, golden eyes desperate, and sweat beading on his light chest hair, his cock coated in a mixture of precum and lube from his hand. He hadn't started working his cock yet, waiting for my permission.

I gave my own erection a few tugs, knowing that

neither of us would last when he finally started to move his hand. "Work that cock for me. I want to watch you come all over yourself."

Elliot moved his hand up his shaft slowly, twisting his fist as he reached the top, only to drag it back down just as slowly. I followed his movements with my own hand, allowing myself to imagine my hand being his ass wrapped tightly around me.

Dammit, I was close.

"Faster, baby. Faster. I want you to lose control and paint that beautiful stomach with your cum."

Elliot pumped his dick faster. He'd managed about a dozen strokes before I saw his thighs tense. "Gonna. Close. Please. Yes."

"That's it. Come for me now." My own orgasm had built to an impossible-to-ignore need in my balls and the base of my spine. Every nerve ending in my body was alight with the need for release, but I was waiting for Elliot to come. I wanted to watch the moment he lost it, his fingers still shoved deep in his ass.

The corded muscles in the hand that was working his hole moved and Elliot let out a yell as his balls tightened. A second later, the first spurt of cum shot from his dick and landed up by his nipple. His chest heaved and his legs twitched as he shot rope after rope of cum across his chest and stomach, and I followed him over the cliff. My own orgasm exploded out of me with a force that shocked me.

Cum landed on my chin and throat as my muscles tensed and pulsed with each spasm.

We were both quiet, our breaths the only thing filling the space for a long time before Elliot removed his fingers from his ass. He let out a little sigh as they came free, and he wiped his hands on the T-shirt I hadn't noticed beside him before he finally picked up the phone from between his legs.

"I thought I was going to be embarrassed after that, but I think I actually shot half of my brain cells from my dick and I'm unable to be embarrassed at this point."

I smiled. "You were gorgeous. I loved watching you." He was worn out enough that his signature blush only tinted his cheeks slightly.

He returned the smile and let out a yawn. "Damn, it's only nine but I feel like it's midnight. I'm exhausted."

"Go get cleaned up and get some sleep. I think I'm going to do the same."

Elliot gave me a lazy, almost sad smile. "I do wish you were here."

"I'll be there in thirty." I knew then that there was no getting Elliot Mitchell out of my system. There never had been and likely never would be.

CHAPTER 24

ELLIOT

Saturday mornings had never felt so good as when I woke up wrapped in Nathan's arms. But there was something that had woken me up and I couldn't figure out what it was. Then the noise came again and I realized it was my phone buzzing on the nightstand. The nightstand where my phone charger had been plugged in for over two weeks now.

Since the night Nathan had come over to my place after we'd had the most amazing phone sex, even though I'd never had any before, we'd spent every night together. By that point, my place had only had a few of my dishes and a few outfits left in it, though even those had been slowly making their way to Nathan's house.

My phone buzzed again and pulled me further from the fog of sleep, and I accepted that whoever was trying to get ahold of me wasn't going to give up.

"Early." Nathan pulled me closer and buried his head into my shoulder as I moved.

I patted the arm that was wrapped tightly around my chest. "Let me just see who's blowing up my phone. It's probably Emma or Austin. I'll tell them to fuck off and we can go back to sleep."

"Mmm. Sleep. Yes." A tired Nathan was nothing like the stern man I worked with or the no-nonsense man that showed up to my office like a swarm of wasps when I forgot to text him for too long.

I moved just enough to grab my phone and unlock it, wincing at the bright home screen. The clock read nine thirty, but with the blackout curtains in Nathan's bedroom, it could have been three in the afternoon and I wouldn't have known it wasn't three in the morning. My phone vibrated again and the message preview popped up.

Four missed texts from Kyle Mitchell.

I stopped breathing for a moment and my finger shook as I went to tap on the notification to open them. I hadn't texted him since he'd texted me to say that Emma and his boyfriend had been on him to contact me. I still owed him an apology, but I'd assumed that I would end up taking it to the grave with me.

So why, nearly six weeks later, was he texting me?

Kyle: *Um, hey. I don't even know where to start with this one. I think I'd like to meet up with you.*

Kyle: *Not because Emma told me to, or Rand.*

Kyle: *Well, that's kind of it. I mean, Emma told me*

you're living in Tennessee and relatively close by. But that's not why I want to meet up. Okay, maybe it is. I mean, since you're close it makes it easier, but if you weren't close, then I'd probably just... I don't know, call? Maybe?

Kyle: *Shit. I'm fucking this up. Sorry. I'm confused. But I've been thinking about it, and I think it's time we talk. Like... um, adults?*

Nathan's lips pressed against my shoulder. "What's wrong, babe? You went stiff as a board."

He'd been calling me babe recently and I liked it. I'd never had a nickname or pet name, and the effortless way he let it slip, even around clients and his family, always warmed my insides. But his lips on my shoulder and his breath ghosting over my skin as he said it had my stomach doing funny little flip-flops.

I dragged in a breath and gathered my thoughts. "It's my brother."

Those three words pulled him from his sleep and he propped himself up on an elbow to look down at me. I rolled so I was on my back looking up into his eyes. I could only see concern in them. "What does he want?"

I held my phone up. "To meet up?" It hadn't been meant as a question, no matter how the sentence had come out.

"And what do you want to do?"

I lifted my hands to indicate I didn't know. "Shit. Part of me says I really want to. It needs to happen, but the other part of me hates the idea. I think the part that hates it is more that I know I'm opening myself up for disappointment and rejection, and I just don't want to go through that."

He hummed in understanding. "I get that. But regardless, it's a door that either needs to be opened or closed, once and for all."

He had a point.

His lip twitched at the corner. "And no matter what the outcome, I'm going to be here for you."

That he would be. There had never been a doubt in my mind. All those confusing feelings I'd had a few weeks ago had eased. There was no longer a question in my mind as to if it was my heart or dick that was in love with Nathan. Sure, my dick loved his hand or mouth wrapped around it, but my heart loved both those things and everything else about him. I might not have known much about relationships before him, but I knew that I'd fallen for Nathan Johnson. I'd fallen for the growls and the smiles, the scowls and the laughs. I just hadn't found a way to tell him yet.

Instead of telling him what was bouncing around in my head, I settled on the next best thing. "Thank you."

"So what are you going to tell him?"

I stared at the phone in my hands a little longer before coming to a conclusion. "That I'll meet up with him."

Nathan smiled down at me. "I think that's a very wise choice. Do you want me to come with you?"

I didn't have to think about the answer to that. "Yeah." I

began tapping a reply to Kyle when my eyes shot up to Nathan. "He has no idea I'm gay. Emma said she's never told him. What do I say?"

Nathan hummed. "Do you want to come out to him over text or in person?"

"In person." That had been an easy, immediate answer and it helped me form my thoughts. I turned back to my phone and tapped out a response.

Me: *I'd like that a lot. Do you mind if I'm not alone? There's someone I want you to meet.*

I hit send and now we waited. The response took nearly five minutes, but eventually my phone buzzed and I looked back down at it.

Kyle: *That's fine, as long as Rand can come.*

While I wasn't looking forward to facing the gruff cowboy after the way I'd behaved back in New York, I knew it wouldn't be fair to tell him no. Instead, I took the mature road and told him that was fine, and set about making plans for the meetup.

An hour and one orgasm later, Nathan and I were dressed and in his SUV heading south to one of the distilleries for lunch with Kyle and Rand. I didn't think there was enough liquor in Tennessee to make this meeting any less awkward, but Nathan remained confident all through our showers and quick breakfast.

My nerves hadn't settled as we climbed into his car. Instead of telling me I was ridiculous and overthinking the entire day, he'd leaned over and pressed a gentle kiss to my lips. "Whatever comes of this, you finally have a chance to tell him you're sorry to his face. And you've got a chance to tell him what happened all those years. Babe, your parents fucked you up. That isn't your fault."

I tried to force a smile, but it didn't come.

Nathan just shook his head at my attempt. "We practice family law. We've both worked in New York. I can't speak for you, but I've seen some pretty fucking shit things happen to kids because of their parents. I don't have any, nor do I want them, but I know that kids find a way to survive, and they'll do just about anything for their parents' acceptance. Kyle wasn't wrong for being himself and you weren't wrong for protecting yourself."

I appreciated the words, but I kept going back to the wedding. "That doesn't excuse my behavior last fall."

Nathan squeezed my thigh. "No. But I think that you were under a lot of stress at the time. You were trying to make partner, you were marrying your best friend, not a girlfriend, and your parents were there breathing down your neck. Excuse? No. Reason? Well, probably. Hopefully, Kyle will be able to see that. If not, you'll have said what you came to say and you'll have tried."

His pep talk kept me going until we pulled off the highway and headed toward the meeting spot.

Outside the distillery's restaurant, a giant man in a cowboy hat stood holding the hand of a guy with the same brown hair as mine. I knew Kyle had grown up and I'd seen him about once a year since we'd both moved out of the house, but for the first time, I saw him as a man. He wasn't my kid brother, wasn't the guy who'd had what I wanted. He was an adult, an equal, and a virtual stranger to me.

Nathan eyed the two, then glanced over at me. "Rand and Kyle?"

I nodded confirmation as he pulled into a spot and killed the engine.

"I'd say they've got balls holding hands out here, but I don't think anyone would think about bothering either of them."

Rand was a tank of a man. I'd noticed that the first time I'd laid eyes on him. Today, he looked even more intimidating. Though a glance at my boyfriend showed a firm-set jaw and frosty eyes. Nathan was ready for battle, but I was pretty sure it wasn't going to come to that. His rigid stance helped relax me. "Don't strike first."

He blinked over in confusion. "What?"

"You look like you're going into an MMA ring. If either of them were going to be violent, they would have decked me back in October."

His pursed lips softened into something that resembled a smile. "Okay. Let's go. This thing turns into a hot box as soon as I turn the engine off."

To that I couldn't disagree. We both opened our doors at the same time and were hit with a muggy late June temperature, but at least the breeze felt better than the stagnant air in the SUV with its black leather seats.

Nathan walked around to my side of the car and linked

his hand in mine, offering a gentle squeeze of reassurance. When he made to release me, I squeezed tighter, a silent request for him to not let go. Thankfully, he took the hint and held on as we rounded the back of the SUV.

Kyle and Rand had been leaning toward each other in conversation as we crossed the street. It took them a moment to recognize me and I knew the moment Kyle did. His eyes widened beneath his ball cap's brim and he elbowed Rand's arm. From fifteen feet away, I could read his lips form the word *Daddy*.

Rand looked over to where Kyle's eyes had become transfixed on us and his eyes widened just as much. He not-so-subtly adjusted his cowboy hat upward to get a better look at us, and the shocked expression on his face did not fade any.

Coming up next to them, I could see that Kyle was the same height as Nathan, but Rand felt like he nearly dwarfed us.

If the situation wasn't awkward enough, the two of them staring between us and our interlinked hands only made it worse. I finally cleared my throat. "Uh, hi."

Kyle never looked away from our hands. "Um. Hi. I..." Rand elbowed Kyle and Kyle looked up at him in confusion.

"They have eyes." He might have been trying to tease Kyle, but his voice was filled with as many questions as Kyle's eyes.

Kyle shook his head like he was trying to clear

cobwebs from it. "Oh. Oh yeah. Um. Hi." That time he met my eyes, but the confusion in them clouded everything.

Nathan cleared his throat and gestured toward the side of the building with his head. "There's a walking path down this way. Maybe a walk before lunch?"

Rand's voice rumbled over the low hum of the restaurant and the parking lot. "I think that would be a very good idea. I like to think I know my boy... and well, I do." He squeezed Kyle's shoulder. "He can get a bit worked up when he's surprised."

Kyle nodded reflexively. "So many questions my brain isn't functioning." He turned his head to look at Rand. "I told you Fred should have come."

Rand chuckled lightly. "Drama queen. There is nothing Fred needs to see here because there isn't going to be drama."

My brother huffed. "That's what you said at the wedding too."

"And there wasn't Oscar-worthy drama there either. You're fine and you can tell Fred about lunch when we get home."

The only thing Oscar-worthy so far was the sigh Kyle gave Rand.

Nathan looked over at me, his raised eyebrow asking who Fred was, but I shook my head, just as confused.

We made it to the path, a wooded trail that led around the grounds the brewery was located on. As we reached the trailhead, Nathan moved his hand from mine and placed it on the small of my back.

The trail cut back into a patch of trees and we were well into the shade before I finally cleared my throat. "Nathan, this is my brother, Kyle, and his boyfriend, Rand." I gestured to each of their backs in turn, then rubbed my neck and steeled myself for a negative reaction at my next words. "Kyle, Rand, this is my boyfriend, Nathan."

I'd been pretty sure that Kyle and Rand had both figured that out by now but questioned myself when Kyle tripped over his own two feet. He recovered quickly and swung around, taking two steps toward me so fast I ended up backing up a step myself.

"Really? You really think I'm going to buy that? Twenty fucking years of you ignoring me and treating me like a pariah and you think I'm suddenly going to believe you're dating a man? All the fucking way to Tennessee just to fuck with me." He shook his head in disgust. "And to think I'd hoped that you were serious when you kept telling me you wanted to work on our relationship." He made to storm off, but Rand grabbed his arm, halting his progress quickly.

I glanced around, thankful we were the only ones in sight on the trail and hoped like hell that our voices weren't carrying and drawing attention from other guests. I looked to Nathan, hoping he'd know what to say or do. All I saw was a ticking in his jaw as he clenched his mouth shut.

He gave a little tug to my waist, pulling me closer to

and slightly behind him. "I think it would be a good idea to take a step back and listen to Elliot."

Rand tugged my brother's arm gently, pulling him closer but eyeing us both with suspicion. "Hear him out, Kyle. We're already here."

It felt awkward to stand there not moving with all the attention on me after spending my entire life with my head down and trying to avoid attention, especially from my family. "Um, do you mind walking while we talk?"

Kyle huffed and flung an arm around, trying to convey something I didn't understand, though I breathed a sigh of relief when he turned on his heels and started walking down the path. "Talk."

Nathan cocked an eyebrow in my direction. "Safewords aren't just for the bedroom." He'd spoken quietly but his voice traveled and my brother heard. He flung around so fast he smacked into Rand's chest and knocked him back a step.

"Safewords? The fuck do you, Mr. *You Are So Fucked Up*, know about safewords?"

This was not going well. Panic was starting to rise in my chest and I looked over at Nathan.

Did I safeword? God, it sounded tempting.

Did I run? That sounded tempting too.

Did I stick it out and lay everything on the line? Well, that idea made me want to puke, even though it was my only real shot of ever having a conversation with my brother again.

CHAPTER 25

NATHAN

Elliot's eyes met mine with fear and uncertainty. Seeing the panic in his face, I knew I had about three seconds to defuse this situation before Elliot bolted. "Yellow?"

I'd whispered the word, but Elliot's voice rose noticeably in response. "Yellow? Try neon-fucking-orange!"

What was with this man and not being able to answer with a normal color? Red, yellow, and green shouldn't have been that hard, but for Elliot, he had to combine them into random colors. All I could say was that at least it wasn't red... yet.

About fifty feet ahead of us was a small seating area. "Let's go take a seat." Walking and talking wasn't going to work if Kyle kept bowling people over every time Elliot opened his mouth.

I was talking mostly to Elliot and a little to Rand, who seemed to be keeping his cool better than Elliot's brother. If I was being honest, I'd expected the meeting to go worse than it had, so I was actually hopeful that we could sit and have a conversation.

Despite no words being exchanged, Rand gripped Kyle's elbow and headed toward the benches. I placed my hand between Elliot's shoulders and gave a gentle push. His feet moved, but I could feel the reluctance in each step.

We closed the distance in painfully slow strides. Halfway there, Elliot leaned toward me and whispered into my ear. "Was this a mistake?"

I rubbed at his back and shook my head. "Not a mistake. Just uncomfortable. I've got you."

Some of the tension eased in his shoulders and he leaned into me. "Thank you."

Turning my head, I let my lips brush against his cheek. Beneath my lips, I could feel his cheek twitch to some approximation of a smile. "There. We're going to talk. We don't even have to eat here. Though I will say they have an amazing burger and my stomach is growling."

Elliot's head dipped down but he was smiling again. "You're impossible."

"It's lunchtime, and I'm hungry."

As we approached the benches, Kyle was looking between us skeptically. "You two really aren't faking this shit, are you?"

To my astonishment, Elliot barked out a laugh. "I totally deserve that."

Some of the fight left Kyle and a small smile played

across his lips. "Yeah. You do. But I *told* you I was bringing Daddy to your wedding, and you *knew* I was gay well before then."

Rand squeezed Kyle's knee in a protective grip. I would have picked up on the protective vibe Rand had with Kyle even if Elliot hadn't told me about their relationship. The two cowboys sitting across from us didn't immediately stick out as a Dom and his sub, but I knew far better than to judge a book by its cover. With those two, it only took a few minutes to see clear as day that Kyle was Rand's submissive.

Part of me wondered if it was that obvious to them that I was Elliot's Dom and if that knowledge would change anything. These two were so far from talking about kinks that the question shouldn't even be in my mind, yet there it was.

My thoughts got interrupted as Elliot lifted a shoulder and began to speak. "I also knew that I was gay long before then too."

Kyle's mouth fell open, and he studied Elliot closely. Elliot looked like the same guy I'd met, but something in his words or his expression had Kyle softening a little more. "You're telling the truth."

Elliot nodded once, his lip slipping between his teeth, and I had to fight the urge to tug it free. Eventually, he heaved a sigh and looked up at his brother. "I can't say sorry enough. And before you say anything, I know it's not enough. I've been an asshole since... well, forever. My excuses are just that, excuses. They were built on fear and frustration. None of that was directly related to you, more like a lot of me hating myself."

Kyle was silent for a long time, staring at Elliot like an alien had taken over his body. He finally looked over at Rand. "I told you I should have brought Fred."

Rand pinched the bridge of his nose but despite his attempt at looking exasperated, he was smiling. "Okay, I'll admit it. That was probably something Fred could have heard firsthand."

Now I was confused. Who the hell was Fred?

Rand actually laughed. It was a rich, deep sound that had me relaxing. "The look on your faces. Sorry, I shouldn't laugh, but I wish you could see yourselves. Fred is Kyle's bear."

Elliot didn't look any less confused, but I began to soften. I was beginning to see a side of Kyle that reminded me a lot of Larson. My brother would deny it to his dying breath, but I knew he still confided in his blanket, and I'd seen the few stuffed animals he kept on his bed. They were special to him in a way none of us could be and I had a feeling Fred was probably that to Kyle. It brought into perspective that Larson was unlikely to give up those connections, even if the perfect Daddy walked into his life next week.

Kyle flushed but didn't dispute Rand's words. "I wanted to take him to your wedding. I expected some crazy ex to jump up or for her to leave you at the altar."

"She damn near did. But it was mostly because neither of us had ever wanted to get married and the week had been a disaster."

I hadn't expected the look of shocked confusion on Kyle's face. Emma and Kyle spoke regularly and she'd had dinner with him while she was in town. "Wait, what?"

Elliot was just as taken aback as I was and he blinked. "The entire thing was... well, it wasn't fake, but it wasn't real either. Emma and I were only together for appearance's sake. Someone overheard a conversation one day and thought we were engaged. Before we could correct it, she had a wedding dress and our wedding was being planned."

Kyle sat unblinking for a long few seconds before he snapped. "If it was all fake, then why the fuck did I have to be there? I never wanted to be the token gay brother for the fucking events you dragged us to. I didn't want to be the center of all the fucking mess."

I moved closer to Elliot, who reached out and gripped my hand tightly enough that his knuckles turned white. This was his moment of truth. We'd talked about it in the car and he'd been nervous about how Kyle would respond. He closed his eyes on an inhale and I could almost watch him counting down from ten as he exhaled slowly.

When his eyes opened again, words came out in a rush. "Because I wanted you there. I wanted to tell you that week that I was gay. I wanted to use that week as a way to get to know you better."

Kyle fell back against the bench, his eyes finding the trees above us. He aggressively scrubbed his face with his hands and let out a frustrated growl that I found impressive. "Yet you spent all fucking week attacking me!"

Elliot deflated. It was the reaction he'd expected and truthfully I had too. Elliot hadn't been right then, or ever, in regards to how he'd treated his brother. He understood as well as I did that he'd made his bed and he now had to lie in it. "Mom and Dad got there before you two did. They hadn't been off the plane for five minutes when it was questions about why I was still in an apartment and not a house, why I hadn't made partner. Hell, they wanted to know why I was in my mid-thirties and didn't have kids yet. My defenses were up before you arrived. I'd already heard that you'd thrown your life away by moving to Tennessee and how at least one of their kids had done something right."

True emotion shone bright in Elliot's eyes as he spoke and I reached my arm around his shoulder, snugging him up as close to me as I could, then reached across my body to grab his hand. Rubbing his shoulder with one hand and the spot between his thumb and forefinger with my other thumb, I felt him relax into me.

A few tears hit my shoulder as he spoke into his lap. "When we were little and I tried to play with you, they chastised me. When I tried to find things you liked, I was told I was being immature and to grow up. So I kept my distance. Before you came out, I knew I was gay. But then you came out and I saw how they treated you. I wanted to tell you then, but I wasn't strong enough."

Kyle was wiping tears from his eyes as Elliot spoke, but I didn't think Elliot could see with how hard he was staring at his lap. "The only thing I had going for me was that I wasn't bucking their wishes. Looking back, that wasn't enough. It never was. I didn't get a high enough GPA. I wasn't top in my class. I'm not a partner at a law firm. I'm not in a major city. I'm not married. I don't have kids. And when they find out I'm not straight? Well, I can just imagine how well that will go over."

Elliot clung to my hand. "It doesn't make how I've treated you right. And I know a relationship is a long way off, but I wanted to tell you face-to-face that I'm sorry. And I wanted you to hear from me that I'm gay."

Kyle shook his head. "I need some time." He got up and started to walk away, Rand standing to follow him.

Elliot looked gutted but not surprised. He leaned more heavily into my side, breathing deeply.

Kyle made it about ten feet before he turned and looked back. "I need time. But, umm, not a lot. Can you give me a few to gather my thoughts?"

Elliot's head popped off my shoulder so fast it nearly collided with my jaw, hope evident in his eyes as he nodded fervently. "Yeah. I-I can do that."

The two disappeared down the path and when they were out of sight, Elliot nearly collapsed onto me. He lay against my shoulder, fingers finding the buttons of my

Henley and rubbing at the fabric. I was getting used to the feeling, his fingers finding something on me to rub when he got nervous. Usually it was the lining of my coat, but today the buttons of my shirt appeared to be the next best thing.

As the minutes stretched on, we sat in silence, my hand rubbing up and down Elliot's back. Every so often a twig broke or voices came down the path, but each time they kept going, never paying the two of us any mind.

Eventually, Elliot sighed. "We'll give them five minutes, then I guess we can go get lunch. Your stomach is rumbling and so is mine."

I laughed at his statement. With his head on my chest, he probably heard and felt my stomach's food demands as much as I did. "Sounds good. The lunch crowd is likely thinning out by now anyway. Getting a table should be easy."

He pushed himself off my chest and I immediately missed the contact. "You know, it went better than I had expected it to. Half of me thought they wouldn't show and the other half of me was sure he'd leave as soon as I introduced you."

"I can't tell you you're wrong. I'm glad he listened as long as he did. Even if they don't come back, it's a step in the right direction."

Our stomachs rumbled again and I couldn't help but chuckle. "Anything sound *not* good to you today?"

"Mushrooms."

"Smartass."

He grinned at me and opened his mouth to speak, but shadows crossed over us and we looked up to see Kyle and Rand standing along the side of the trail. Kyle's cheeks were red and he was clutching Rand's hand with a death grip noticeable from eight feet away. When he spoke, his words were rushed but clear, and I could tell how much he'd thought about them on their walk.

"Thank you for telling me that. That couldn't have been easy to be honest with me, but I'm glad I got to hear that from you." He glanced down at his feet and dug the toe of his boot into the dirt. "I'm not really sure where this leaves us overall, but for now we're all here and it would be a shame not to at least eat."

Tension bled from Elliot's shoulders and I felt him sit a little taller as his hand dropped from my shirt. "I'd like that." His face showed hesitancy, but his eyes sparkled with hope.

As we stood, I looked between Elliot and Kyle, really taking his brother in for the first time. Kyle was bigger and bulkier than Elliot, but their faces were nearly identical. They both had the same golden brown eyes and hair that didn't quite want to be tamed. Kyle looked younger, but I didn't think it had as much to do with his appearance as his personality. Even during a serious conversation, I could see a spark of mischief lurking right below the surface that Elliot didn't possess.

We walked toward the building, Kyle and Elliot doing their best to ignore the other while Rand and I stayed close to our men. Kyle and Rand led the way up the path and I got a clear picture of Kyle's natural submission. It was second nature to him. He held Rand's hand the entire way, letting him make the first move at each turn and waiting for him to open the door.

I'd been right. There were still people eating, but the restaurant wasn't full and the hostess was able to seat us quickly. Elliot didn't bother picking up the menu that had been set in front of him as I looked through the offerings in my own menu. A warm hand came to rest on my thigh and I smiled over at him.

"Want a drink with lunch?"

Elliot smiled at me. "Well, we are at a distillery. It would probably be criminal not to." Then he chewed on his lip and looked toward his brother. "Uh, is that okay?"

Kyle had been fiddling with a spoon before Elliot spoke to him and he looked confused for a moment. I saw the moment he figured out what his brother had asked because his eyes widened. "Oh, yeah, that's fine." He looked toward Rand, his brows turned downward in silent question.

Rand's lip twitched and he nodded. "Yeah, you too, little one."

Kyle's cheeks turned pink at the endearment and I felt Elliot grip my thigh a little tighter, his own silent question about if or how he should respond.

In an attempt to ease some of the discomfort at the table, I spoke mostly to Rand. "You guys are fine. Believe me, there is nothing you could say or do that would surprise me." I placed my hand on top of Elliot's and gave a little squeeze of reassurance. "And as long as it doesn't involve whips or paddles, you can basically say or do anything around him too."

Well, at the very least, I'd stunned the entire table into silence. Elliot was blushing, Kyle was gawking, and Rand was blinking like he hadn't fully processed the statement. The poor waiter showed up at that moment, making the others have to focus more on him than on whatever was going through their heads.

I gave the guy a smile, ordered two old fashioneds, then tipped my head to Rand, who managed to shake himself out of his shock long enough to order himself and Kyle drinks.

When the waiter disappeared, Kyle narrowed his eyes at Elliot. "First, you're talking about safewords; now he's telling me that I'm not going to shock you? That doesn't sound like the guy from a few months back."

"Kyle." Rand's low grumble made Kyle look over toward him and I watched as Rand shook his head slowly. Kyle snapped his mouth shut and glowered.

Elliot cleared his throat, getting ready to speak when the waiter appeared with a smile on his face. "Slow time for the bartenders. Three of them standing back there right now. You lucked out." He set our drinks on the table, then looked around. "Do you gentlemen know what you'd like to eat?"

Rand looked over toward us. "Go ahead and order. We'll be ready when you're done."

That was easy enough. I ordered a burger and fries for myself and a barbecue chicken sandwich with a salad for Elliot. He'd inevitably eat a few of my fries, but he'd never eat an entire order and he loved salads. I verified there were no mushrooms on anything, then ordered a side of their house ranch for his salad. I'd been here enough and was certain Elliot would love it.

I looked over at Rand just as he put the menu down. Kyle was staring at the two of us in surprise, not even listening as Rand ordered for both of them. The waiter's back had barely been turned when Kyle couldn't hold his thoughts in any longer.

"You. You. He." He pointed between us. "He ordered for you. And you, you didn't tell him what you wanted. Safewords, and okay with me, and Nathan ordering for you. And, holy shit, you're *kinky*!" He hissed the words so no one around us heard, and given that we were in public, I was quite thankful he had.

Elliot turned red, but I nodded. "Guilty as charged. I think it is safe to say that Elliot has expanded his horizons."

Elliot looked over at me with relief in his eyes and mouthed the words "Thank you."

The look he gave me paired with the words had my own smile breaking out, probably for a reason he wouldn't know or understand. I was the one who gave him that peace.

Me and no one else.

Elliot turned toward Kyle and gave him an awkward shrug. "Things changed for me when I moved to Nashville. Emma made me promise her that I'd do something for myself: for once in my life, I'd stop living for Mom and Dad and be happy." He looked back at me, his features softening and his eyes warming. "I did that. For once, I did it. And I'm happy."

CHAPTER 26

ELLIOT

THE TENSION between Kyle and me gradually lessened the longer we sat at lunch. He had even managed to smile and laugh a few times as we ate. Once the ice broke, we kept the conversation light, never circling back to the past or even our current relationships.

When Nathan paid the bill and we headed toward the car, I knew that Kyle and I still had a lot to talk out and was hopeful that we'd find a way to have those conversations sooner rather than later. Even with things left unsaid, I was feeling better than I had in months. Nathan's hand was on the small of my back, I'd had a conversation with my brother that didn't end in my yelling at him, and my belly was full from a delicious sandwich.

Rand bowed his head slightly as we parted ways to go to our respective vehicles. "Drive safe."

Nathan stuck out his hand, a smile on his face. "Will

do. You too." To Kyle, he turned and gave a dip of his head. "It was good to meet you. Thank you for inviting us."

My brother's cheeks pinked slightly. "Thank you for coming."

My hands were jammed awkwardly into the pockets of my jeans. I'd never been good at social interactions with my family. The Johnson family showed affection easily with hugs and kisses and laughs. The Mitchell family had never been like that. I didn't even get a handshake from my dad when I arrived or left the house. Figuring out what was expected of me in this situation—the one where I was being civil with my brother for the first time—wasn't easy.

Did I wave? Did I shake his hand? Was I expected to do that half handshake slash hug thing? Hell, should I give him a hug? I had no idea, so my hands stayed shoved in my pockets while I took my cues from him.

Of course, Kyle was glued to Rand's side, looking equally as uncomfortable as I was. I was the older brother and I was the one who had gotten us to this position in the first place, so it was up to me to make the first attempt. I didn't pull my hands out of my pockets, but I did look to Kyle. "It was good to see you again. I hope we'll see you again soon."

To my surprise I meant the words, and Kyle must have sensed as much because some of the tension eased from his body at my words. "I'm glad I came. And thank you for opening up."

He yawned and Rand shifted slightly, a nearly imperceptible change coming over him but there nonetheless. "Come on, little one, you've had a crazy day. Let's get you home for a nap."

Kyle leaned his head against Rand's shoulder, mumbling something inaudible as they headed toward a big truck at the far end of the lot.

"You too. I bet you could use a nap. It's been a crazy morning." Nathan's hand slid from the small of my back to my waist and he gently tugged me toward the SUV. As he moved, my T-shirt slid up and his palm made contact with my skin.

While I knew the touch wasn't meant to be erotic, the feel of his hand sliding just above my jeans sent a jolt of pleasure south. Goosebumps pebbled my skin as I fought a shiver. "I don't know that sleep is what I need right now."

Nathan looked toward me, his eyebrow raised in question. My only response was to look down to where my dick was beginning to fill in my jeans. It wasn't much more than a slightly rounded bulge but was growing quickly the longer his fingers lingered just above my belt.

Nathan's eyes dilated despite the afternoon sun overhead. "Well, that's going to get mighty uncomfortable in a hurry and we've got quite a drive ahead of us."

An hour wasn't long under normal circumstances—in New York, there had been times it would have taken an hour or more to go from Upper Manhattan to Lower Manhattan—but wearing snug jeans and facing an hour or more car ride back to Nashville was going to test my patience levels. The mischievous look in Nathan's eyes told me that he had something planned and the smirk that twisted his lips should have made me nervous.

Logic had left the building because I found myself eager to figure out what that look was, not at all worried about what it might mean for me.

With a press of a button, Nathan had the doors unlocked. I'd heard him start it as soon as we'd stepped out of the restaurant, so hopefully it would be cooling off by now. Getting into a car with a black leather interior could be unbearable and I'd already learned that Tennessee heat was a very different heat than I'd known in New York and Chicago. His remote start was a lifesaver in this weather.

Nathan led me to the passenger side door and opened it for me. As I climbed in, his fingers effortlessly found my half-hard cock and rubbed along the bulge. My knees buckled and I collapsed onto the seat with a gasp. My dick didn't care that it was confined inside unforgiving denim and decided it was ready to play.

The lengthening of my cock caused me to moan in discomfort and wiggle around to find a more comfortable position. Nathan stepped back to shut the door at the same time I reached out to adjust myself. He cleared his throat, shooting me a hard stare. "No. Mine."

My hand stopped moving immediately and he finally shut the door. I didn't think he could actually see me past the hood of the car, but he kept his eyes trained on my position as he rounded the front to get in, effectively thwarting my attempts at making myself more comfortable.

He was enjoying himself way too much as he grinned at my discomfort. "So fucking beautiful." His words were nothing more than a murmur that could have been said more to himself than me, but they made my insides somersault around. "You're being such good boy."

I bit my lip to try to hold the moan in that was trying to escape at his words. There was no question about it. I was a sucker for the praise Nathan gave so freely.

"Let's make you more comfortable." He adjusted himself in his seat so he could reach over the center console. In seconds, my zipper was down, my underwear maneuvered below my balls, and my dick had been worked through the fly. It hadn't necessarily been easy to get me freed but the effort he'd taken was well worth it, though looking down was a bit comical.

Nathan hummed in appreciation as he resettled into the driver's seat. "Here's the deal. I don't want you to get soft the entire way home, but you can't come."

I gaped at him in surprise. "That's an *hour* from here!"

He inclined his head. It could have come across as dismissive had it not been for the obvious bulge in his pants and the slight flare of his nostrils. "And if you can manage to stay hard and not come, your reward will be your choice."

My choice? I already knew exactly what I wanted. I'd

known for a long time, but I hadn't been able to find the words to ask. "Anything?"

Nathan was already pulling onto the highway and paying more attention to the road than me, but he managed a response as he glanced in his side mirror. "You name it."

My cock twitched as I thought about lying on the bed, watching Nathan between my legs as he stretched me in preparation for his cock. His fingers stretching me wasn't new at this point. He'd become well acquainted with my ass and prostate over the last few weeks, but I'd yet to feel his cock inside me. With the promise of any reward I wanted, I was going to rectify that today.

Thinking about Nathan inside of me was enough to keep my dick hard for nearly fifteen minutes, but not touching myself was making my erection slowly fade. I glanced down to see myself at half-mast. "What are the stipulations on ways to keep myself hard?"

Nathan gave me a side-eye that fell to my exposed dick. "Oh, that will be a problem soon, won't it?"

Well, it would have been until I caught sight of him eyeing it. It seemed as though the only thing I needed was to have him look at my dick for it to go fully hard again. A muscle in his jaw twitched as he thought and I wondered if I was going to have to stay hard with thoughts alone. I was horny enough that it would be possible, but it would be much easier with some form of stimulation.

Nathan chuckled. "I'm an ass but I'm not cruel. You can stay hard however you need to—you just can't come."

Thank fuck. My hand wrapped around the base of my cock and I could feel myself beginning to lengthen in my grip. "Mmm. Much better."

"Have you figured out what your reward will be?" Nathan asked the question casually, but I saw him palm his cock through his jeans. I might have been more exposed than I had ever been in all my life but at least I wasn't pinched in my tight jeans still. If he got pulled over, I was going to have to cover up but from everything I'd seen so far, the odds of that happening were slim to none. Nathan was an exceedingly safe driver, though at the current moment, I wouldn't mind if he'd go just a bit faster.

I flicked my thumb over my slit. "I have." I didn't elaborate. I wasn't sure if it was because I'd meant to drag my response out or if I was just so caught up in my own arousal that I'd forgotten to say more.

"And?"

Nathan wasn't going to give up that easily.

I had to release my dick in order to respond. "You. Inside me."

It took about three seconds for the words to sink into Nathan, and I took pleasure in watching his eyes widen in surprise and the speedometer climb to six over. *At least we'd be getting home quickly.*

When he glanced over at me, I could see the want and desire in his expression. "You sure?"

As if to prove a point, a bead of precum pooled on my

tip. I gathered it with two fingers and rubbed it around the underside of my head. "So sure."

The statement had Nathan focusing more on the road and allowed me to focus more on my promise to be good, stay hard, and not come. Only thirty more minutes to go.

We fell into silence as Nathan concentrated on his driving. I smiled a few times as I saw him file in behind the row of faster-moving cars, eager to get home as quickly as possible. He'd definitely shaved a handful of minutes off the trip. As we were approaching his area of town, I was happy at the thought that I'd fulfilled my end of the bargain, so Nathan's growl surprised me.

"You've got to stop making those noises if you want me to last long enough to sink into you."

Now we were both at risk of coming in the car. I pulled my hand away, allowing my cock to pulse and twitch with desire before finally calming down slightly. Slightly, not completely, because I was still hard as a rock as we pulled into his driveway.

Nathan's seatbelt was undone before we'd made it into the garage and he killed the ignition as soon as the car was in park. The garage door hadn't made it all the way down when he turned to me. "Out. Upstairs. Jesus, I need to touch you and be inside of you."

As if driving through Tennessee with my cock hanging out of my pants wasn't awkward enough, my dick hanging out as I climbed out of the SUV, then walked through his house and up to his room was even more awkward. My dick was usually only out of my pants to pee and I definitely wasn't in a bathroom as I walked through the kitchen and toward the steps.

Nathan was hot on my heels and if he could have, I was pretty sure he'd have scooped me up and carried me to his room. I turned to fall back on his bed, still fully clothed, to find Nathan completely naked. I wasn't going to get tired of seeing his body, but seeing it fully naked at that moment surprised me and I had to know. "Where did your clothes go?"

He gave a vague wave toward the hallway as he shook his head at me, disbelief in his eyes and voice. "I have no idea what it is about you, but this is not the first time since meeting you that I've lost my clothes on the way to my bedroom."

I did that. Pride and awe swirled in my stomach. I'd turned my organized-to-the-point-of-obsession boyfriend into someone who dropped his clothes haphazardly through the house. He was sexy all flustered like this and I realized with a sense of satisfaction that he was all mine.

Nathan stepped between my legs and reached for my jeans. "One day I'll take my time undressing you, but right now I just need you naked."

I wasn't going to argue, raising my hips to allow Nathan to remove my pants and underwear easily, then sitting myself up for him to pull my shirt over my head. Nathan followed me as I fell back on the bed, his body hovering over mine. He rocked his hips, dragging his cock alongside mine and pulling moans from both of us.

"Fuck." He pulled back with a gasp. "I want to taste you and touch you all over, but I'm not going to last. I need in you."

"You're not going to last? I've been hard since we got in the car to come home." I swatted at the nightstand, hoping to find the lube but only managing to knock the bottle across the room.

Nathan chased after it, his dick bouncing, and I couldn't help but stare. It was a gorgeous dick, especially with the head just beginning to peek out from his foreskin. As he bent to snatch the bottle from the floor, I rolled over and fished through the bedside drawer where I had stashed a box of condoms earlier in the week.

When he stood up, I was holding a condom packet out to him. He grabbed it, though questions were written all over his face. I pointed at the drawer. "Got them from there." When that only left him more confused, I clarified. "I've been anxiously waiting for this."

I hadn't been blushing as much recently, but I felt my face heat with my words. Nathan's confusion turned to a fondness I'd never seen on him before. Hell, no one had ever looked at me like that before. "You're so damn cute. You should have said something."

Easier said than done. Though I didn't have to say anything because Nathan was already coating his fingers in lube. His finger trailed behind my balls, down my taint, and finally slid into my ass. Far from uncomfortable, the feeling brought a sense of belonging and need: the need for more, the need for him.

My breath caught in my throat. It wasn't just the need to be fucked, wasn't the need for his cock—it was the need for Nathan. I needed Nathan but not just in that moment. I needed Nathan for the long haul.

A second finger slid into me and I rocked down to meet his hand, needing more. I'd always been slow when prepping myself, but knowing that Nathan was getting ready to enter me, my body was demanding more, opening quickly to him. Nathan didn't rush, though, and when he stretched his fingers apart, stars danced behind my eyelids.

"More." My plea came out breathy, somewhere between a gasp and a moan.

Nathan pumped his fingers a few more times, making sure I was loose, then entered me with a third. My cock jumped as he nailed my prostate. I was just going to ignore the whimpering noises I was making as he worked his fingers in and out of me because they were nothing compared to the keening sound I made when he pulled his fingers from me.

He splayed his hand across my stomach, barely avoiding my dick. "Give me a second. I need to get the condom on. Grab a pillow. It's going to feel better."

By the time I had a pillow shoved beneath my hips, Nathan had rolled the condom over his length and had grabbed the bottle of lube again. Another small squirt into his hand and he coated the condom, then used the rest for my ass.

Instinctively, I lifted my legs as Nathan climbed onto the bed and settled near my ass. "Tell me if I hurt you."

I knew he wouldn't but nodded my head anyway as I adjusted so my calves were resting on his shoulders. With an arm wrapped around my thigh, Nathan pressed his tip against my opening, which suddenly wasn't as sure about the intrusion.

Unbothered, Nathan reached down, circling my rim with his thumb and gently coaxing the muscles to relax. After just a few circles, he pressed his hips forward again. That time the head of his cock slid in effortlessly.

I was pretty sure we both stopped breathing for a moment and Nathan struggled to get words out. "That's it. Fuck, Elliot, you're perfect."

I told myself I was not going to cry as Nathan pushed his dick farther into my ass, but the words and the reverence in his voice let me know they weren't just words to him. He meant it. In all my years, I had never been enough for anyone. Leave it to the grouchy attorney who hadn't even wanted me there to be the one who tore my walls down and made me feel complete for the first time ever.

"More. Please." I needed to feel more if I was going to keep myself from breaking down with his dick in my ass.

He paused for a moment, looking down at me with concern. "Are you okay?"

I nodded forcefully and swallowed the lump in my

throat. "Need you to move." It wasn't a lie. I needed him to move. I needed to feel him inside me, to know that I was his.

Shit. I was his. He was mine.

His balls meeting my ass was what finally pulled me from my thoughts and brought me back to what we were doing. I refused to get so lost in my head that I missed this moment.

I reached up and ran a finger down Nathan's chest where sweat had begun to break out on his smooth skin. He rolled his hips, pulling out and pressing back inside in a hypnotic rhythm. His chest moved, the dark tattoo there rippling with his muscles.

After a few thrusts, our bodies moved together. Not that I'd had a lot of experience to pull from, but sex had never felt like this before. Hell, nothing in my life had felt like what it felt like with Nathan. Emotions entangled with feelings that became nearly indistinguishable from our pants and moans.

There was nothing fast about this, no matter what either of us had said. We were moving together like we'd done this hundreds of times and like we had all the time in the world ahead of us. But when Nathan gave a slight buck of his hips and nailed my prostate, I knew one of us wasn't going to last.

That person was me.

"Nathan!" His name came out sounding like it had been run over gravel, but I was desperate.

Without my needing to say anything else, Nathan reached down and gripped my dick. He pumped it twice and my back arched off the bed. "Need... to... come." I had no idea how I got those three words out between the babbling and moaning I had begun to do as he worked both my cock and ass in perfect time.

His hand untangled from its resting spot around my leg and he leaned forward, bracing himself near my head. The position opened me wider, but thankfully the slight burn of muscles I seldom used pulled me back from exploding right then. He pumped the hand on my cock again. Then he leaned forward, his mouth just inches from my ear, and whispered the words I'd been dying to hear. "Come for me."

My orgasm rolled through me at the same time his lips made contact with the sensitive skin at my collar bone. He sucked a mark there as cum spilled between us and over his hand, but his hips never lost their rhythm. He rocked into me, steady and controlled, as I rode out the waves of my orgasm, never faltering until my cock was spent, my heart racing, and my body limp. He pulled back, let go of my dick, and gripped both of my knees for support as he thrust into me fast and hard.

Just before it became too much and I became too sensitive, Nathan's head fell back, exposing the long line of his neck. If I'd had more energy, I would've found a way to kiss that spot, but at the moment, I was unable to move.

Nathan's movement faltered and on the next thrust, he

buried himself deep inside me as he came. I could feel his cock pulse a few times and I wanted nothing more than to pull him closer to me. I squeezed my ass, sensitive muscles protesting the movement, and drew a guttural noise from Nathan at the additional stimulation.

Eventually, he pulled out of me and expertly tied the condom. I didn't know where it went, nor did I care. All I knew was that he pulled me toward him, spooning me tightly against his chest. Between the kisses he peppered along my hairline and shoulders, he promised to clean me up as soon as he'd caught his breath.

I couldn't have cared less about getting cleaned up. The man I loved was holding me in his arms. I'd never felt better in my life. Who knew that falling apart could put me back together?

"I love you."

It took a few seconds for me to realize the voice had been mine. And the longer we lay there without Nathan saying anything, the more I began to freak out.

When he spoke, his voice was barely more than a whisper. "Do you mean that? Or is that the sex talking?"

I could hear the attempt at humor in his words, but it had fallen painfully flat. I refused to roll over and see his face. There was every chance I'd just fucked this up, but I wasn't going to take the words back now. I swallowed harder than I'd intended before speaking. "I love you, Nathan. I know right after sex is the worst time to say it, but it's not sex or hormones talking. No one has ever seen me. No one has ever made me feel the way you do. No one has taken the time to get to know me and still wanted to be with me. No one has ever been the first person I thought of in the morning and the last person I think of at night. No one has made me want to leave work at work and look forward to tomorrow. All those feelings that I'm feeling right now, they are all because of you."

Nathan reached up, cum-covered hand be damned, and rubbed his thumb over my cheek. He wiped away tears I hadn't known were there. "I love you too." He hummed. "I love you, Elliot. I think it kind of snuck up on me. But you're right. No one has ever made me want to change or take a step back. I have spent my life being this serious, driven guy that is always thinking about the future. Everything had to be in order and in place. Then you got dropped into my life, and there's suddenly chaos and clothes dropped all over my house." He laughed and kissed my shoulder. "But more importantly, there's you. And work isn't so important, the future isn't all I think about, and there are laughs and smiles that have never been there before. Hell, now I don't even want to kill Austin most days. And that's because of you."

My heart swelled and I fought to keep more tears at bay. I loved Nathan, but more importantly, he loved me too. I was in love. A warm washcloth over cold, drying cum couldn't beat this feeling—nothing could.

CHAPTER 27

NATHAN

"WHATEVER THAT MAN of yours is doing to you, we need to make sure he keeps it up."

I put my phone down and glowered at Seth. "Don't you have something better to do with your time?"

Seth grinned at me, black-brown eyes sparkling, and I knew then that I was in for the long haul that day. "Nope! But since I haven't seen you or your man in over a week, I thought I'd stop by to see if you're both still alive. He paid me for next month and I honestly can't figure out why."

The thought hadn't crossed my mind, but I saw his point. Elliot had spent every day at my house for the last few weeks, only heading to his place to grab something he'd left. Usually a pot or a pan. Hell, there couldn't have been much left there. He'd only moved in with a carload of things and I swore he'd brought a lot over to my place already.

"You hadn't even realized he'd basically moved in with you, had you?"

I hadn't. Not at all. It had happened so effortlessly I hadn't even thought about it. "Huh." My mouth opened and closed a few times as I racked my brain trying to pinpoint a time that his coming home with me had become natural. It was probably at the point that we'd started bringing my car to work and leaving his in my garage. That had been how long ago? Two, three weeks earlier?

Seth kept himself composed for longer than I had expected him to before he broke out in laughter. "Man, your face. It's priceless!"

"Shut up. I'm processing over here."

"You're cute." He downright cackled at the statement. "Wow, I never thought I could call you cute, but that's exactly what you are right now. You're a goner for him."

I stuck my middle finger up at Seth but didn't deny his statement. "I love him."

Seth stopped laughing instantly and his mouth hung open in shock. It was rare that I could stun any of my siblings into silence, but I'd managed. I should probably write this day in the calendar. "Have you told him?"

"Yes, asshole. He knows. But beyond falling in love with him, I think he's the one."

Seth adjusted himself in his chair so he could level me with his dark eyes. "Even though he's not into the heavier BDSM? Seriously, I don't think I've ever heard him call you Sir. And I know he's not into whips or spankings."

How the hell did Seth know this stuff? My confusion must have been evident because Seth lifted a shoulder and tilted his head to the side. "We used to sit by the pool and chat in the evenings."

That made more sense, but it also made me a little sad for Seth. He was surrounded by people every day, but he didn't have a lot of people in his life that he was comfortable relaxing around and just talking to, especially people that weren't our family members. He had apparently been working on that with Elliot but now Elliot had moved in with me.

"Don't make this about me, idiot." I balked at this and he rolled his eyes. "It's written all over your face. I asked you a question and I really do want an answer because that man has so many insecurities, the last thing he needs is you changing your mind in a few months because you need more."

I held my hands up. "No, no. We've talked about it. Honestly, Seth, I don't miss it at all. I like control and Elliot gives me that in subtle ways." I picked up my phone and shook it slightly. "When you walked in, he'd texted me to let me know that the case he'd taken for me was over and had gone well and the judge sided with us. But he also wanted to know what I wanted for lunch, then asked me what he should get."

I looked at my phone and smiled to myself at the last text I'd sent him. It was cute to watch him come out of his shell around the office and around members from the club who came in, yet still hesitate to ask for things for himself. Today had been no exception when he'd asked me what he should get himself. The stumbling text had tugged at my heart, leaving me smiling like an idiot when Seth had walked into my office.

"And while Elliot might be mortified with my saying so, the night he texted me to see if he could jerk himself off was the hottest fucking thing of my life. So much sexier than any flogging or spanking I've ever taken part in."

Seth sat, mouth slightly parted in shock, staring at me. "Whoa." He shook his head as though trying to clear it. "You're actually serious. I never thought I'd see the day."

"We've discussed it. It was a point of concern for Elliot. Hell, we don't even have a formal contract."

Seth's mouth fell open as he gawked at me. "Jesus, don't tell Mom and Dad that."

"I've tried to make one. Elliot's not comfortable with it. We've got safewords... for what they're worth. Every time I ask him what color he is, he makes one up."

Seth barked out a laugh. "What the hell does that mean?"

"One night, he was chartreuse."

Seth nearly fell off his chair as he laughed. "Oh god, that's great. Like, epically great." He pulled himself together slightly, though he was still chuckling as he spoke. "You've needed someone like him for a long time. I'm glad you got your head out of your ass. I loved you when you were stern and growly and super serious, but I like you a lot more when you smile and laugh like you have been lately."

The truth was I liked myself more like this as well. The only thing I had to say for myself was that it was all thanks to Elliot and the way his shy awkwardness got under my skin. I'd never known that what I needed hadn't been the masochistic submissive, but the sweet one who was desperate for affection and acceptance. I'd been able to give him both and it had warmed something inside of me that had been frozen for longer than I could remember.

Before I could get too sappy, I changed the subject. "Do you want lunch? It's not too late to ask Elliot and Austin to bring something back for you."

Seth shook his head, shooting me a wink. "Nope. I'm actually heading off to meet someone in about fifteen minutes. I'd really just stopped by to harass you, then ask if you were going to be at family dinner this week."

I hadn't thought about it. We'd gone a few times at Mom and Dad's house, but dinner was going to be back at DASH that week. Dad and Gram had to work Wednesday night, so we'd meet early in the evening, have dinner in the community room, then everyone would split up. Elliot and I hadn't talked about going back after his first, and only, visit had ended so catastrophically.

Would he even want to go?

"I haven't asked Elliot. I'll have to talk to him tonight."

The corner of Seth's lip twitched upward and I could tell before he opened his mouth that he was about to drop something surprising on me. "You know, it's littles' night tomorrow night. I think Zander, Noah, and Larson are going to be there. It's a pretty quiet evening overall and nothing too intense ever happens those nights. Dad doesn't even have a demonstration planned. Maybe it would be a good night to let Elliot actually experience the club. You know, without someone going caveman possessive on him out of nowhere."

I'd just taken a sip of water and choked. "I have no idea *what* you're talking about."

"Right." Seth stood up, grinning down at me. "I need to get going, Caveman. I see your mate walking in, anyway." He winked and left my office, leaving me sitting there with my mouth hanging open.

I watched as Seth headed out the door and toward his beast of an SUV, stopping for a moment to say hi to Elliot, then give Austin a hug. Elliot headed into the building a moment later, two bags of food in his hand, while Austin and Seth chatted in the parking lot.

A few seconds later, Elliot was turning the corner into my office. I'd already stood up and was halfway to the door to meet him. I greeted him with a kiss and kicked the door shut with my foot as we headed toward my desk to eat.

When I'd first started working, my desk was covered in files all the time. Now it was rare that I had to move anything out of the way to make room for a meal and today was no exception.

We made it halfway through the meal, discussing a

little about the case and how it went overall. When a break in our conversation happened naturally, I finally broached dinner. "How do you feel about going to dinner with my family tomorrow?"

Elliot's shoulders sagged slightly, a tension I hadn't known he was holding suddenly gone. "I've been wondering if you were going to ask. I'd like to go."

When my brows furrowed in question, Elliot gave me a bashful smile. "Austin was talking about it yesterday and today. He'd been talking about it as though it was a foregone conclusion I'd be there, but you hadn't mentioned anything."

Embarrassment stained my cheeks and caused me to rub at the back of my neck. "Sorry. I should have talked to you about it sooner. I honestly didn't know if you'd want to go since it's going to be at DASH. I didn't want to make you uncomfortable."

Elliot tried to look stern but he came across more tender than anything else. "I appreciate that, but please let me decide what I'm comfortable with and not."

"Consider me properly scolded. Are you comfortable going?"

He considered for a moment while he chewed his last bite of sandwich, then nodded. "Yeah. As long as no one comes charging at me unexpectedly."

"Hey, it worked out in the end."

To that, Elliot laughed. "I guess it did. Though I nearly crapped my pants first."

"In all seriousness, I'm sorry for that. It was way out of line. Maybe I can make it up to you after family dinner?"

His eyes narrowed at me, clearly wondering what I was talking about. I decided to put him out of his misery before he had to ask. "It's littles' night at the club tomorrow night. Seth told me that Larson, Zander, and Noah are going to go, but it's usually pretty quiet. Dad doesn't have any demonstrations scheduled and very few people show up that aren't littles or Daddies. The ones that do keep things quiet or in private rooms. I was thinking we could give you a taste of the club as my submissive."

Elliot's eyes widened in surprise. "I. You. What about your family?"

Logical worry, but in our family, it would be weird to not know each other's kinks. "I've seen my dad kneel for the guy I grew up calling Uncle. Believe me, my family won't care."

Elliot stared at me with his mouth hanging open and eyes unblinking. He didn't speak until I'd reached across the desk and used my finger to shut his jaw. "You know, that's an image of your parents I'd rather not have in my head."

The man had a point and I hadn't necessarily wanted to see that either. Of course, that night had taught me a lot about assumptions and expectations about anyone. It had also been a wake-up call about just how hard it was for Larson to be seen as a submissive when he didn't fit the mold. I'd changed a lot of my interactions with him after that night.

"Yeah, there's not enough brain bleach to erase those images. But I'm also glad that I know my dad is comfortable enough to express that part of himself, even around us kids. We all get that everyone has kinks and no one in our family is going to shame anyone for them. DASH has members who play for the professional sports teams, are politicians, and in police and fire departments. Believe me, we get it."

Elliot worried his lip for a moment before nodding slowly. "Okay. I'll do it." He nodded again, that time more forcefully. "Yeah. I'd like that. I think you're right. It's the perfect time to try out submitting outside of the house."

I wasn't sure if he was convincing himself or me, but I had to remind myself that he had his safewords, whatever color of the rainbow he chose each time.

CHAPTER 28

ELLIOT

Emma: *Oh! That sounds exciting. I can't believe we didn't talk about this while I was there!*

Me: *I am not talking about this in person. Dammit, woman, you're worse than Austin!*

I hadn't wanted to talk about it over text either, but I needed someone to mildly freak out to. It wasn't a full-on panic attack. It wasn't even a half panic attack. It was just my natural anxiety rearing its ugly head and making me question if I was making the right choice.

The last experience at DASH had been shitty from the moment I'd walked in until the moment I threw my phone at Nathan—however unintentional that might have been. I still maintained that he shouldn't have been lurking around outside my house in the dark.

This was a chance to change it into something positive.

Emma: *What are you going to wear?*

Me: *Umm, jeans and a T-shirt?*

Right? Isn't that what I should wear?

I put the phone down and called into the bathroom where Nathan was doing his hair. The man took forever to get the little bit of length at the top of his head to look perfectly unstyled. "What should I wear tonight?"

Nathan's head popped out of the bathroom and he looked me up and down. "That's fine for dinner."

Ugh, for dinner, yes, but I was talking about after. "Not dinner. I mean *after*."

He disappeared back into the bathroom where I could just see shadows of him messing with his hair. "Don't worry about that. I've got something for you to change into."

My eyes widened. What was he planning?

Me: *Apparently, he's got something for me for later tonight.*

Emma: *Oh! Pics or it didn't happen!!!*

Thank fuck there was a no technology rule at the club.

Me: *Nope. Can't. No phones in the club.*

I gave a satisfied grin as I hit send and turned my screen off. I was ready and it sounded like Nathan was finally washing his hands. My phone buzzed again and I looked down expecting to see a text from Emma but was surprised to see Kyle's name. I swiped my finger across the screen and read the text.

Kyle: *I thought you might like this. I found it in a suitcase today. No clue how it got there or how long it's been there.*

Attached was a picture of the two of us. I couldn't have

been much more than four or five, making Kyle only a toddler. We'd been at my grandparents' farm at the time and both of us were covered in mud and laughing. I had no memory of the picture, but I knew that Kyle had always had fond memories of the farm. My memories revolved mostly around my parents being pissed that we always came home with stains on our clothes and dirt on our cheeks. In order to avoid the complaints, I'd stopped going when I was about ten while at the same time Kyle had started spending every summer with them.

Me: *Wow, we were cute.*

Kyle: *Speak for yourself, I'm* still *cute.*

I couldn't help but laugh.

Me: *Don't flatter yourself. You doing okay?*

The text took a moment to come in, but when it did, it felt genuine.

Kyle: *Yeah. We're heading up to Nashville in a few weeks. There's a club up there we want to go to. Would you want to meet up while we're in town?*

I couldn't help but wonder if he was talking about DASH, but finding out was far lower on the list than what he'd said. He'd asked if we wanted to meet up.

Me: *I'd love to. Yeah. That would be great.*

Kyle: *Awesome. I'm getting called to the barn, but I'll let you know our plans when I know better. Have a good one.*

Me: *Yeah, you too.*

"Who was that?" Nathan was leaning against the doorframe between the bedroom and the bathroom looking sexy enough to take to bed, not to a family dinner.

"Kyle. He said that they are going to be here in a few weeks and wanted to know if we wanted to meet up."

Nathan smiled. "Great. We'll make sure we're available."

"Thanks."

Nathan crossed the room, grabbing a small bag from the dresser that I hadn't noticed earlier. I couldn't help but wonder what was in it, but he went to great lengths to keep it shut and out of my view. "Ready?"

"I don't know, am I?"

Nathan pulled me to my feet and tugged me close to his body. Leaning in, he placed a kiss on my lips that quickly turned deeper. When his hand reached around and cupped my ass, I gasped and he took the opportunity to slip his tongue into my mouth. The longer we stood kissing, the harder my dick became, and the harder my dick became, the more pronounced the bulge in Nathan's slacks became.

He finally pulled back, looking at me with kiss-swollen lips, and scrubbed a hand down his face. "Fuck. We're supposed to be leaving and all I want to do is take you to bed."

I wouldn't complain about that, but I also knew that Nathan wanted to get to DASH and see his family. Family dinner was still such a foreign concept to me, but the Smith-Johnson family had welcomed me into the fold without question, and after a number of dinners, it wasn't as awkward as the first had been. Of course, this was the first one at DASH, so who knew how awkward I'd end up being.

"Come on. We need to get going."

I groaned but followed him out the door and to the car.

For some reason, I hadn't realized how close DASH was to Nathan's house. Living outside the city, I'd assumed it would take longer to get there, but it ended up being a straight shot up the highway. Getting into Nashville just before five on a Wednesday was a hell of a lot easier than getting out of Nashville. We didn't hit any traffic until we made it into the warehouse district.

I took a deep breath as we pulled into the parking lot and Nathan looked over in concern. "You okay?"

My head bobbed up and down but Nathan wasn't convinced. "What color are you?"

"Green."

I'd answered without hesitation and I'd been completely truthful, so I couldn't figure out why Nathan was looking at me like I'd grown a second head. He reached out and put the back of his hand to my forehead and hummed. "No fever."

"What the hell?"

Nathan stared at me in shock. "You answered with one of the stoplight colors. Until now, it's always been some random combination of them. I was expecting you to come out with violet and me to need to decipher what the hell it meant."

I snorted in surprise. "Green, yellow, and red can be a little constrictive."

"Clearly." He rolled his eyes with the word, but he was smiling. "Come on, let's get in there. Dinners here tend to be chaotic and rushed. Every nonmember needs to be out and Gram needs to be at the front desk by seven."

It was still weird that Nathan's grandmother was the old lady that had greeted me the first—and only—time I'd ever been to DASH. The tiny white-haired woman had taken me by surprise when I'd walked in. Now that I knew her a little better, I knew she was sweet and funny but had a look she'd give her son and grandkids that made them all shape up quickly and made me just a little scared of her.

Nathan used a key to enter through the emergency exit. "It's just us!"

Heads popped out of a room down the hallway to see who *us* was. A few smiles, a few greetings, and then the heads disappeared back into the room before we got there. We rounded the corner into the meeting room to find the counter on the far wall filled with food, and paper plates and cups at the table.

Nathan and I had just taken a seat across from Noah and Zander when Seth walked in. He was wearing slacks and a dress shirt and grabbed a small plate of food before taking a seat on the other side of Noah.

I opened my mouth to say hi, but my eyes caught on

the subtle sparkle above his eyes, the darker pink on his cheeks, and the glossy sheen to his lips. There was no question that Seth was a good-looking guy, but there was something about the way the light makeup softened his dark beard and eyes. "Oh wow, you look amazing." My mouth had worked without my brain's input and I felt myself flush.

Seth grinned at me. "Thanks. I've got a date after this. I thought I'd dress up a bit."

Nathan looked over and nodded hello to his brother. I caught a small wink before he spoke. "Good to see some things don't change. I was starting to worry you'd forgotten how to put your face on. I haven't seen it in forever."

Seth stuck his middle finger up at him. "Shut up. You know I won't leave the house in this during the season. Now that the season's been over a few weeks, media's died down some."

Nathan just nodded. "Looks good." He got sucked back into a conversation with one of his siblings and left Seth alone.

Seth turned back to me and spoke quietly. "Sometimes I like feeling pretty. I'm the picture of masculinity on the ice and for the team, but off the ice, I don't always feel like being *that* guy. The guy I'm going out with tonight doesn't mind either."

I didn't know if he was trying to defend himself or simply letting me into a piece of his life. Either way, while it had been a shock at first, I'd meant the words. "You're very pretty. I like the colors you chose."

Seth beamed, a dimple appearing above his well-trimmed beard. "Thanks." He ate a few bites before he spoke again. "You know, you didn't have to pay rent for next month. You've hardly been at the house. Hell, you really didn't need to pay it this month."

I poked at the spaghetti on my plate for a moment before looking up again. "Yeah, well, it's still new. Nathan might get tired of me midway through next month."

Seth choked on his dinner roll but recovered quickly. "If you think that asshole is going to get tired of you, you're sorely mistaken. I've never seen that man so fucking smitten. You're like some magic pill that turns him from scowly pants to sunshine. I think there's a better chance of you getting tired of him."

Peeking over at Nathan, I saw him scowling at something his sister had said. When he turned his head and caught me looking at him, his features softened and he gave me a smile. "You good?" he mouthed more than said.

I nodded, a smile spreading over my face. "I'm good."

He turned back to his sister, but the scowl didn't come back.

Seth laughed. "Yeah. That. That's exactly what I'm talking about."

"He's pretty awesome."

"All I can say is you must have a magic dick."

My eyes widened at the statement and then even more

as Zander reached across Noah and cracked Seth on the back of the head. "Behave yourself. Seriously, don't give them a complex. Nate's actually happy for once. They're clearly good for each other."

Seth rubbed at the back of his head. "I was teasing."

Zander growled at him. "Just behave yourself. Don't go scaring Elliot off." Before Seth could say anything else, Zander's attention turned to Larson and they started speaking quietly.

Seth gave me an apologetic look. "I wasn't trying to make you uncomfortable."

A few months earlier, having someone say something like that to me probably would have made me crawl under the table and hide. Tonight, I was grinning. "It's okay. I like knowing I've given him something he's never experienced before. Everything is new to me, so I guess it kind of feels like I've leveled the playing field a bit."

"I like that. Whatever it is, it's working for you two, so keep it up."

Pride swirled in my stomach as I glanced around the table. People were already finishing their meals and cleaning up, and to my surprise, my plate was nearly empty and I was full. A glance at the clock on the wall showed we'd been there for over ninety minutes by then and I had no idea how. DASH would be opening to the public in under thirty minutes, so dinner was wrapping up.

Nathan stood and took my plate just as his grandmother stood up. "If you're staying, hand your cards over."

She was looking mostly at Zander and Noah, but Larson turned bright red as he reached for his wallet to hand over his card. When Nathan reached into his pocket and pulled out his wallet to get our membership cards, she looked surprised for a moment.

Nathan stared down at her, trying to sound stern but only managing to sound amused. "Opinions to yourself, Gram."

She raised a shoulder and gave him big innocent eyes. "Did you hear me say a thing?"

A number of amused noises came from around the room. Nathan turned to his dad, pouting in a way I hadn't known he was capable of. "Dad, Gram's being ornery! Can't you make her behave?"

Zachary held his hands up and backed up a few steps. "Nathan, you're nearly thirty-five years old. Have you *ever* known me to be able to make your grandma behave? You're better off cleaning up and keeping your head down."

Alice went around to the family who weren't staying, planting smacking kisses on their cheeks, leaving lipstick marks on them all. Though when she reached Seth, she barely brushed his beard, leaving no trace of her pink lipstick. They were close enough to me that I heard her quietly tell him that he looked "fabulous" before she moved on to the next person. The blush Seth was wearing did nothing to hide his natural blush as he ducked his head and left the room.

"Come on, Elliot. Let's go get you ready before Larson

gets in the changing room. He's not going to want us to see him."

In the hustle and bustle of everyone cleaning up, I'd nearly forgotten that we were going to be staying. And I had forgotten all about the outfit that Nathan had for me. "Oh. Yeah."

He winked as he placed his hand at the small of my back and led me to the changing room. Just inside the door, he handed me a bag. "Go on. I'll wait."

I looked at the bag like it was a bomb that might explode at any second.

"Go." Nathan reached down and adjusted his dick that was already filling. "I can't wait to see what you look like."

I groaned but headed toward the bathroom stall. I needed to pee and I really didn't want any of his brothers to see me naked. They overshared enough as it was.

A few seconds into changing, Nathan called out to me. "I'm going to help Dad and Zander set up for the evening. It will only take a few minutes. I left our locker open. We all share one, so you can toss your stuff in there when you're dressed. You can wait for me to come back or come out when you're ready."

I heard him leave, and after relieving my bladder and stripping my clothes off, I turned my focus to unpacking what he'd given me. The bag was light, so I didn't know why I was shocked to see that it had only contained a pair of blue shorts. I held them up, marveling at the lack of material. They weren't underwear, but there wasn't much more to them.

They were going to hug my thighs and wouldn't cover much. As I turned them around, my heart thudded in my chest. The rainbow stripe on the back pocket with the letters P-R-I-D-E stitched above sent emotions running through me that I hadn't expected. I kind of wished that I'd been out in the main room where there was a bench to sit down on.

Thirty-five years and I'd never owned a single rainbow item. I'd avoided them like the plague for years, scared that someone would see it and figure it out. To me, these were the ultimate announcement of my sexuality, even more than calling Nathan my boyfriend. I knew Nathan had no idea how much that little stripe meant to me because, until that moment, I hadn't realized how much it would mean to me either.

I ran my finger over the letters and smiled to myself as my confidence swelled. Nathan wanted to see me in these shorts. These were mine.

My shorts, my boyfriend, my life, my truth.

I slid them up my legs and tucked my half-hard cock into a comfortable position, then looked down at my body. I wasn't as muscular as Nathan, nowhere near as muscular as most of his brothers, but the pants fit me well and I felt even sexier in them because Nathan had bought them for me.

Stepping out of the stall, I felt more confident than I

had going in. I quickly found the locker, placed my clothes in it, and shut it, then headed toward the entrance of the locker room.

In the few minutes I'd been in the locker room, the entire place had been changed. All the normal tables, benches, and crosses had been moved to the sides of the room and in their place a toy store had exploded. Blocks, stuffed animals, trains, and books were everywhere. It felt warm and inviting, nothing like the uncertainty I'd felt the first night.

As my unease lifted, something else settled into place. A peace and a certainty like I hadn't experienced before. I was ready for tonight—I just needed to find my Dom.

CHAPTER 29

NATHAN

ELLIOT WALKED from the locker room with a confidence I couldn't describe. He'd always had a slight hunch to his shoulders, like he was ready to tuck into himself like a turtle at the slightest sign of stress. The man who'd gone into the stall had been that same man I'd known but the one who came out had his shoulders up and his head held high.

He didn't even try to hide the half-chub he was sporting in his snug blue shorts. Noah's eyes went big when he spotted Elliot. "Wow. You look hot!" He clamped his mouth shut and looked over at me as pink rose in his cheeks.

I smiled and called to Zander. "Your boy is taking a liking to mine."

Zander shook his head, walking over from where he'd just pushed the last St. Andrew's cross to a temporary resting place along the far wall. "I can see why. Your boyfriend is looking downright edible." He wrapped an arm around Noah, pulling him close. "But then again, so are you. And you, darling, need to go get changed as well."

Noah sighed dramatically. "Yes, Daddy."

He huffed and puffed but headed out of the main space, giving Zander a moment to look over at Elliot. "I hope he didn't make you uncomfortable."

Elliot was still standing tall. "No, Sir. I'm fine."

I felt my eyebrows creep up my forehead. Who was this confident man, and where had my bashful boyfriend gone? Zander didn't pick up on my confusion as he nodded his head. "Glad to hear it. I'm going to go check on my boy. See you two soon."

We both waved and I turned to look at Elliot, who was standing there smiling at me. "You like?" There was a brief moment of hesitation in Elliot's words, but the way my eyes raked over his body, lingering at his crotch, was all the confirmation he needed.

"Oh, I love."

He leaned in for a kiss but waited for me to completely close the distance. As I pulled back, Elliot licked his lips and averted his eyes for a moment, a sweet, innocent gesture that had my blood rushing south. "Thank you, Sir. I like them too."

This newfound confidence gave Elliot an entirely different sex appeal that I liked. I had no idea what had caused the change, but his submission was evident in every interaction we were having.

"Come on, let's go find a spot to sit." Because if we didn't find a spot to sit down quickly, I was going to be looking for a private room and I didn't want Elliot to get pulled from this headspace he'd found.

In an uncharacteristic show of affection, at least from me, I took Elliot's hand in mine and walked us toward a comfortable couch. It was next to where Zander had placed the backpack he'd brought with him and there was plenty of space for the two of us and our guys. Though I suspected Noah and Elliot would be kneeling at our feet. "Wait here for just a second."

I placed a kiss to Elliot's temple and jogged over to the storage closet for two large floor cushions for Elliot and Noah to kneel on. I was back in less than a minute to find that Elliot hadn't moved but had watched me the entire way. "Thank you." I enjoyed how Elliot shivered at my words.

With the pillows tossed on either side of the couch, I directed Elliot to one as I took a seat. He sank to his knees in seconds and laid his head on my lap. I tangled my hands in his hair, much the same way I'd seen the Dom Elliot had been watching that first night do to his sub. Elliot hummed and I felt his body go slack.

The arrival of Larson, Noah, and Zander didn't disturb him either. I was the one who had to try not to stare at Larson as he sat down near the toys at Zander's feet, with a stuffed Dalmatian and his blanket in his hand.

Larson didn't regress often and I'd always made myself

scarce when he had. Not that I'd been bothered by it, but I hadn't wanted to make him uncomfortable with my presence. With Elliot at my side, it didn't feel awkward.

Zander had an innate ability to multitask while helping Noah and Larson, though I got the impression Larson was getting more attention than Noah. I'd heard enough snippets of the hushed conversations he'd been having with Noah to know that Noah would be the center of Zander's world once they left DASH.

I glanced down at Elliot once everyone had settled and Larson had found some dump trucks and cars he was interested in. Elliot's face was turned toward the room, but from what I could see from my vantage point, his eyes were unfocused.

He was perfection.

My eyes found the St. Andrew's cross against the wall and I studied it for a long moment. I zoned out until I heard Zander's voice in my ear. "Penny for your thoughts?"

Tuning back into my surroundings, I noticed the club had filled with a number of new boys and Daddies. To my surprise, Larson was playing with a few. Though I wasn't sure if *play* was the right word. Two littles were near him and playing together while Larson was occasionally sending a toy their way. I got the distinct impression that they knew one another, but I had no idea how. The pup playing nearby seemed somehow connected to them all but was keeping a safe distance from my brother.

Weird.

Then I remembered Zander's question. "It's nothing really. I was just thinking about all the times I've been here for a scene. All the floggings and paddlings, intense sensory play, etc. I've done a lot here and I've always enjoyed it."

Zander hummed, a gentle encouragement to continue.

My lip twitched, the feel of a relaxed smile no longer so foreign. "It's funny. In all those visits, I never knew that I would be happiest as the guy sitting along the wall, watching everything going on with my boy kneeling beside me."

I ran my hand over Elliot's shoulders and his eyes came up to meet mine. His voice was scratchy, telling me he'd been in a very different place for quite a while too. "Funny. I knew I wanted to be here the first time I discovered submission, and I saw you as the man I was kneeling for. I just never thought it would happen."

Zander cleared his throat, though I was fairly certain I'd heard a low "Aww" come before then. I used my free hand to flick my brother's knee, then turned my attention back to the man on the ground.

Emotion caused my throat to tighten and I had to clear it a few times before sound came out. "Come here, Elliot." I held my arms out and Elliot got up to straddle my lap. I couldn't keep my eyes off his crotch as he moved, his dick hard and straining against the material, a wet spot in the front from precum. If there had been any question about if he'd kept his underwear on, it would have been erased at the perfect outline of his cock—to the point that I could see the head clearly through the material.

He didn't care if he gave half the room a show as he wiggled his way to a comfortable position over me, his ass resting against my cock, his erection running along my stomach. I leaned up to kiss his lips and he kissed me back, hungry and urgent. My fingers snaked into his waistband above his ass and I gripped his butt, eliciting a little moan from him.

"Behave." Zander's growl was serious and I looked around to see we'd caught the attention of some of the littles and Daddies in the room.

"Oops." I pulled my hands out and patted Elliot's ass. "We need to behave for a bit longer." I nipped at his jaw and Elliot surprised me as he leaned down to place his head on my shoulder.

"Love you." His voice was barely a whisper, but I'd heard it loud and clear.

"Love you too."

I'd happily stay in that position the rest of my life—hard and aching—as long as it was with Elliot in my arms. Maybe my mom had been right all this time—I'd needed to lose the vinegar. I didn't know if I'd found honey or something else, because I'd always known I hadn't been looking to attract a fly. I'd wanted a unicorn and the man resting in my arms was just that.

Elliot was my everything: my submissive, my boyfriend, my partner. My unicorn.

~*~

Not ready to say goodbye? I wasn't either! Grab a free bonus short where Elliot goes to Untamed to see Kyle—and the horses. Click Here!

Coming July, 2021: Submission, Undisclosed Book 4. Pre-order now to meet Canyon and Larson on release day!

If this is your first visit to the middle of Tennessee with me, then welcome. Here's a list of books in which the side characters from this book appear.

Meet Rand, Kyle, and Fred in *Untamed.* A fake boyfriend, fake Daddy, friends to lovers romance. It's shocking the lengths Kyle is willing to go to in order to make Elliot and his parents uncomfortable in New York. Join them as they discover something the two friends have been missing all long. Pick up your copy *Untamed* now.

. . .

Larson and James first appeared in the *Undisclosed* Series. After meeting in college, this group of men have become closer than friends; they're family. Fall in love with each of them when you pick up *Desires, Curiosity, and Attraction.*

Zander has appeared in many books in the past. From the *Curiosity* and *Attraction* to *At Home*, but he finally found his happily ever after in *Zander, Johnson Family Rules Book 1*. Laugh and cringe with Zander as Noah figures out how to interact with Zander and the whole Johnson family by picking up *Zander* now.

A NOTE FROM CARLY

Dear Reader,

Thank you for picking up *Nathan.* If you enjoyed reading about Nathan and Elliot, as well as meeting the entire—*crazy*—Johnson family, please consider leaving a review here. Reviews are invaluable to independent authors, and even a few short words can help others discover this book.

Up next, Larson will get his happily ever after with the Daddy he didn't think existed. Make sure to join my Facebook reader group, Carly's Crew, to find out the latest on the Johnson family and everything coming up!

Peace, Love, and Happily Ever After,

Carly

ABOUT THE AUTHOR

Carly Marie has had stories, characters, and plot bunnies bouncing around in her head as long as she can remember. Today, she is a USA Today Bestselling author, lover of all things romance, and avid reader.

Carly spends her days writing sweet, kinky stories about men who love each other and her nights as a wife, mother, and chauffeur. She spends far too much time reading books, or in hockey rinks or driving between them, and far too little time cleaning her house.

Carly lives in Ohio with her husband, four kids, two cats, and has lost count of the number of chickens in the backyard. The numerous plot bunnies that run through her head on a daily basis ensure that she will continue to write and share her stories for years to come.

Keep up to date on all the latest by following me at:

Mailing List: Carly's Connection

Website: www.authorcarlymarie.com

Made in the USA
Monee, IL
15 August 2023

41048864R00226